Song of George

Portrait of an Unlikely Holy Man

Jesse S. Hanson

Song of George

Copyright © 2010 by Jesse S. Hanson

ISBN: 978-0-9846154-1-4

Library of Congress Control Number: 2010909362

Illustrations by Christine Sherwood

Original Cover Photo by: Cheryl Guthrie

Cover Design by: All Things That Matter Press

Published in 2010 by All Things That Matter Press

Dedicated to my benefactor, Ajaib Singh Ji Maharaj
(Sant Ji)
Who literally rescued me
from my own self-destructive way of life

Acknowledgments

Thanks to my wife Lilasuka and my daughter Audrey and the many uncomplaining hours they have spent reading and re-reading and listening to me read the manuscript. Thanks to the fact that they allowed me the necessary freedoms and obsessions to write and re-write and still be part of the family, the manuscript was completed. I can never thank them sufficiently.

A special thank you to my very dear friend Helen Perkins, who really bolstered my confidence regarding the message of "Song of George". Without her kind help, I would possibly be circling within the shoulds and shouldn'ts of literary neuroticism to this day.

Another special thank you to yet another dear friend, Dr. Sylvia Sholar, who read the manuscript, only slightly interrupted by appendectomy surgery, and then offered invaluable insights and her special point of view as well.

Many thanks to other kind friends and associates who read or listened to me read parts and gave feedback.

Thank you to my illustrator, Christine Sherwood.

And of course, thanks to All Things That Matter Press for giving me a "leg up" in an industry typified by closed doors.

Author's Note

Out of empathy with the many unfortunate souls, incarcerated with long sentences in prisons, for behavior they are incapable of amending, and who are in need of thoughtful and *careful* treatment, in more appropriate institutions, I have chosen to imagine the character of George. My beloved Master, Ajaib Singh, used to say, "God comes as a man. If he came as an animal we would not be able to understand his language. If he came as a ghost we could not see him."

The imprisoned characters in this story are men. There are those who would call some of them less than men, or perhaps even call a few of them other than men. But men they are. Men who for one reason or another cannot understand or cannot conform to mainstream society, and therefore cannot survive in any mainstream society. If God came to them as a man of any mainstream society, it is possible they would not be able to understand him. If he came as a ghost, some of them *may* be able to see him, but the understanding issue would likely still exist.

In my enthusiasm to write this story, if I have created any offense, unwittingly or otherwise, to the very great spiritual personalities to whom I endeavor to pay tribute, I beg their forgiveness. I would also like to mention here that I have been given no sanction, neither do I have any authority whatsoever to represent the teachings or views of any person or spiritual tradition or organization, past or present. Every aspect of Song of George is fictional, allegorical if you will, with the exception of quotations that are so noted.

PART ONE: GEORGE ON THE INSIDE

Heaven lies about us in our infancy,
Shades of the prison-house begin to close upon the growing boy.
Earth fills her lap with pleasures of her own;
Yearning she hath in her own natural kind,
And even with something of a mother' mind, and no unworthy aim,
The homely nurse doth all she can,
To make her foster child, her inmate Man, forget the glories he hath known,
And that imperial palace whence he came.
                                        —Wordsworth

When there was no dream of mine, You dreamed of me.
                        —Hunter/Garcia   Attics of My Life

"The people seem to come out of nowhere. I don't seek them out, all these strangers. I don't find it all that comforting to have lifelong strangers. They don't like me—not really. Sure, I can impress them in certain ways. Sometimes please them, somehow. But they sure as hell don't like me. Not all of me. They don't think like me. They don't feel like I do. Who are they anyway, these people that have come out of the void?"
—George

ONE: George gives the message that is later referred to as "The Great Separation"

Bascomb (Jesús)

"George and I, we were just coming up the stairs is why I am breathing a little bit heavy. We do it for the exercise and also because, well, on the outside the elevator gets to be such a drag, you know. People standing and staring at the doors. Nobody speaking. And if you do dare to break the silence after a few floors, everybody is like relieved, but they don' admit it. They pretend that it is perfectly normal to talk in the elevator, where you are all squeezed in together with perfect strangers, and you are taking up everyone's space with your big mouth talking. In a way, we are preparing ourselves for when we get out. To avoid stress and to be healthy, you know—clean cut.

"So George and I and a few of the others, we're not lazy anymore. We take the stairs and we yak. Yak yak yak. Forty-first floor to the thirty-first. Some of us good behavior cases, we get passes, two of us at a time, and they will let us visit the other floors of the mental unit. We got a *beeeg nanny* tagging along with us the whole time of course."

"I'm impressed that they let you go," says the young man with the recording device.

"It is only for one hour a day, and just the main rooms, not the cell blocks, but it is a change of scenery, so we go. Coming back up we talk a little less, though. We have to catch our breath once in a while."

"Do inmates from the other floors come up here, as well?"

"Oh, no. I've never heard of that," Bascomb replies.

At this point, the friendly and gregarious Latino prisoner with the odd name and the intensely expressive blue eyes puts his hands on the edge of the table at which they sit, looks carefully around to see that no one is listening. There is, in fact, a guard standing about thirty feet away against the wall, but Bascomb seems satisfied with that distance. The guard is not obviously looking at them and shows no apparent interest in the conversation. Then, in a very serious tone, and with his voice lowered, "Listen, dude, if you fellows are going to hang around, I just want you to get something straight from the beginning, before you hear it different, from maybe a less reliable source. Because there is a bad rumor going around about something George said to one of these damned nursemaids of ours when he was having one of his seizures." He glances over at the guard as he says this.

"It sure ain' my place to correct George, but he is wrong if he said that people don' like him. Well, maybe he is right about 'not everybody', not all the time. But he is loveable, that George. We love him."

message of George – I
~ The Great Separation ~
Ansel

He's pacing back and forth in the middle of the great hall before an assembly of devotees, an old black leather bound book in his right hand. You'd never guess they were devotees if, unawares, you walked into the room. Most likely you'd see just another crazy preacher, like the ones you come across on the street corners that everyone's trying to ignore. In fact, the people in the hall are just lounging around all over the place. No lined up chairs. No prayer mats or meditation cushions supporting respectful postures supporting attentive faces.

But their attention he has. Most of them, at least. When he begins to speak he shifts the book to his left hand and then back and forth as he continues, sometimes shaking it at his followers in a gesture reminiscent of the puritan preachers of old, as they would personally call forth the fire and brimstone.

***

"And the Lord said, 'Let there be separation'—and in that way He separated all from Himself. On the first day, He created separation. And in the days following he created pain and confusion and fear. And He created the beings and He set them against one another, that they should hurt each other in myriad ways. And he laid traps and the tangled webs, that all who would do good should be tripped up. He baited the traps and the webs with desires and with hunger. And all the beings were thus coerced to use each other and to devour each other.

"The Lord was beautiful, and he was mad. He was terrible in His madness and He took no rest. But in the world He created the need for rest. He created the need for rest and said, 'Let all who are weary come to me and I will deceive you and make fools of you and you will consider yourselves the righteous ones. Dwellers of the human bodies, you will find peace and tranquility and

superiority over all beings that live in this beautiful world of my creation, before you die and I send you to the hells and then back into the world again. For ages upon ages I will have sport with you and you will call me God and Allah and Krishna and many other names of glorification. You will depend on me and I will depend upon you. For I take my life from your lives. It matters not that I am arrogant and violent. You will worship me and you will dwell in utter misery as do I.' Thus sayeth the Lord."

He puts down the book, leaves it lay on a table – he has not looked at it anyway – and pauses after the gospel of George. *"Capital letters and all, my crazies. That's the way we learned it. It's not what the teachers and the preachers told us, but that's the way we learned it. Sorry; I guess I'm not helping here. But I figure, what's the difference? We're all nuts here anyhoo. I've come here not to preach to you, but to agree with you. Just like you, I also can't figure out how anyone can call themselves sane, let alone be sane."*

Milton

"We got all kinds here. Criminal addicts take five floors all to themselves; the bottom two for women and three above for the men. No offense, but I think they're dumb. I mean, they make themselves dumb, shooting that stuff into their veins, smoking that crack and angel dust and all that. They're the lucky devils, though; they keep 'em mostly doped up even in here," he says, laughing. "Thirty-six is the most serious noids; nonstop freakin' out, man. They should just hook up with the addicts and mellow out, you know what I mean? Thirty-seven, who knows? The elevator don't stop. There's no door to it in the stairwell. Some people figure it's just administration, but who knows? Maybe they do some kinda dark experiments in there on the psychos.

"Hell, no, we ain't all psycho, thank you very much. We're sicko; we ain't psycho. Hmm, now that you mention it, I see where you could get the terminology twisted. Put it this way: on this floor we're mostly harmless, physically anyway. Just like the normal folks outside, we hurt each other in all the usual ways.

"The names? It was Horatio's idea. His real name is Harold. It's just a game. Harold had the notion that, as George's followers, we should take on spiritual names, you know, like initiated names, but when George wouldn't give us any we just came up with our own. Mostly we picked names of poets and philosophers, although some are just kind of highbrow names.

"My given? It's Raja Santhanam. But everybody calls me Milton.

"Once in a while they send some preacher or other up here. Or down here, when they fly 'em in. And to be fair, it's not just Christian preachers, although we do have the regular Bible study groups, of course.

But sometimes the guys they send in are some of my guys – I mean, that look like me, minus the scar, of course—from the old country, right? Yogis, swamis, gurus. And it ain't like they don't get some converts now and again. I notice they don't go to no thirty-seven neither, though. But George is our man. We don't really need no outside guys. George goes to thirty-seven, too. Won't tell us about it, though.

"Anyway, on thirty-eight are the wackos that never come around; they got a fella down there that shoves whole loaves of bread down his throat all at once. That's a sight you don't wanna miss. I don't even get it, why they're in here. They got half of 'em tied up just so they don't chew on themselves. How can you commit a crime when you don't even know if you're coming or going, for God's sake. On thirty-nine and forty they're just plain depressed. And the top four, drum roll please ... the top four reasons to eat more fresh vegetables when you're pregnant—the just plain crazy and dysfunctional, otherwise known as the delusional hallucinatorians. We got chemical imbalances, we got psychic phenomena, anxieties comin out the wazoo, grandeur, you name it. And that's just our floor. Upstairs is the bad guys. The real special psychos, you know? The beasty boys.

"Listen, I gotta git. I gotta go pray or something."

Bascomb

"Well, if you are interested in my background as a kid, I'll tell you straight out, in my family, I'm the only one that's *off*." Bascomb points at his temple, makes a funny face with his eyebrows raised, as he says "off". "My dad was a shoe salesman; and our Mom raised us and she worked part time for the high school office in our neighborhood. Albuquerque being a small city allowed us kids a lot of freedom without having to worry for our safety all the time. We saw our Dad only a few days each month when he came in off the road. He covered stores for his company all across the western US, except California.

"There were three of us kids, my older brother and my baby sister. My brother and I were close in age but we ran with different crowds. I had a tendency, even then, to attract, I guess you would say bad company, although I don' think, really bad. Maybe they did not have that much respect for their elders, or maybe a little shoplifting and that kind of stuff. I never thought they were bad. Not like people who mean harm. People like that, I cannot imagine where they come from.

"Here is an example. One day after school, with my buddy Juan, we are fourteen or fifteen I guess and we were just walking aroun', looking for stuff to do. We were cutting across the flea market grounds, which were almost always empty except on the weekend, you know. This guy comes out of the outdoor john just as we were passing and he hits us up for a smoke. I was out, but Juan, he gives him one, and when he's handing him the cigarette, the guy says, 'What the hell, just gimme the whole pack.' So Juan snaps back the one he was going to give to him and say's something like 'I guess not', cool like, ya know? But the guy pulls out a gun, points it right at Juan's head. I'm going, 'Juan, give him the smokes, man!' But the guy don' seem to care about the smokes anymore and he knocks them out of Juan's hand onto the ground when he tries to give them to him.

"Oh, I don' know, he was probably in his early thirties, I suppose. "He tells Juan to go into the john and when he says that I start running. It sounds stupid, but I was zigzagging as I ran, thinking the guy might miss when he shot at me, but he never bothered.

"So I ran and I tried to find a cop, but, naturally, I couldn' find one when I needed one. Finally I did but it had to be at least twenty minutes 'til we got back there. I stayed in the car, because he told me to. When he came out I was yelling at him, 'Is he in there? Is Juan in there?' but the cop, he wouldn' answer me at first. An' then this cop, he was a young guy, you know, like I said, and he walks off a little ways and he gets down on the sand on all fours and gets sick, and I hear him retching and his body's convulsing an all that. Then he's wiping his hands on a little bush, but when he comes back he's still got some on his hands and on his shirt cuffs.

"That cop didn' tell me anything. He wouldn' talk at all. Just drove me down to the station. They interrogated the shit out of me. Didn' matter that my friend had just been decapitated in an outhouse, which I found out as we went. Those cops didn't give a crap about me. It's all about the dead folks, I guess. The living can go to hell, apparently. Which is pretty much where I went after that. Which is pretty much where I am still. There's a lot of different versions. Different plots in the story of a land people call Hell. But some people's eyes are not open, that's all. That is why they don' get it—the real nature of things. They don' see it."

~ The Great Separation ~
Ansel
-continued-

He walks around in a little circle with his head down. He stops and looks around at all of us, all over the room. Makes a couple of more circles.

"But if there was a way to put a stop to it," he says, more sincerely now, in a softer, normal speaking voice and without the former visual embellishments, without the book. *"If there was a way to be certain—because*

of something you knew in your life—that you would not have to go through it ever again, would you want to? Wouldn't it appeal to you?

"Because I think it's not God that I've just described at all. That we've been duped, all along. I know it sounds crazy, but what if God really does love us? Is waiting for us, like an anxious father waits for his teenage daughter to come home when it has gotten very late? And we know that that father is justified in worrying about his daughter, don't we?

After all, we know who the world has made a bargain with."

He is just standing there now, looking long, and I can only describe it as lovingly, like a patriarch of a large family might look lovingly around a room where that family is gathered, his eyes expressing much more than any words could convey. It is a surprising impression, given that he is a young man, but a powerful one, nevertheless. After a time he goes on.

"I don't know how I got into this. I met a man. He gave me something to eat. I was homeless. He took me in. He showed me love. And he gave me something for you, dears. A message. A plea. 'Never again. Go home. Don't come back here again. There's nothing for you here.'"

And then George sits down in the middle of that room and cries. He cries for some time. What could we do? I think almost everyone cried, those who were beyond shrieks and moans. I even thought I saw one of the guards trying to wipe his eyes, trying to hide it, trying to maintain his composure. Maybe it was my imagination.

Later, after George left the room, I went over to the table where he left the book lying, picked it up. *The Journeyman Electrician's Resource.*

Stephen

"It was a red day. They say it's pollution but I've always felt that there was more to the color of a day than just some physiological phenomena. And a red day gives an uncertain quality. I'm not saying necessarily ominous, just uncertain. However, we got word, about ten a.m., one of the ladies down below died, one of the heroin addicts. They wouldn't tell us what it was she died of.

"Around ten thirty, I went through the floor and the dead folks were all sitting on the next floor down. That's why I never go down there. They were sitting there, thousands of 'em, naked, and I had to sit among 'em, and folks were crying, stifled kinda sobbing, and we were all so hungry and chilled, but nobody had anything, just thousands of cold dead people crowded together, sitting on the cold hard floor. There's nothing else at all in that whole room, just big high, dirty white walls like a warehouse. We didn't stand up or move around, because we were embarrassed at being naked. I saw 'em bring that lady in, the heroin addict. There was some shuffling noise in the back of the room, behind me, so I turned to look and I saw two guards throwing that poor lady in through the door like she was a dead fish or something. Her flimsy, skinny, naked body landed on some of the folks sitting there and knocked them around some, cause they weren't looking when them guards threw her. But they just kind of murmured in surprise and then she had to sit down among 'em as they made a little space for her. I don't know how I knew it was her. I just figured it was her I guess.

"And you know about the gnashing of the teeth and you know about the Goddamnation! I sat on that floor below us for maybe only a few hours, though it felt eternal, but it wasn't.

"When the stairwell door opened and George walked in, the whole moaning room went silent. From the door there were a few concrete steps down onto the floor with a black metal handrail on one side, and everyone turned and watched him come down those steps, and I knew they did, though I only watched him myself and didn't look elsewhere. And the room became warmer, and some of the people stood up, and then we all stood, and we weren't embarrassed. George stepped down onto the floor and the people parted and as he came through the people to me. And I cried when I saw him coming, and, as I cried, he took my hand and led me out of there without a word.

"Outside the door, in the stairwell, there were large cardboard boxes, hundreds of them, full of some kind of white food, and I knew it was prashad because I'd heard of prashad, and there were healthy women there, with beautiful faces but dressed with modesty. I saw them as they began to carry the boxes into the room, and George and I went up the stairs to this floor.

"I'm not one of George's gang, you know. Those party guys. But I love George, all right. I can't even say."

TWO: Ansel explains The Project

Why do ye not understand my speech? Even because ye cannot hear my Word.

—*John 8:43*

Ansel
- hanging out -

"We were hanging out to *little purpose,* as my mother used to call it, when she was unable to see any tangible results of an activity. We'd taken an apartment in the Day Dream district of the University sponsored housing, after graduating. Fancy degrees, as my father called them, we had. It was careers that we had cold feet about. Not that we were afraid of the work. Well, I can't speak for Jeff or Ozwald, but for myself I was just afraid of starting down the *wrong* career. Hell, I don't know, maybe I was afraid of any career at all. I mean, when you look around it seems like they suck the life out of most people. You can't really succeed in one without giving it your all, and, if you give a career your all, how can you succeed in your life? Maybe that sounds crazy to you but it's probably something that rubbed off on me from association with my best friend, Ozwald.

"We met each other our first year at the University and although we came from such different backgrounds, in many ways we were so alike that we could have been brothers. I mean we are brothers. That's the way we see it. You see, Oz was raised a Hare Krishna, out in the country in West Virginia, and although he was given these opportunities, just as I was, for education and success in the world, he told me that somehow he was always taught on some deeper level that that was not top priority. Not from his parents, necessarily, who apparently always kept a balance. Oz likes to mimic them in a kind of sarcastically affectionate way. '"Hands to work, hearts to God" and all that', he's always saying. I used to tell him that maybe he just hung out too much with the sanyasis down at the temple. I went with him many times to the *farm* on breaks from school, so I had some idea what I was talking about. I never converted, exactly, but the Krishna devotees have certainly been an important influence for me.

"Then there's Jeff. We actually met him at a bar. Oz and I were kind of far-gone that night but, even so, it wasn't hard to see how brilliant he was, not to mention that he kept us laughing for hours. Well, Jeff was in some kind of similar place, philosophically speaking, as Ozwald and I anyway, even if not exactly. I mean, although he's always been more cynical by nature, I guess he figures there's more to the whole thing, somehow. It was originally Jeff's idea, the project. His cousin had been sent to the joint for some fairly petty crimes complimented by the fellow's very heavy attitude. He wasn't actually in the mental unit, but he'd gotten wind of some things from the general population rumors.

"Jeff was telling us about it one evening over a few beers—he was telling us about a guru in the prison mental ward—and we were letting our imaginations run into some pretty far-fetched and rather sarcastic places. Then about a month later, there was a little story in the University paper about it. Up to that point, it had been only joke material for us. But with that article, we really started thinking. I mean it was very basic, didn't even mention George's name, but it peaked our interest. As things have turned out, our far-fetched fictional imaginings didn't even scratch the surface of the kinds of realities that were later revealed to us.

"We had to do some serious legwork, preceded by some serious brainstorming to get in. If that place is impossible to get out of, it's also all but inconceivable to get in, short of being sentenced or gaining employment there; God save me from either one of those options, *ever*. But we started at the top and worked our way down to the prison authorities and finally to the mental unit authorities.

"Amazing Ozwald got an audience with the Governor; I took the mayor and the city council. Jeff approached the psychology community of the world, basically. He worked tirelessly, I mean we all did, but he had all these incredible, or I should say highly credible, scientists from all different countries putting in the good word for us. We had to stand damn strong, though, to keep from getting undercut by any number of hotshots. But that was partly where Ozwald's and my work paid off, because our government folks knew we got there first. I don't know how we managed, or were lucky enough, really, to keep the news hounds from getting the drift, but that was a real blessing. I don't think it could've been half as *real*, and I know it's somehow politically incorrect to use the word *real* like that, but I don't really give a damn; I like the ambiguity of it as well as the potential for a kind of slang clarity. I don't think the project would have been half as *real* with the press involved.

"We were given two months. We were to come and go, putting in eight-hour shifts, just like a day job. We were allowed to mingle freely with the population of floor number forty one, which is the floor on which George was held. The ever-present guards were not to interfere with our observations or our interviews unless there was a threat to our safety. We were allowed audio recording devices, but not cameras. It was a remarkably liberal arrangement. Perhaps entirely unique."

***

"When we finally completed our report, or I should say, when we finally quit working on it, it was a small hit with the paranormal world. We're getting all these job offers now, of course. I suppose I'll take something. Got one from a major psychology journal, headquartered in the UK. It'd be doing similar work. Reporting with a psyche angle. How bad could it be? Making a living just talking to people. The guy told me, 'You just have to ask the right questions. Then you let people draw their own conclusions.' Well, that's what we did in the mental unit. Everyone's gonna have a different opinion.

"But I'm not so sure I'll take the job. The project affected—no, George affected us. Confidentially speaking, our objectivity was broken down. There was no escaping it, no escaping him. He made no efforts to convince us of anything, or to approach us with any agenda whatsoever. Hardly gave us the time of day, you know. At the end of it all, though, I'm even less interested in the career thing than I was before. At the risk of sounding melodramatic, I'd say I'm less interested in the world altogether, its allurement. You know how people used to talk about the young Hare Krishna kids being brainwashed? Their founder and Guru, Srila Prapupada, used to have an answer for that. Something like, 'Yes, we are washing their brains.' I find myself daydreaming. And what do I dream about? I think about the things George taught us. You won't believe it, but I swear I see Krishna in George. I mean the guy is insane. Well, there's no explaining it after all.

"I remember the first day they let us in. It was an extreme shock to the system."

Horatio's story
Ansel

"When I was in my early thirties, one day they just opened up the doors and shooed us all out into the streets. A lot of us, anyway." Horatio's very favorable reputation regarding his personality has preceded him. His rather daunting physical presence hasn't. But this huge, powerful looking, African American man immediately puts me at ease with his amiable nature and his engaging conversation. "Said they couldn't hold us no more 'cause we weren't dangerous to nobody, 'cept areselves. Missus Ford said the new law'ed set us free.

"I guess I wusn' ready for that. Hell, I hardly knew what a street was. I mean I knew the look of it but I didn' have no idea about the life of it. Seemed to have no order, nor rhyme, nor reason. An' I didn' know how to act. Kept gettin' in trouble for little things. Things that were the way you did stuff in the hospital, well, you'd get in trouble for doin' the same way on the street. Like if you were in a line to get your food, you had to take your turn. Or if you were lucky 'nuff to have some tape player or somethin', you had ta play it soft so's not ta disturb other folk's space. Things like that. But out on the street, seemed like nobody was fair to the other, hardly never. I guess it got ta me an' made me pritty edgy, 'cause after awhile I started in havin' more of my seizures again. An' then sometimes I started tryin' to enforce the rules myself, an' that din't work too well.

"There was this young man that came runnin' down the walk one day, pushin' people outa the way if they hadn't already got outa his way. Well, he was getting pritty close to me and, be darned if he din't knock a liddle ol' man right down. So I caught him up when he come up by me, an' I took him over to that ol' man an I was tryin to git 'im to 'pologize an' to offer to help that ol' man. I found out quick if you laid a hand on somebody on the street, even if they was cheatin' plain as day, yu'd not only end up in a tussel with 'em but also the cops'd be down on ya before ya knew what was happnin'.

"So I got some pritty good talkins to by them cops all right. I think it also had to do with my size. Know what I mean?"

I answer that I think I do. He explains anyway, and I find that I'm glad when he does.

"Sometimes it seems like folks like to trouble a big fella. I notice it, but I don't know the exact reason for it, 'cause I don't go showin' off my strength. Nothin' like that.

"What got me back in deep trouble, though, was this poor lady I foun' in the alley. She was bein' molested by a couple of bad guys an' I went in there to help her, but as I was holdin' her when the cops showed up they put the blame on me. Well, that was pritty much it for me. Powers that be decided I wasn' harmless after all, an' after some doin's in the courts they got me up in prison."

Ansel
- recording George -

"I decided to record George's public talks, insofar as I was available for them. By public, I mean talks that he would give to the general population of the forty first floor. Most of these occurred quite impromptu and informally in the main hall. His words, I believe I have transcribed accurately, as the recordings were usually of good quality. In cases where it was not entirely clear what was said, I have so noted and left them out of the transcriptions entirely, rather than risk misquoting him. I have taken the liberty of including my observations, with the intention of portraying the varying moods of George and the others as well as giving my impressions of the effect of these talks upon those present, including the staff and my colleagues and myself. I admit the potential for bias in such observations and impressions, yet I am convinced that George was speaking intentionally and specifically to the audience that he had, so I thought it to be in order to attempt to present the whole mix, so to speak.

"I have labeled these transcriptions, "message of George," and numbered them chronologically, beginning from the time we first came to the floor and began the project. I've also taken the liberty of giving them my own titles, referring to their content. The titles simply make it easier to reference any given talk."

message of George – II
~ Don't Believe in God ~

"Don't believe in God. We're all fools believing in God. How in the hell can we believe in God, unless we know who that is?

"We don't know who we are. We don't know who the devil is. Alright, alright, y'all think you know who the devil is. You don't know who the devil is. Otherwise he-slash-she wouldn't be the devil, if we could figger it out. You might of seen something of the devil, some aspect, or aspects. But does anybody really believe it's as simple as that?

"Maybe you've seen some part of God. Maybe you have, maybe you have." He's sitting down now.

"Well out there," he makes a sweeping gesture toward the barred windows, *" out there they say that God demands responsibility. Some say that. But in here,"* he places his hand over his heart, *"we plead insanity."*

Someone starts screaming from a corner of the hall. George says, *"I gotta go. It's a Goddamned nuthouse in here."*

message of George – III
~ Vegetarianism ~

"I want to ask you dear people to be vegetarian. I don't have no big speech today. We pay hell, 'cause we make hell. We commit all manner of violence and horror upon the innocent animals. And they suffer no less fear and pain than we humans would if another species was in the habit of sending us to the slaughterhouse, then going to the store and buying our body parts to eat. Think

about it, when and if you can. Dwell on it, please," and George walks out of the room.

message of George – IV
~ Why Don't God Make Us Good? ~

"Why do you people listen to me? Haven't you suffered enough?" He doesn't smile at his little joke. No one else does, either.

"You know, I'm married to a wonderful woman and I don't know when I'll ever see her again. I know some of you have already been up in here for a long time. Others have arrived more recently, and the future is very bleak. Some are serving one, even two lives. Anything can happen. Myself, I have two kids. I should be serving their lives." He doesn't smile at that either. Nor do they. He paces. *"The laws are hard—unforgiving."* He paces, silently, for some time.

When he stops pacing, he asks without looking up, *"What if there was no devil? Some folks would say that's sacrilege. 'Course they'd most likely say every word out of my mouth is sacrilege. Probly right. But what if the devil is just some poor crazy son of a bitch, child of God on steroids? 'Cause I've heard that.*

"Aw, I'm just as confused as you are. Why don't God make us good? I don't see the problem with that. If God is good, how can He make bad? But there's some things going (two words omitted that are unclear) *over our heads, I expect."* He does smile at that. Nobody else does, though. *"I'm lucky to have you, my friends. You're all very dear to me."* That produces a few subtle smiles, which George doesn't appear to see as he walks out.

THREE: The troubles of The Man on the Street

Watch out now, take care
Beware of the thoughts that linger
Winding up inside your head
The hopelessness around you
In the dead of night
            —*George Harrison, Beware of Darkness*

the man on the street

He doesn't recognize the street that he wakes up on. The light of the day didn't wake him. Neither did the sirens or the roaring and horn blaring stream of traffic or the jazz band that set up no more than fifty feet from him. The people step over him on the sidewalk. The police haven't found him worth the effort. What has woken him is that someone is repeating a word, or some sound, "Is it a name, or what is it?," repeating it over and over. It grows loud and insistent. Somehow, it's infusing his lifelessness with some life. In his still muddled waking, his experience is that he sees the sound of it, and he sees it as a many colored sound. The color of it is sweet and beautiful in timbre. "Oh, it's a dream," he says regretfully, and his head screams in pain from the sound of his voice. But the word is repeated, and his pain is quieted as it is repeated.

The man sits up. His body again cries out in pain but he ignores it, captivated as he is. Looking around he can find no source of the word that is being repeated. The concrete rises up two feet from the lake side of the sidewalk, forming an edging upon which there is a hand rail of stainless steel tubing against the drop off to the tunnel below. He reaches for the railing and pulls himself upright as the foot traffic detours around him, carefully avoiding the hectic traffic of the street. Out on the lake the ferries are coming and going and on the dock, the mob waiting with some sufficient decorum for a turn, for a portion of the island's afternoon promises. But for him the lifeline is now fading. No one is there. The street, the walk, the dock, teeming with people. Who is it? No one is there.

He walks. He doesn't know where to walk to. He doesn't talk to anyone. His head begins to throb. It's gone. It was such a beautiful dream. How could it be a dream? No, *now* he's fallen into the dream, into the nightmare, where noise and confusion and pain rule the world of the dream. As he walks, he is so clumsy. He stumbles against the buildings, into people. They push him off, some of them carefully, some cursing and rough. After three blocks or so he's moved out of the tourist traffic, but not out of the traffic. The sun is not allowed here for most of the day. The tall buildings guard the street jealously and coldly. The people crowd the walks in the business of their city. In the business of their city lives. A drunken bum is an obstacle in a world of obstacles.

His head is reeling. His mind in a stupor. The backs of his hands, cut and bruised. Someone's missteps. "Oh, sorry buddy." But it didn't wake him. He's gradually tumbling and bumbling his way down the fourth block, just going. He knows he has to go somewhere. Where? When he falls into the street, people gasp. Some cars screech to a stop. One car swerves, narrowly avoids tragedy with the next lane traffic. But his arm goes out to break his fall. When the braking front wheel goes over his forearm he cries out so, but as the rear wheel goes over a moment later twisting his already broken limb, his cry is drowned out by the shrieking brakes and the honking horns.

***

He opens his eyes but no light comes into them. There is no sound, save his own breathing. His arm does not respond to the message from his brain so he sends the same message to the other arm and he touches his face to determine if it is there—to learn if the arm and the hand are there as well, puts out his tongue and touches it to a finger. These tactile sensations give him some little aspect of physical dimension in the complete darkness, the total silence.

There is no other sensory input coming to him. No pressure anywhere on his back or either side as if he were lying down, on his feet, were he is standing, or anywhere else, were he somehow suspended. His face and one arm only. And neither his arm or his hair seem to fall one way or the other to give him any knowledge of his position.

Suddenly he surprises himself by calling out. "Aaaah." He told himself to call out, yet he was surprised by the sound of it when he did. Clear and loud the voice left him, but it did not return. He tries it again, "George!" and then he is listening carefully, noting there is no reverberation, the sound manifests and then it is gone.

He thinks, *am I vertical or horizontal?* and then, *compared to what?*
He assumes he is alive because he is breathing. "Is that the test? Does one who is dead not breathe? Does one who is dead think? Like this?
Is there no wisdom in death?

He exists now in the darkness. He is aware of himself existing. He has the odd thought that maybe God existed like this, without dimension or form or company, and so decided to create.

If I were God, what would I create first? What would I create at all? He is toying with the idea, existing in the darkness. In the void.

He becomes aware that he is not alone. His face burns in sudden panic. There is now *such* an ominous presence. All too familiar, yet utterly unknown. Surrounded by fear, he becomes absorbed in fear. He feels the hot breath of fear—the cold chill of fear. He remembers with increasing alarm that there is no dimension in fear. There is no relation to anything known in fear. There is no help.

With nowhere to go, fear is the substance of a boy's creation. All of the horrors of the hells exist and live. The light does not make them go away or show them to be only phantoms of the imagination. Horrors committed to the mother, committed to the son. Those protectors of children, they are the horrors of the children. With demands and curses, sharp instruments and dull instruments, and ugly parts of themselves and ugly parts of you. And the horrible tooth and the horrible claw. And the preaching of God and the rules so hard and the punishment, regardless of the obeying or not obeying. Oh God, you horror! You beast. You *murderer*.

The tears are running down his cheeks and they bring some little softness to him in his fear. And he realizes, the tears are running down his face to his neck. And he thinks of perspective, of relation. The tears stream down his face. He must be vertical, in relation to something.

Hope. He knows how fickle is this thing called hope. He mistrusts it. Very much mistrusts it. But just like the slave who is driven here and then driven there at the will of his cruel master, he acts. Just as he must react hopelessly to the fear, he must also react helplessly to the hope. Even if, especially if, it is only a tool, an instrument, of the fear, only so slightly abated.

And he imagines that in the distance, provided there is a distance, that in the distance he sees a light, and it is soft and white and very faint. But it is something, real or imagined, to look at in the utter darkness.

After a time the light strengthens a little. Or the imagination strengthens a little. How does it matter, suspended here? And he hears the faint rhythm of a drum as if from miles in the distance. He puts his attention on that light and looks and he listens and as he does, the horrors of his mind begin to gradually diminish, and his fear is slowly subdued. He is long in his looking and his listening, though he has no consciousness of how long.

When the light draws nearer he sees, somehow, that it was perhaps never far off after all. Out of the light and out of the sound of the drum come the deep and pure strains of some ethereal cello in expression of utter melancholy. And as that comes forth he begins to imagine that the light is looking at him, even as he is looking at the light. After awhile he begins to see what appears to be the white beard of a man and after a little while longer, he comes to recognize that beard, that face, as the source of the light. Gazing at that self-luminescent face, though it is not entirely clear, and listening to the most sweet sadness from the strings, he becomes conscious of a compassion. It is as if he is aware of the suffering of all existence at that moment. He can see the face more clearly now and in the eyes of the face, he is witness to an empathy with all things.

But after a time incalculable, the light begins to fade until he can no longer make out the face or the beard of light and the sound retreats to, once again, a distant drum, and then, in that state of loss and anxiety, his heart breaks.

***

When he awakes he finds himself lying in a bed, his upper body elevated, in some kind of small and noisy room, instruments beeping, people talking and laughing, which he soon recognizes as coming from a television program, the recognition of which comes just before he realizes he's in a hospital room. What has awakened him is physical pain.

When the nurse comes in he is informed about his having had heart surgery. When he asks about his arm, she tells him that he was hit by a car. "Where was I when all of this happened?" "Only you can answer that, I guess," she tells him, smiling, changing the bag of fluids containing his pain medication, electrolytes, etc.

***

When he wakes again he is being arrested. There are several people in the room standing around his bed, talking loudly. Most of them seem to be men but there is also a woman who seems to be arguing with the men. She is telling them they cannot just barge in and disturb her patient like this, but they seem to be ignoring her as they speak roughly to him. He concludes that it is nighttime. Then it seems as if one of the men is reading him his rights, he is informed that his room will be under federal occupation, and he is under house arrest.

***

Within the same week he is released by the hospital and received by the Hennington County Jail, where he is to be held until his trial. That turns out to be a period of eleven months. He learns from his court appointed lawyer that he apparently broke through the glass doors of a Federal Building and vandalized an office there, miraculously avoiding the law enforcement units that arrived within five minutes of the building's alarm call. To top that off, when he fell into the street the morning following the break in, there was a four-car collision directly related to his fall. Fortunately, no one was seriously injured, other than George himself. During the first two weeks of his stay at the jail, he is examined daily by the medical staff and given what treatment and medication determined by them as appropriate for his recovery. He is allowed a cell with only one cellmate. At the end of those two weeks, his medical attention is reduced to once per week and he is put in a cell with three other men.

***

At his trial the judge makes it clear to him that, although he has been diagnosed with paranoid schizophrenia, further complicated with symptoms of severe manic depression, aka bipolar disease, (all of which is surprising news to him, he was not aware of having undergone any psychiatric evaluation) he, being a danger to society as well as to himself, and for the multiple and habitual crime of reckless endangerment, as well as destruction of federal property, will be confined to the Wade Federal Correctional Institute; specifically to the mental ward of that institution for a period of five years, the sentence to be evaluated annually after the completion of the first two years.

head in the clouds

"When the fog rolls in we sit up here above the clouds with only the other skyscrapers. The city disappears completely. I've been up on the roof in the fog like that more'n once. It would be beautiful, but--you know--it just increases the feeling of how we're separated from everthing. All these odd boxes floating on fluff, completely isolated from one another. Once in awhile you can see some tiny people out on one of the other roofs or maybe on a balcony, but we're not allowed any binoculars or anything so they look more like bugs than people.

We had a fellow here who was into bugs, but he died a couple of years ago. He'd been a bug scientist on the outside. He told me he was respected as a bug scientist. It was interesting listening to him. It seems that when you love something, it's interesting. Like George says about the attention. That's the problem with most of us here, though. We have very little control over our attention. Myself, I'll be focused on something, really into it, ya know and then, wham! I'm in another place altogether."

"Where are you then?" Ansel says.

"I expect you'd have to axe me that when I'm there, wherever the hell it is."

"Sorry, I guess it wasn't such a good question."

"Naw, it's alright. Besides, I guess that's with everbody that they drift off, but I assume it's a little more subtle, wouldn't that be right, Ansel?"

"I'd say you're about right, Horatio."

"It's worse with some of us. Of course there's the drugs, but then it's the land of the zombies, you know? But when George talks, he gets my attention. Don't know what it is. I don't even know if he knows what it is. He talks like a crazy man and we listen. Go figure, man. We could listen to 'im all day. Well, maybe that's a stretch. I guess he don't really talk so very long.

You know, I guess right now I shore got off the track. I was talking about the fog. I meant to say how it's all about point a view.

"Horatio pauses for a little bit and seems distracted, so Ansel attempts to bring him back on topic.

"I'm not sure I follow you Horatio—about the fog and point of view."

"Oh, I'm sorry. I was just thinking about something, happened a long time ago. Oh yeah, point a view. Well we might have philosopher's names, you know, but I guess things'd be in a sorry state if we were the philosophers of the world for real."

"Things appear to *be* in a pretty sorry state to me."

"Oh well, I reckon you're a philosopher too, then, my man, welcome to the club."

"Thanks, are there dues to pay?"

"Hell, you can't afford the dues. Nobody can afford the dues," Horatio says with a soft laugh.

"I suppose I can't then," Ansel replies, smiling along with Horatio's laugh.

Horatio is in a pretty good mood, Ansel thinks to himself. But then he's almost always in a pretty good mood. But he wants to know, so he asks; says, "I hate to keep bringing it up, Horatio, but what about the fog and point of view?"

"Oh ya, that. Well, the way I see it is pretty simple. I mean when you're in the fog, it's disorienting; it's a little bit eerie. You know what I mean?"

Ansel nods.

"When the fog is above you or below you, it's called clouds. Then they're kind of romantic, sometimes beautiful, sometimes awesome and even threatening. Often inspiring."

Then Horatio goes into another lengthy pause. Ansel is trying his best to be patient, but he wonders where this thing is going. Finally he says, "Horatio?"

"Yes?"

"Where are you going with this fog and point of view thing, if you don't mind my asking?"

Horatio smiles at him. Finally he says, "I don't know. I guess I ain't never known two men in the fog to have the same point a view."

He doesn't say any more.

"Oh," says Ansel.

"It ain't much of a philosophy, huh?"

"I have to think about it."

"It's the only one I got though."

"Alright," Ansel says.

"Alright," Horatio says.

"Thanks" Ansel says.

"You're welcome," says Horatio.

ancestors of children of ancestors
a poem

From the tops of these once verdant hills
I witnessed the works of a great species
their barefoot running paths through the forest
their marks and their recognitions and their challenges.
Colorful and gaily attired
clever in hiding
clever in pursuit
brilliant in display.
Social, generous, brave, honest, connected
reverent of life, grateful unto death
humble and majestic.
Fierce, cunning, deadly
they wear the clothes of their prey.
Creators of art,
believers of destiny
hearers of voices
seers of visions,
Ever adaptable
ancestors of children of ancestors.

I turn my face to the great star of fire
I turn to the pale moon of relief
and even the strong beasts have come under their spells
and even the ancient towers of the forest fall down at their feet
and come up round them
and protect them
and shelter them from the terrible winds.
And the food of life grows where they will it
they kill to protect it
to hoard it.
Harnessing dog and ox and horse and fire
and even the wind upon the waters
and even their enemy's wives and daughters.
Wanderers and fearsome travelers abound
Wagon wheels and boot heels all o'er the ground
roads ongoing
and bridges across.
Fruitful
Multiplying
ancestors of children of ancestors

I hear the great bell, celestial wonder in tolling
the pulse of the drum, eternal, thunderous, rolling.
My job is the watching from these heavens
These stony pinnacle retreats
now I must be ascending
relinquishing the hills to the retreat of others
lion, wolf, and bear
the herds and the flocks come there
to avoid the clamor, the noise of things unsettlin
engines roarin, horns ablowin, guns ablazin
hordes aclashin, blood's aspillin.
Steel shines and cuts and stretches across the plain
wheels that whine and saw and rumble
black highways upon which their hooves will stumble
great beasts of metal come hurtling down
crashing, slashing at everything around.
Even mountains tremble with explosions
the whales are pulled right out of the oceans.
They pile their stuff up to the sky
they even get into things that fly
they've forgot about things that live and die.

invasive
predatory
ancestors of children of ancestors

I've had to forgo this un-heavenly body
it was all used up, too frail and shoddy
and looking out from behind this veil of illusion
I don't understand, I'm beset by confusion
Afraid of what I see
There's no place left of good earthly stuff for me to be
Poisoned and blackened
The mountains broke and flattened
The sea's so high and churnin
and mostly empty
The forest so low and burnin.
There's just too many
Too many roads
Too many bridges
Too many wheels
Too many ditches
Too many ships
Too many wings
Too many metals
Too many plastics
Too many chemicals
Too many things
Too many man made materials
Too many winners
Too many wanters
Too many hooks and ladders
Too many almighty dollars
Too many sex parlors
Too many laws
Too many lawyers
Too many scientific theories
Too many made for television series
Too many doctors
Too many diagnoses
Too many neuroses
Too many psychoses
Too many drugs
Too many thugs
Too many intellectuals

Too many leaders
Too many goin down the highway speeders
Too many false prophets
Too many entertainments
Too many false profits
Too many shady arrangements
Too many computers
Too many viruses
Too many pirateses
Too many guns
Too many dead
Too many lies up in the head
There's just Too goddamned many people
the ancestors of children of ancestors

FOUR: George tells the inmates that they have an unfair advantage

If the mystical truth that comes to a man proves to be a force that he can live by, what mandate have we of the majority to order him to live in another way? We can throw him into a prison or madhouse, but we cannot change his mind...
—William James   in The Varieties of Religious Experience

A mother has to prattle like a baby to make her baby understand her.
—Sawan Singh

Ozwald and the philosopher

All three members of this somewhat avant-garde research team have been observing a surprising aspect of the project, regarding the level of eloquence of many of the patient/inmates. Although there are certainly those who appear to be veritable bundles of inhibition, there is a tendency among many to be uninhibited in many ways. Whether this lack of inhibition is due to a consciousness of 'What have I got to lose?' or a genuine lack of concern for the opinions of others, or even a complete lack of objectivity regarding the perceptions of others, is obviously a complex and perhaps inexact analysis. The fact is some of these seemingly broken and captive spirits speak with, not only a poetical flair, but also in a genuinely thoughtful and insightful manner.

Ozwald's conversation with Carol J., who is serving a six-year sentence for two separate counts of assaulting police officers for no apparent reason, is a case in point. Hearsay has it that Horatio, in his good-natured humor, once called Carol J., *Confucius*, because of his propensity for "philosophizing", but it almost immediately became *Confuse Us* to the general population. That notwithstanding, Ozwald has already recognized Confuse Us's ability to express himself from a bit of previous association with him.

***

"If you were to write a biography of yourself, Carol J., what would be the main focus or the slant of it," Ozwald asks.

"Well, first of all, I'd never write a book, especially one about myself."

"Why?"

"Because I haven't the attention span for it. I may have the endurance for it, but not the attention. I suppose that is because I have no interest in any of the forms of this society, neither in its art nor its science, nor its history, nor any other function or pursuit or endeavor of it. I've never read a book."

"Never?"

"*Never*. Not in any existence that I'm aware of."

"You seem well educated."

"Education is a very relative term, is it not? Like intelligence. Like luck."

Ozwald then asks him if he would, nevertheless, mind telling something about himself, if only in a very brief manner.

"I will tell you that I am a being with no connection to my current physical existence. I live in the distant past, though I inhabit this foreign body."

Then Carol J. does a thing that seems a direct contradiction of what he has just said regarding art forms.

"If you'll excuse me for a minute I'll go to my quarters and get something that may address the topic of which you inquire."

Ozwald agrees and when Carol J. returns he has a piece of paper. He lays it on the table before him, smoothes it out with great care, and begins to read.

"My mind is a rock face descending into dark water. There are so many colors, but they are of subtle differences. Ancient shapes of intelligence, deep and terrible are manifest in the pools far below. They look up into my existence as if in recognition, and though I would disown them, I cannot. Beasts, fantastic beyond the imagination, form the incarnations of my past. Great cascades of thundering white water fall off the edges of my sanity, crashing down over the layers upon layers of black rock and pound upon these creatures of the depths of me, but to no avail. They are unassailable. They are as invincible as the present.

"The eyes of great intelligence are akin to the eyes of ignorant violence. Petrified ghosts, they look at me, with their great heads above the water, peering through the gray mist, and I am always lost in their gazing. The profound eye of the Narwhal and the Sperm, the porpoise and the turtle, the cold blunt eye of the shark, the shy hypnotic glances of the dragon and the ray and the squid, and the crazed absurdity of the piranha and the barracuda.

"In your world, there are some souls that fly around in the air, others run over the plain or dwell in the forest or in the mountains, or even in the frozen places of ice and snow. In any case there is light in balance with darkness. But in my world it is only the old and the deep, though I apparently share this space with you."

Here he stops. He is looking around nervously. Then he leans over and whispers his question, as if he is putting his trust in the young man, just as one would take a therapist into his confidence.

"What do you think I am, dear Ozwald? Only a man with a mental disorder? That is the simplistic diagnosis, born of ignorance and self preservation by these foolish children that are called doctors."

Ozwald has no answer, only shakes his head.

"So, in lieu of other competence, I diagnose myself. And although my approach is quite divergent, it at least addresses my experience. I cannot accept that I am man, disturbed or otherwise."

"It is very troubling to me to think, 'Am I only a link of evolution, not really one thing, but also not another?', but that is the possibility that I entertain. 'Could I be an experiment of cruel, mindless nature? Or am I simply an aberration, a defective product of the creator that, because of his having had something else in mind, was rejected and thrown into this bin of rejects?'"

Ozwald still doesn't answer, so Carol J. goes on.

"Some say the world is altogether insane. But if it is so, it seems that most of the created have one saving grace, namely the blissful ignorance born of familiarity. They belong to a species."

"I've read that the eastern mystics claim there are eight million, four hundred thousand species in creation, at any given time. Surely you could be one of them if, as you say, you are not one of us?"

"Maybe so. Maybe so. But I'm afraid I'm a species of one."

He looks around the hall and invites Ozwald to do the same with the sweep of his arm.

"Indeed some of *these* do appear to be exceptions of the human race, at best, dear Ozwald. I think that many of the others here share only that fate with me. Perhaps we have fallen between the cracks in the creator's design."

"It would take a liberal conception of a creator, to allow for such error." Ozwald says, but immediately realizes the narrowness of his statement. "But I suppose it's a fairly common concept after all."

Carol J. only raises his eyebrows, tips his head forward, and stares at the young man as if in disbelief. Ozwald assumes he has been judged stupid or naïve and can only wait to hear what comes next. But his concern is for naught, as the fellow responds seriously to the idea.

"It's true, in one sense, that the idea of a God who makes mistakes is no idea of God at all."

"So are you saying that if there's a God, there is a reason for everything," Ozwald asks, somehow relieved to not be thought quite stupid after all.

The philosopher/patient/inmate leans back, runs his hands through his hair, inhales and exhales deeply, shakes his head slowly. "Well, after all, these are just thoughts, young fellow. I don't place a lot of stock in them. Do you?"

Ozwald is a little taken back with that. He just sits for a minute looking down at the table, looking at his hands on his notebook, next to his recorder. Finally, he looks up at Carol J. who is looking out across the room. He decides that maybe he *was* taking the conversation too seriously. He tells Carol J. as much. Gets no noticeable response.

Then he says to him, "Carol J., you're not saying that the things you just told me were just passing thoughts?"

Carol J. looks at him. "Could you believe me any less if I told you they *were* only passing thoughts?"

"Well, yes. I could believe you less," Ozwald says after a moment of reflection.

"Oh really?"

"Yes"

Carol J. looks out across the room again. It occurs to Ozwald to ask him if he is bothered that some of the others call him Confuse Us.

"They're men, after all, dear Ozwald."

Ozwald isn't quite sure what he means by that, but he doesn't say so. Instead he says, "If you are really a non-species, I guess others could care about you anyway."

"I could give a flying fuck," says Confuse Us, looking out across the room. And with that the philosopher/poet, in denial/ornery old cuss, refuses to even look at his interviewer again.

Ozwald gets up and walks out from between the tables, toward the service elevator. The guard is smiling at him as he approaches.

"How was your chat with ol' Confuse Us, Ozwald?"

"I could give a flying fuck," says Ozwald.

he doesn't has no mahners
a poem

he doesn't has no mahners
   he sits in the middle
      he makes mountains out of drivel
when the world awakens there's a sound
   it's the sound of him approaching
      it's the sound of him encroaching

he doesn't has no mahners
   he's a trouble with time

his, a philosophy sublime
on the teetering edge he suspended
these days from a gossamer thread
he plays like a philosopher in dread

he doesn't has no mahners
when they raise the curtain
oh, he's a player certain
he's so fine, he's so pretty pretty
got his big teeth well hid, he does
but underneath, what he is, not what he was

these are the chapters, these are the pages
first come the actors, then come the sages
it's all a great mystery played out in time
shrouded and whispery secrets and rhyme
poets, philosophers, pundits and fools
teachers and preachers and judges and rules
elephants, monkeys, lions, and snakes
scientists who make no mistakes
this way and that way and all roads the same
coming and going and back again

Oh bad world, oh bitter land
world without an honest man
inheritance of disease and death
in and out the acrid breath

From the hill I saw the teeming masses
men like beasts in the misty poison gases
all condemning one the other
You ain't my kin—you're not my brother
You're a karmi son of a bitch
You're a sheep led into the ditch
and a trillion other useless curses
and empty bowls and big fat purses
no end, no end to such examples
faithless love and tainted samples

he doesn't has no mahners
even with the children seeing
even with the enemy fleeing
run them down and slay them cruelly

like toys for his own satisfaction
like boys who crave such constant action

message of George – V
~ An Unfair Advantage ~

"We have an unfair advantage over the people outside, when it comes to matters of the spirit, my friends. There's a saying, 'Spirit speaks to spirit.' and that's good for us in a couple'a ways. We don't take as much convincing about the reality of things of the spirit, now do we?" he says with a wink and a smile. *"But even more important, we got a whole lot less to lose. You can't very well get free when you won't let go of all you got."*

Ahmed the doctor

"There's no reason why I can't have my medical kit. I could help, but they deprive me of everything. Psychiatry? I have no interest in their so-called psychiatry. But people hurt themselves regularly here and get no attention, whatsoever. Yes, yes, but I am not a fool to let them steal my instruments. Or at least I could have a small room. Even a cellar room. They get no attention and they suffer greatly, many of them."

He sits down at the table, puts his head in his hands, fretting. Then he shakes his head sorrowfully.

"Often the soldiers interrogate. They wear the metal plates on their faces and in their hands they hold the tools of their trade. Only when the planes fly low do they repair to their caves and leave us in peace for a few days. And the women, I'm afraid they've exterminated the women. There are no women.

"I am going to ask him. Yes, I'm going to ask him. Have you seen him? The beautiful one. Please ask him for me if you see him. Ask him to come and help us. I'm afraid for all the women and I'm afraid for myself too. I am ashamed to say it but I am. When he comes I am not afraid. He is tall as a mountain and strong, so that no one can stand against him. And his voice is melodious with the expressive qualities of the Nay but also it carries the power and the rhythm of the Tabl. His face is attractive and his beard is long and flowing, as pure as the mountain snow.

"Now you must take our plight to him. We cannot hold out much longer here. We are poor people and have not the weapons. If only they would give me back my kit, I could help. I could be of some service. They seem to think me a fool."

dead man
Ansel

There's a man in a bed in a room who is severely emaciated. His appearance is that of a grey skin of dry leather covering a skeleton. He cannot be persuaded or coerced to eat by any means so far attempted. He is attached permanently to an intravenous feeding apparatus and that is the only source of nutrition he receives. I have been informed that he has been incarcerated here for three years, at least half of which has been spent in solitary confinement and the other half on forty one.

Miraculously he is able and willing to speak, albeit in a rather pinched and frail voice, so I sit down with him and I am able to conduct a rather engaging interview with him.

***

"When I was in my twenties, a friend and I drove up into the mountains after eating some orange sunshine. We were fairly sensitive and aware guys for our time, I think. Considered ourselves, rather flatteringly now, I believe, seekers after truth. This friend of mine had more education than I did. Could generally express himself better in a conversation. But I was an artist, a musician, a writer. Expressed myself that way. But like so many of our time, we were naïve enough, gullible enough, to look for our knowledge in some damned dangerous places. Places like little tiny orange barrels, that came from who in the hell knows what or where. We stopped at a place near the ski slopes and had a couple a beers. It was getting to be dusk and we were in those spaced out early stages where it's like anxiety and speedy energy, but you're not really trippin yet. We started driving through the pass. Not really going anywhere, just checkin' out the view. Just drivin'. I was driving, but I remember telling him at one point that the road was going right into the mountain, or some such nonsense, and we both agreed I should pull over. I was hesitant to just sit there, worrying about cops, you know, but I really couldn't do much else. And wouldn't you know it, before long, there's one pulls up right behind us, lights a'doin that wacko thing they do, blindin' everybody in sight and makin' a goddam spectacle out of themselves and whoever or whatever they're dealin' with. So, I tell my friend, 'I can't talk to him. He'll know I'm a raving lunatic and haul me off to the friggin nut house.' So my friend says he'll talk to 'im. And I don't know how that worked, because they never let you get out of your car, you know, but that's what he did and he talked to that cop outside. I don't know what he told him, but he left us alone, and we sat there. We sat there and we talked."

The man is obviously tired from talking so much. He shuts his eyes and for that time, looks for all the world as if he has left his body. But after a while he opens his eyes, which make contact with me and then he goes on.

"There's a point, and I remember my friend even marveling that I was brilliant in my observations that night, which was really the acid talking on his part, I have no doubt, but there's a point where you think so damned much and so hard and it all comes to nothing because there's a flip side to every thought you can have that makes just as much sense on the level of the intellect. It's one thing to say that or even to realize that, my friend, but it's quite another to be existing at that place with the core of you there and it's like a balloon that's blown up too damn far and it might make it, but if there's any little blemish, the tiniest flaw," he puts his leather thumb and his leather index finger together and makes the softest little snap.

"Sometimes I think a strong person holds on out of sheer will, while a weak person gives up. Goes over. Or you could say, 'Goes under.' I know it's a sorry weakness. I never could bring myself up to take another breath of life. I floated down. And down to the bottom. And after a few unsuccessful attempts at resuscitation they let me be. I been dead for a long time. I like it. It's all I want."

After awhile I asked him if he could remember what they had talked about that night.

"We didn't talk small talk. Sometimes big things are on your mind, you know, but you talk about small things. Seems like the right thing. To talk about big things makes 'em seem small, right? At least it makes the talker seem small."

His breath is labored here and he rests again for a little bit until it calms. Then he starts again, somewhat slower now.

"But there's other times when you're in it that far and somebody's in it with you, small talk can't even get there. So what do you talk about?"

He pauses. I wait. Then it occurs to me, "You're asking me?"

He gives me one of those flat, straight-lipped, squint-eyed, non-smiles that says, *Yes, What did you think?*

"I don't know. I don't know what you talk about."

"You talk about death. What else is there in life to talk about? Small talk or death."

"What about your families, your wife or children, or the beauty of the natural world or ways to help people or do good, or, what about God? Talking about God or no God. That kind of stuff. Not small talk." I give him the flat, straight-lipped, squint-eyed thing at that point because I've got him.

He takes kind of a big sigh. Especially for such a shallow breather. "I suppose you're right, Ansel. Who am I to argue with a psychology educated fella like you? I'm a dead man and you're living. Living a full young life. Got a family, good friends; after your stint here you'll land a great job, maybe get married, travel, you name it."

I don't know where this crazy dead guy is going with this, but I somehow have the slightest tremor in my confidence as he goes on.

"I'm sure you'll have many great and stimulating important conversations in your life with your colleagues and all your important connections. The merits of this and the problems with that. Whether 'tis nobler to save the planet or to save your soul, and then the souls of others.

"Yes, what about God? What about God? Let's see—the planet. Save it from what, Ansel? And your soul, should you decide to have one— and then to save it. Do you mean save it, like in a piggy-bank? No, you mean save it, from *what?*"

I don't know if he's just being dramatic or what, but his voice is just a dry crackling whisper now.

"God," he says. "We have to deal with God, don't we? Okay, Ansel, you talk about God. I'm a lost soul. I don't know what to talk about God. The God created the life which is the process of death. I've always seen God as the harbinger of Death. So you tell me."

I feel that on some level he really wants me to tell him. But I'm at a loss. He's right, everything has a flip side. So I let go of it.

Then I ask him, "What about George? Have you talked to George about God—or anything?"

"George doesn't have the time of day for me," he says in a way that strikes me as very bitter.

"Besides, that's the last thing I need is some fucking nut case guru to represent me to God. I'd sooner hire some two bit lawyer from Market Street to do the job."

"He's made quite an impression on a lot of people around here," I tell him.

"Yeah, so'd Jim Jones impress a lot a people. So'd Elvis."

"He's made an impression on me," I suddenly admit.

"I ain't easily impressed, no more."

"No; I see you're not."

I get up. "I appreciate the interview."

"Yuh"

Before I turn to leave he closes his paper eyelids. He's an unwrapped mummy by all appearances. But as I am going out the door he has something more to say.

"Ansel."

"Yes"

"Do you know what I'm in for?"

I confess that I don't.

"I shot an FBI agent."

I wait in the doorway to see if there's more.

"The son of a bitch thought he was God."

I ask the dead man if he is being facetious. He asks me what I mean. I ask him if he really meant to compare an arrogant cop to George. He tells me the cop wasn't arrogant; that he really thought he was God. He told the dead man as much. He tells me the cop was already a dead man. He just didn't know it.

"I sent him to hell. He's interred at the County Hospital. Lays there in a bed like me. Doesn't know who he is, they say. Well, anyway, if he still thinks he's God he don't say. I shot 'im in the throat."

like bones
a poem

we lay like scattered bones on the floor of her lair, mother earth
some broken, splintered things, white against the dirt
the pain is gone
most of the flesh is gone
concern is gone
There's something left undone
some faraway fear, the faintest line, a distant tease of a nerve
worried red
        irritation

some birds come down when she is out
they walk around and peck at us and quarrel about
they fly into panic when she comes padding back in
some frayed threads still bind us here like sin
like an old desire's song?
the pain is gone
memory's gone
concern is gone
did someone forget about us?
maybe start something and forget what it was?

first comes light and then comes darkness
put us together and tear us apartness
the clouds go by and we stay put
with the rubble under the mountain's foot
no sense of time though I suppose it passes
we lay like bones among the masses

which came first, love or song
wear away is a prayer so long
the pain is gone
fear is gone
concern is gone
she who felled us lies among us, and he who felled her too
time will tell and makes a promise, and time is a lover all untrue

FIVE: The sad story of a lady from West Virginia

If he had ever been anything else, weak or sentimental or loving or kind, there was no trace left now, no trace at all.
— Howard Fast from The American

Horatio the troubleshooter

"The new *head* doc must be some kinda music 'ficionado 'cause we been goin' over this Guthrie Library a Congress all morning. Seems like some kinda differ'n't Christmas to me, but I guess it's better'n them Santa's Comin to Town crap we useta get treated to. Only thing is, if ya ask me that Guthrie is a sort of rabble rouser. Course, nobody seemin' to get too riled up, I guess.

"I useta work for the docs, you know. At the other place, before I come here. They treated me alright an' I helped 'em out by kinda lookin' out for trouble, I guess you could say. Sometimes a fair amount of trouble was averted, I believe, because a my payin' 'tention. But here they're careful not to set nobody against nobody. So my job's been phased out."

Ozwald in West Virginia with Ella

"It was forty-five degrees Fahrenheit the night he died. Well, it was morning, really. Somewhere's between two and five a.m. I'd guess. It was the hypothermia got 'im. I found him in the front yard no more'n ten feet from the porch when I went out to do the morning chores. He lay there all curled up, like in the fetal position, just a cold lump of flesh. Whatever was the man that was in 'im had flew off some bit of time before I got there. Funny thing a person could chill up like that, all full a alcohol. Too drunk to come on in, he just lay there until his body quit runnin', I'd say. Well he generally had been throwin' it all down the tube from the first, ya know. He was a sweet lover man but he waran't no other use to me and George 'cept to worry us. Oh, he didn' get up after us like some men of the bottle, though; I suppose we got that to be thankful for. Later on, I'd pine sorrowly to have that man back.

"After him, I was stupid enough. Got me a man a the cloth. Thought I'd go thataway. Now that'n was mean. He was strict with George. Goddam strict, if you take what I'm gittin at. Caught 'im of a morning fooling with hisself one time, at least he accused him of it, an he shamed poor little George as if he was the worst boy ever to of done it. That's how he did at first. He hurt ya with words. Big high an mighty words of the Lord they was supposed to be, but they sounded as much like they was from the lord of hell to me. Later on he took to the tortures of the flesh. Hung 'im up by 'is ankles from the ceiling joist one time, naked, to hang there all morning. Dragged 'im out a bed in a fit. Poor Georgie cryin' and carryin' on seemed to please the devil. I tried to get 'im down but he prevented me. Had 'is way with me on the table right there in front of George with him hangin' there like that. Used to more less rape me whenever he felt up to it, then put the shame on me. Sometimes right on a Sunday morn before draggin' us off to the church so's he could preach the sermon of righteousness.

"Three years of that and I finally got Verna, my only neighbor friend, to help me and we run out. We hit the road and never did stop til we made Chicago. Even then, with two states between us, I was scared they wasn' enough, but he never found us. Truth is, it was too late for us, though. I was not pretty no more and couldn' get no help or break from nobody outside the mission. In my misery I took to sellin' myself to poor men for what little I could get. And Georgie, he was already gone. All up inside 'imself he was. And when he would let any out he was wild and embarrassing to hisself. My poor George. Them men and me, we ruin't 'im. When he started to come at me with hammers and scissors and such implements I had to turn 'im over to the ward. I figure I'm goin' to hell. But then I also figure, how much worse can it be?"

"He's not the same George now, Ella. He's risen above all of that," Ozwald tells her.

"I've heard the rumors, but I been too ashamed to ever git up there to see 'im."

friend of a friend
Jeff

I noticed that somebody had been coming regularly to visit Ahmed. One day, I got permission to go out to the visiting room. His visitor was a tall black man, maybe in his late fifties. Looked like they were good friends. After their visit, I approached the man and explained briefly who I was, asked if I could ask him a few questions about their relationship. He said he had to run, but the next time he came, which he told me was every Thursday, he would allow some time for it. I asked his name and he told me it was Stook. I took him up on the offer of next time, and when the next Thursday came around Stook proved good to his word.

The following is a transcription of our recorded conversation, from that same Thursday, after his visit with Ahmed:

***

Stook began, "You see, it's very bad for him to be here. He is not bad. He may be mad, well he is mad of course, but he is not bad."

"I suppose they can't allow people to practice without a license though," I said in some kind of half-hearted defense of the system.

"Maybe not, but there's them with licenses out there that ought more to be in here than that good doctor. I mean, he was a, he was actually a very knowledgeable and competent holistic type doctor. He just didn't believe in the licensing system."

"I didn't know any of that. I'll have to accept your opinion on his merits as a doctor. They'll never let him have a chance at it again, of course."

"Well he ain't the same no more."

"Can you share anything of your friendship with him? Has he been delusional as long as you knew him?"

"Oh no. No, no. I suppose there were some signs. But God, he could say the same about me, I know.

"There was this group we had. We had all been medics. Different wars. Same job. Who else could we talk to? Who else could have a clue? Most of us were about the same age but there were a couple of guys from the old wars. It was old Sal brought us together. Sal and Bony had been part of a group for a long time. But they were dyin' off, ya know; their pals, I mean. Never even did know how they got started, but anyway, Sal reached out to us and pulled us together. In time we became, not only fond of each other, but, I'd say, quite dependent upon each other."

We were sitting in the sterile little room where visitors wait to be called for their visits with the inmates. Stook was sitting back with his long legs out in front of him, kind of slouching onto his elbow on the right side wooden arm of his chair. His thumb braced against his temple, he rubbed his forehead with the tips of his fingers as he said, "The details that mark the true character of a man are the details that most people don't see. Only a brother that's been there might see some of that. We'd been gettin' together for about, oh, say three years when Ahmed first came to the group. I liked him; thought he was a interesting guy. His family came from the old country. We learned some stuff from him. But it was a funny thing. Sal was prejudiced against 'im. Only on account of his being Islamic. Never saw that from Sal before. And Sal's pretty sharp. So I 's'pose his opinion affected some other people's opinions. But for me, if anything, I reacted against it, and Ahmed and I became pretty damn close. We hung out outside of the group. Went to the movies and stuff."

"He didn't exhibit any signs of mental illness at that point?" I asked.

"There wasn't a one of us that didn't exhibit any signs of mental illness. Truth be told, it's only the difference of a missed turn or a detour here or there that gets a man off the main road anyway, the way I see it. And often as not it's them that always look to see the best in everybody, that get broke down when all they really see is the worst."

"Ahmed was one of those that looked for the best?"

"Yes he was."

"I'm sorry. It's just that he seems kind of cynical now," I explained.

"Well, I guess he ain't responsible for that no more, now."

"I think I agree with you that he's not," I said, then, thinking about it more, I added, "When I think about it, I guess cynical is the wrong word. I imagine he's just frustrated."

"I guess he's all the way back in it, huh?" Stook said.

"You mean the war?"

"Yeah"

"Seems to be. But there's a bright spot."

To which Stook said, "Yeah? What's that?"

"He's been inspired by a kind of holy man."

"No kiddin."

"No kiddin."

"In the joint? He's done told me about that plenty, but I figured it was just his imagination. Damn, it's for real."

"Yes. There's a man here, a patient, an inmate who seems to inspire many of the others."

"And you too, I guess."

"I'm just telling you about it," I told him.

"Well, I guess that's alright. I wouldn't expect Ahmed to be gullible, that's one thing, even like he is. So maybe there's something really is special about the man. Some Indian guy or what?"

"No, he's Caucasian."

Stook said firmly, "Well, I won't judge him."

"Ahmed gave me that opinion about you."

"That's my man, Ahmed."

I didn't say anything to that, and then Stook asked, "Does he say anything else about me?"

"He has you in the war with him."

"I suppose he does. That's okay, too. I still got the war in me. Listen Jeff, I'm supposed to meet somebody. Hope you got what you needed."

"Yes," I said, then added, "Now that I've met you, I at least know one of the characters in Ahmed's war life."

"Funny though, we were in different wars. We only met as civilians."

"Well, you're important to him. I'm sure that's why you're in there."

"Thanks. It's good to see it ain't all bad for him."

"I'll tell him."
"I'll hold you to it."
"Okay"

Wary
a song

 A little bit of medicine
come on you wary one
let somebody help
you been through bloody hell too

The circumstances aren't clear
we know you had to bury one
child of God in you
we'd all but forgotten you too

          In the sky there's a ball of fire
          but it's cool and shady in the forest deep
            All of the animals have to retire;
          a careful sigh and then give in to sleep

"Please say what you've come to say
everywhere is enemy
i don't have time to think
i think I'm the missing link too

You wish that you could help me see
but you know it was meant to be;
too much government
an you don't know what we went through"

          In the sky there's a ball of fire
          but it's cool and shady in the forest deep
            All of the animals have to retire;
          a careful sigh and then give in to sleep

"You find me neath this lonely sun
so who knows where i can run?
up on some windy peak
or down to some troubled sea too"

Your mother called me on the phone, said

"Tell him, my only one,
'I know you're in good hands
off in those foreign lands of you' "

SIX: George Moonlighting

… Night had fallen. I dropped my tools. What did I care about my hammer, about my bolt, about thirst and death? There was, on one star, on one planet, on mine, the Earth, a little prince to be consoled! I took him in my arms. I rocked him. I told him, "The flower you love is not in danger… I'll draw you a muzzle for your sheep… I'll draw you a fence for your flower…"
—Antoine de Saint-Exupery (narrator) in The Little Prince

the beholder

There's a face in a small window, high up in a small gable of a very large house. The right side upper corner of the forehead resting on the pane, the lower and left portions of the glass clouding over in a crescent of fog and then clearing, in concert with the breathing, against the outer early morning cold. The eyes in the face are casting their gaze out across the distance. And what returns to the eyes of the beholder?

There is a storm portending at the horizon. There are a few subtle streaks of grey laid against the pale blue depth of the inverted sea, wherein small birds swim in apparent "waters of oblivion" and delight. The tops of the trees are the floor of her perspective, their dense, feathery tufts providing shelter and protection for small creatures from those silent gliders, angels of death, of the open waters. Shining little silver fish go by afar, shooting out white stuff streamers behind. They play at their painting, going up and away and then crossing and turning.

Often on bright sunny days there are big balloons of bright colors and pretty patterns just over the ocean floor, with little dark shapes hanging from them. Most of the time they are suspended there motionless until the light goes dim. That's when they drop down below the ocean floor. But on occasion, very rarely, a balloon will drift very slowly across the way from one side to the other, or from the other side and across.

Sometimes one or two or three little birds will follow a big bird and peck at it and worry it for a long time and without any fear, it seems. Up and down they go and this way and that. And at those times the big bird will seem confused and afraid, and in the eyes of the beholder there is compassion for the big bird.

It is morning and from behind her the floor opens, and when she looks back, she sees eyes that shine from the darkness beneath the trap door. A bowl is set just beyond the opening. Eyes meet eyes and hold each other's gaze for a few seconds. Then the door descends and the floor is sealed again.

After a time she climbs down from the wooden ledge by the window and crosses over to the bowl, the front of the too large flannel night gown bunched up in her hands before her. She is very small, about two and a half feet tall, with legs and arms like broom handles, with doll's feet, and with hands like the feet of a small bird. The eyes are big and the face is small, gaunt, and so pale, like the transparent membranous skin of some tropical fish.

She stoops down and takes up the bowl along with the flannel and crosses back to the ledge. She takes her breakfast at the window, methodically lifting the spoon to the thin, bluish-grey lips, mechanically swallowing the unknown mashed up substance.

The window warms with the day, so she stays back a few inches from the glass. The clouds gather from the distance. As they come together they become darker and very powerful looking. She watches as the blue sea/sky takes color from the clouds and all becomes grey and full of energy. Jagged streaks of bright light shoot out of the dark mass of cloud and down into the hiding places of the birds and she worries about them. She shakes and trembles with each big crashing sound after the streaks of light and she feels the terrible strong vibration in the room.

The storm lasts for almost an hour and as the rain continues after, she puts her head against the pane to feel the padding of the rain and its coolness through the glass.

When it passes altogether she is glad to see the birds come swimming back up through the blue and across the enchanting band of colors that arc through the now serene firmament.

The day passes and as summer's light fades the face maintains the vigil. Only a very few of the flying things are now coming across. A few swallows still flit here and there, alighting and teetering back and forth occasionally in groups of three to five on the wires, but at last light there are small grey gossamer-like fleeting shadows that replace them. They swarm down from the top of the view in great numbers, fanning out and dispersing before going out of sight. The stars and the moon now become the objects of devotion, by the face.

***

So the cycles come and they go. The light gives way to the dark and the dark gives way to the light. Some time back she began to mark the cycles on the wall with the handles of the spoons, before returning the bowls to the edge of the door. There are many marks now. They mean little to her. She cannot count. She cannot read, or even speak. No one ever taught her. She has never seen another room that she can remember. She has never seen the earth, the ground, nor tree, nor hill, nor river, nor street, nor road. She cannot remember seeing another human being. Only the eyes or a shadow's glimpse of a face when the door is lifted.

But she watches. Things happen. Things change. The weather, the temperature, the precipitation, the light, the dark. And she feels. She is concerned for the birds, though she has no name for them. She is not concerned for the balloons, though she enjoys them. She is afraid of the clouds but only when they get together and become dark.

Most of all she is sad. She doesn't know anything else but still, she is sad for something else. She has no words to think about it or to express it, even if there was anyone to express it to. Nevertheless, she is sad. Her eyes are sad. Her self is sad.

She sits through the night. There is a little child's mattress below and to the side of the ledge. When she becomes completely exhausted she goes to it, covers herself with the big old tattered quilt. But she has no schedule for sleeping or waking. So she sits in the window and the moon is near full and the stars are also lit, and she can see into the vastness of the heavens.

When she first knows that someone is sitting with her she is not frightened, though she cannot ever remember ever seeing anyone before. The man is watching the moon with her and she is watching the moon in his company. After a time he looks at her and she in turn looks back at him. In his eyes is the sadness and in her eyes is the sadness. And she begins to cry. And as she does he gently puts his hand on her cheek and wipes the tears away with his thumb.

She sees the man's long dark hair and his short dark beard. She sees his soft features and his soft white shirt and his soft kind smile, and she reaches out to him with her little arms with her bird's feet hands and he takes her in his strong arms and holds her. And they sit and watch the moon and the stars. When the gossamer fleeting shadows return and the first sunlight replaces the moonlight and as she sleeps, he lays her down on the little mattress and covers her with the big tattered quilt.

George moonlighting with the beholder

Jesse S. Hanson

SEVEN: Some stories of men

He tried to do his best, but he could not.
— *Neil Young - from Tired Eyes*

Eugene
- family ties (the weight) -
Ansel

"Oh I can't complain about my upbringing, you know, or my family. They were, I mean they are, because most of 'em are still living, I assume, well they're good people. Moderately educated I'd say. Not highbrow education, mind you. But well read, worldly people.

"It's funny because I used to have a high opinion of that state of being a worldly person. It meant like someone who'd been around the block, you know, somebody who had a larger view of the world, say than a real local yokel type. Whereas now when I think of worldly I think of all of us damned worldly fools. There's nothing to the world it seems now. It seems like a scene from a movie or a chapter from a book. That's not it exactly. It's more like an epic poem, really, or in many cases, an epic dirge--but it only takes its life from that part of it that goes on. Came here from before and goes on after. You see what I'm saying.

"Growing up we had it pretty good. We had land, we had freedom to run, although we had our chores as well. I was the fourth in line of five. People were having medium sized families those days, of course. That generation before us now they had some families, ten, twelve on average, I'd guess. Must have been some dynamics there. But we had our dynamics, I'll say. Oh yeah. We had our dynamics.

"Son, you wouldn't have another one of those smokes, would you? I like to talk, but you know it makes me want a damn smoke. Goddamn if that ain't the hell of it, the shit we gotta go through to live in this fuckin' hole. I could fuckin' tear 'em a new asshole, those Goddamn freaks runnin this sewer. They'll get theirs and they'll know they ain't no better'n me or my kind. Big city rednecks is all they are. Ignorant motherfuckers anyway."

He's breathing very hard and shaking after his tirade and then he is gasping for breath. I get one of the staff who comes over and looks at him. He assesses the situation. "He'll be alright. Always gets like this after his outbursts. He'll come around in a minute." He walks back to his post by the door.

And he does come around in just a few minutes. I ask him if he's okay to go on.

"Oh yes, I'm alright. I just have a bit of asthma." He starts up again without further reference to the *outburst*. "Let's see now, where was I? Oh yes, the family. I was the third, as I was saying. Hand-me-down clothes and hand-me-down expectations. The folks, they treated us pretty darn equal. Or they tried to anyway. But the trouble comes in life that every single one of us is different, huh? So that's the problem parents have. What we learn from raising one isn't much education for raising the next, and so on down the line.

"The thing is, I never could figure out who I was. So I suppose it's no wonder my parents couldn't, or my brother and sisters, let alone the whole rest of the extended family. Oh yes, we got together with Mom's side and Pops's side and as the family grew we got together with both sides of each side's families. Besides our two grandmas and one grandpoppa, there was the aunts and uncles and cousins and eventually the cousins' spouses and our kids and their kids and then their kids' kids until I couldn't even tell you all their names. I plum got tired of it all. Where's the life, you know. The whole life is one big birthday party?

"Anyway, I'm getting ahead of myself. My sister Coreen was the oldest. She was good mostly to all of us younger ones, but self-absorbed also, as is natural for young people raised in our culture. Then Silvie, Molly, and Paula. It was my brother before me, set my standards the most when I was young, though. Trying to live up to his accomplishments wasn't easy. He was confident, good looking, not a smooth operator I don't mean, but just a real together and purposeful guy. Still is, I'd be willing to venture, provided the Lord's left him out there still. Ben. His name is Ben. I do love him. But I lost a lot of ground trying to be little Ben. Because Ben had direction. Even in indecision he was in charge. He'd eventually come to a decision and off he'd go. Blazing a trail. Hacking through the jungle with confidence that he was getting somewhere. Finished high school and marched on through college, almost taking up the way of an educator, but then turning to med school.

"At one point we took to fighting. I suppose we always had disagreements but there was a time there for a while when it was some pretty bad battles between Ben and I. He'd be trying to keep me in line and I don't even know why but I couldn't be kept so. Sometimes I threw things at him. Sometimes dangerous stuff. I think he was afraid of what I'd do, but he was always stronger and more athletic than me and he'd get the better of me. I can't for the life of me remember why I even was ever mad at him. He was good to me. All in all he was generally always good to me. But I began to resent him. And that resentment from him just

50

pushed me back. And like sheets of glass the barriers came up between us, one after another and I could see him but I was lost to him. And pretty soon I realized it wasn't just him. It was all of them. Mom and Pop, my sisters too. Separated by things I didn't understand. I didn't want to be alone. Wanted to be part of the family. I guess I was about sixteen years old at the time and I had my first realization of isolation. I was surrounded by people and nobody knew me and I didn't know anybody."

Eugene stops talking at this point and I'm wondering if there's going to be another *outburst*. I give him time. He's looking around and I notice his shoulders sort of trembling. But then he clenches his fist, apparently to pull himself together, because then he begins again.

"I was always trying too hard, maybe. Trying to be accepted, recognized. I was always smart. But I didn't get such good grades. I had talents. But my ego was always my enemy. I could fool people. I could almost fool myself. I could confuse people. But that only won their disdain. Like I said, I just never knew who I was, though I put many identity labels on myself. I've been able to convince people who I am, wearing those so-called identities. But I never have convinced myself. Not for long anyway.

"Hung around with bad company a lot of my life, I have. Most of that company wasn't so awful bad but some of it was. Always had a soft spot for bad company. Always had a critical eye for the straight and narrow. Always seem to be able to see the sliver of hypocrite in my brother's eye, but I don't notice the log of degenerate in my own eye. One day, when I was still in those young years, I did notice it, though. And it was as if everything I ever despised in other people, I saw as the material I was made of. Words cannot fully describe emotions. And I think people generally view depression as a state of getting so low that one has no feelings, no emotions, because that is how it appears. It manifests to the observer, family member or friend, what have you, as if the depressed person doesn't care. I can't speak for anyone else, but my experience with depression is a weight of pain so heavy that it's impossible to move. I'm just recently come up here from the depression ward, you know. But I was saying, It's an emotion. An emotion powerful enough to immobilize the victim. The victim." Eugene shakes his head. "The victim cannot become more than the victim. The weight is only taken off by some other something that is greater or it is not taken off. I'll stand by that.

"Think about how big it all is. You can't think about how big it all is, because it's too big. The whole creation, son. Usually we get bogged down puddling around in some little mud hole, you know, but when we lift up our eyes and look, provided we got eyes that work. I mean we can't even see hardly any of it, couldn't in a billion lifetimes with all the telescopes and spaceships in Star Trek. And then I've heard George say that it's small compared to the inner worlds, the spiritual worlds. There's only two ways of looking at it. Either we're under the weight of it, or we're lifted high up in the majesty of it.

"What would you say? Are you under the weight of it or are you lifted up?"

I start to say that I'm somewhere in the middle but he doesn't let me go on.

"Ya, ya, that's what everybody says. But I say, 'If you're not lifted up you're under the weight. Now, when you begin to feel the pain, to feel the weight, to become so depressed, so hopeless, then maybe you're being pulled out. It hurts. There's no words for emotions."

He turns away then, but I see that his eyes are wet with tears. In a minute he continues.

"I was sitting in the infirmary one day, when I first came up here, getting doctored for bites I'd self inflicted. That's why I'm all trussed up like I am. Cause I bite myself. Sometimes I bite other people. Mostly I bite myself though. Anyway, I was sitting there waiting for them to get my prescription, and this guy, it was George, but I didn't know anything about George at that time, well this guy is brought in by two of those big toughs and he's putting up a fuss and they've just barely got him under control. When they drag him by me, he's throwing his head from side to side and when he looks at me, I can't explain it but I start crying inside and then pretty soon I start crying outside. I cried for three days. I'd go to bed crying and I'd wake up crying if I slept at all. Couldn't eat. Good thing I'm in this nuthouse. Nobody thought too much of it. But I've never stopped thinking about it. Words can't touch emotions. George uses words. But even he gets confused by them. It's in the eyes. That's where it's at. And it's not for everybody. I don't care."

Walt Whitman

One sort of part-time member of George's little group is fastened to the back wall in the big room. Ozwald establishes a ready rapport with him as the man, Walt, is easy going and friendly. Oddly, despite that friendly nature, Walt has the quality of attempting suicide whenever he's not restrained. He'll get a running start and ram his head onto or into any hard thing he can find, the wall, cell bars, corner of a table, you name it. So they keep him tied to the wall on a very short cable attached to a harness around his upper torso. The wall behind him is well padded. He has about the same arrangement in his cell at night.

Walt is intelligent and humorous and when the boys come around they treat him as a comrade. Ozwald learns that Walt is in for rape. It seems that he is a confirmed rapist, and considered beyond rehabilitation. His suicidal nature is assumed, or rather declared, to be connected with guilt over his deviant sexual behavior.

Ozwald observes over time that although the "boys" of George's group appreciate and interact regularly with Walt, George himself never comes up to him and seems not to communicate with him on any level. Ozwald is a pretty sensitive guy, but also straightforward, and so, very tactfully, he questions Walt about George's aloofness to him.

"George gives me the cold shoulder alright. It hurts, I have to admit. But this I know, Ozwald. George not only cares for me but he cares for every damn perverted son of a bitch in this place. He did tell me that one time. He did speak to me one time. But he can't abide that I'm a sex addict. He came right up to me and he told me he cares about me, not to think he don't. That's the only time he ever once talked to me, but it was enough. I have a strong impression that ol' George has some big pain from his past. Maybe bigger'n mine. I never heard him mention it, though. I ask the other fellas and they tell it the same. George don't talk about his past. Ain't nobody seem to know nothing about George before here. Not that it matters. It don't."

What's your story, Eugene?

"What's your story Eugene?" Jeff asks him.

"My story?"

Eugene seems to take immediate offence to Jeff's question.

"How do you do it? How do you and all them folks do it, son? I mean how do you divide us up? These sonsabitches are crazy and these others ain't. Cause it looks like we're the ones who *aren't* crazy, I gotta say. How can you get a look at the way things are and continue to play the sanity game? We're all ghosts in a collective nightmare. Man you people freak me out. Think it's real. You think it's real. You real stupid people, you look real stupid. But I suspect it's fear, not stupidness. Don't wanna see. Like little girls protected from the harsh realities."

Jeff has had a rough morning. The subjects he had planned to interview today have proved particularly reticent. In frustration he's turned to Eugene. His notion is readily confirmed that it's really not that hard to get an interview from Eugene.

"I'll tell you about me. Started with me having trouble with the growing old. Grow old and can't do shit. Get weaker and weaker. Weak in the body, weak in the head. Everything hurts. Spend your whole life trying to figure it out, life you know, and you keep learning, and you appear to be getting wiser and all that and come around a corner and there's a mirror. Hell, you're going backwards. Turning into a helpless lump of crap. Racin' rats. Racin' rats to the finish line. How'd ya like the prize, Harry. You won the race, huh? Well worth the anxiety, I'm sure. Damn site insane ain't ya Larry? No better'n me."

"I suppose you have some valid points," says Jeff.

"That's kind of you, Jeff."

"Well we have to function, don't we? If we were all to just fall apart and end up in prisons or other institutions, who would take care of us? It seems as if there's a certain responsibility."

"You think so?"

"It seems that way to me," Jeff says.

"You know what I think?" Eugene says to him.

"You told me you think everybody's crazy, if I understood you right."

"Yeah, well, outside a that I was goin' ta say, 'I think your quite the dumb shit."

"That's a good argument, Eugene."

"Thanks"

"What about what I said about responsibility?"

"What about it?"

"What do you think about it."

"Okay, I'll tell ya what I think about *reesponsibility*," Eugene says with a kind of snooty shake of his head and an obvious sneer. "About half the guys in here are in for small amounts of contraband. They wasn't hurtin' nobody. Your *reesponsibility* put the poor sonsabitches in here. The bad guys are out there runnin the frickin' governments. Sendin' the boys off to battles they didn' start. Girls too, nowadays. Them what don' fit their particular definitions of patriots, they get branded."

Eugene looks pretty frazzled at this point. Ansel has overheard most of the conversation, from where he was sitting farther down the table, and he comes up now to suggest that Jeff take it easy.

"What's the matter, worried that I might be right?" Jeff accuses Ansel.

"You studid fuck!" Eugene says, and it's kind of hard to tell whether the remark is directed at Jeff or Ansel.

"I just don't think you should experiment with therapy, that's all. It's not what we're here for." Ansel answers Jeff's question, as he tries to sort of bridge over Eugene's comment.

"Who's fucking idea was this, anyway, Ansel? Don't tell me how to interview."

"Goddamned good for nuthin' asshole mutherfucker," says Eugene.

"FUCK YOU, Eugene you pathetic copout!" Jeff yells back at him as he scoops up his notebook and storms away.

Ansel looks at Eugene to see how he will react. Eugene tells Ansel to "Go to Hell. Go fuck your mother. Eat shit. I'll kill you. You wait. I'll kill you, you little interuptin' fucker."

the roommate
Jeff

My first interview with George's roommate was notable. A small, thin, nervous type, I probably approached him at a bad moment.

"We're writing about George and his followers. We were told that you were among the flock. Would you mind talking for a little while?"

"Like I told ya, but these ones here that like to eat vvvvv - oh I think I need a vacation Listen son, can you lend me a d-dollar for the paper, I'm short but like I told ya, they're half crazy that bunch, vvvv get back get back are you blind? I'm, I'm, I'm, um, um, um, um ..."

"Do you remember George at all?"

"Well, like I told ya, um, um, um, um, um ... Geor, Geor, Geor, George Where's George? I seen you comin', but George?" "Yes, George?"

But there was no more information forthcoming and Anthony walked away, withdrawn.

EIGHT: Toby and the dead man

Saints and Mahatmas, the Beloveds of God, come in every age; They come in every religion. Saints and Mahatmas do not come to break any of the existing religions, nor do They come to form any new religion.

— *Ajaib Singh*

Toby
- an old story -
Ozwald

There is yet another entity secured to the wall in the great hall. The one they call Toby. One morning, before beginning his talk to the inmates, we observed George approach the amber colored *thing* and stand before it, appearing to communicate with it for a period of perhaps ten minutes, finally bending down and actually embracing the creature, even kissing the top of its rather broad, flat head, the head that has prompted many of the other inmates to refer to him, mockingly, as Pumpkin Head.

Naturally, after the talk, which was a long one for George, lasting easily twenty minutes, I paid a visit.

As I approached the man—he appeared to be a man in many respects—I could feel the awareness of him. It was a strong impression. This was no senseless beast, but a being of some powerful intelligence. That was my thought, and my thought was confirmed readily as I interviewed him.

His bonds were of 3/16" inch steel cable, encased in plastic lining to protect, I assume, from any sharp broken strands, eventually inherent in any such cable. Protection I assume for the staff as well as the detainee. There were three cables in all. From a wide and heavy steel band at each wrist, the cables ran out to their fastenings on the wall, which were located about waist high to a standing person, and at least five feet to either side of their captive. His hands and arms had full freedom of movement, but we had observed that the cables were adjustable at the fasteners. Whenever the staff brought him food or had any other necessary dealings with him, they would pull the cables through so his arms were open wide against the wall, a maneuver to which he complied willingly by opening his arms for them. The cable around his neck was also secured to the wall at a length of approximately one foot.

The fellow's skin had a dark amber coloration with green hues showing through in certain areas such as the temples, around the eyes, the inner sides of his wrists, anywhere the skin was more transparent. He had rather large bulging veins at his neck and at his ankles which were exposed beneath the pale blue leggings of his issued jump suit. His head was large, but low, and flat on top, thinly overlaid in all areas including the face, with limp dark hairs, three to four inches in length. The overall shape of the head could be compared to a half inflated basketball someone has sat upon. The ears were round and quite human-like, the mouth and nearly nonexistent chin located on the lower curve of the ball shape.

When I introduced myself and explained my purpose he responded in a gurgling, watery baritone voice, speaking slowly and thoughtfully, but without hesitation. His unusual accent, soft and fluid, almost never pronouncing the sound of the letter t, and only softly the d, seemed often to not differentiate between the past and the present tense; but it may well have been attributable to the accent itself.

He said he was aware of our project and had been observing us in our interviews with many of the inmates and that he had noticed our presence at some of George's recent talks. There was neither any resentment nor malice in his tone, yet I felt a confused sense of foreboding in his presence. I admit, it may only have been due to his extreme physical appearance, but as he related his history, the feeling grew more profound. In any case I sat with my chair no less than six feet before him, in deference to the most powerful looking hands I've ever seen, adorned with nails that more closely resemble claws.

He began by describing his most recent home on the outside, which was apparently a sheer cliff in the beautiful and primitive Unicoi Mountain Range of North Carolina."

"Idh took a consehderable amoun of didermination from each an ever shree thadh live on thadh wall of sdone from the varr beginnin of idh's life. Oh, you couldh say the connitions were acshually perfec I suppose, even in thadh ausdare location, or idh couldh na of happen, their growin. In the grayiht kaleidoscope of nadeshure, there ha to've been all the cahrec elemends, includin daihny cracks in the sdone for the liddle roots do cling do, the prauper nushriends, prauper sunlayiht, prauper shayihde, fresh ahr, enough moihschure from rayin, the hardhy sdrain of the species idself, so thadh idh happen—so idh couldh na have na happen—was inevidable. But thadh's na the kine of didermination I mean."

Already I'm thinking, *I can't believe I'm hearing this from this very strange being.*

"They have such a will power, dear frien. Idh's the will of the shree idself do grow, and do grow where idh will. People don' think a shree can have idh, bud people are wrong, and they're ignoran of shrees."

I don't know what to say, so I feign understanding and tell him that we have never been taught these things. "I don't think they're easy for us to accept," I say.

"Some of my bes friens are shrees and I'm sahrry do say thadh there's millions of 'em bein darture and slaghder ever day in the ignorance of almaighdy mankahine."

Here Toby leaves off instructing me, regarding the virtues of trees, and begins to relate a rather fantastic and yet fascinating account of his own history.

"Idh was in the year three thousan, one hunner an dwelve B.C., of your dime when I firsd crawl oudh from unner a rock. You'll have drouble swallowin thadh as well."

When he says 'as well', because of his strange articulation, I think he's calling me by my name, Ozwald, but later, when he says 'as well' again, I understand.

"But I dell you, they don' have no recordh of my birth, they don' have no knowledge of my race, and they generally don' know wha do maike of me.

"They've hel' me laihke this since ninedeen-fordy-three, budh I dell you, I've been in mos all their prison houses an their nudh houses, here and mos' aroun the globe as well. They've often drahyid to dehspose of me, budh do ill effeck, undil they jus' give up I guess.

"I've been given me so many nayihmes down through the ages. The Indyiahns call me *Akkāl-dehānt*, do the Africans I'm known as *Isibungu*, 'the worm'. On the islans I was *Hara Popa'a*, the shame, or 'the wrong doin foreigner'. I spendh two hunner years ad the boddom of the Indiyahn Ocean, an to the denizens of the deep I was *Ofo Ogo*, the long live ghosdh. Finally Swumpa, the King of the giandh squid, cridicize me and thereby free me from thadh bondage. I came then do dwell in the dark wahders an the wedlands of the deep south of this condinendh many hunners of years while the many nayihtions populade an esdablish their sovereigny. When the Europeans came, the Spaniars an the French, I survive through them as they harry an darture me.

"I came do those moundains of which we were speakin less than a cenjury ago. Adh the base of the cliff I dwel. Idh was there thadh I was given the knowledge of separation. Before thadh, in all my ignorance, I hadh no compulsion in the world but do survive. I fedh on the death of the things of the worl an I foughd or di na fighd, whichever was do my advandage. Wha came do me I dook. Wha was daken from me, I di na mourn, budh wen on withou. I was never condend, budh neither was I wahning. I undersdoodh thadh death gave me life and I di na know thadh death ha no life do give.

"Budh in the moundains I was given a fleedin but unforgedable experience thadh insdill in me the notion thadh somethin was wrong. Somethin was amiss. More aply, somethin was missin.

"They pudh me in the asylum in North Carolina when they foun me in the liddle graveyardh where I ha maihde a cerdain mess, if you will forgive the image. Budh they couldh na condaihn me there so I was dransferr do the prison sysdem. Idh may be bad how I live, how I have live. Budh I have no consciousness of righd or wrong. I have some consciousness of the curse thadh was pudh on me. An I know thadh you couldh even say thadh a curse is upon us all, however mine may be a darker curse. I am na a murdrer. I am na a threadh to these people, though they dake these precautions. Of course I know they cannah help their fears.

"You couldh say that all the correc elemends of nadeshure have broughd me here, the crimes they accuse me of, the monerization of the worl, the exac amoun of darkness an evil, the adhministration of securidhy an of jusdhice, budh I tell you, idh is will power. Laihke the shrees. From within myself I ha the dhesire do come here do this buildin. I have the desire do en my creepin upon the earth. My comin here and my goin there. I have the bodhy of a human idh is drue. But I have taken on many forms, forms uncoundhable. I am ol'. I am as ol' as the oldes. In my weariness and my ol' age I have come to meedh George—an I have medh him. An he has shown me love. Even I, *Akkāl-dehānt*, 'the gluddonous eadher of death'. Budh I am na thadh any more, now George has made me a vegedharian."

"So you're where you want to be, even shackled to the wall, and with no basic freedoms whatsoever?" I say.

"There is na freedhom in this worl', Ozwal. Another kine of freedomn I seek."

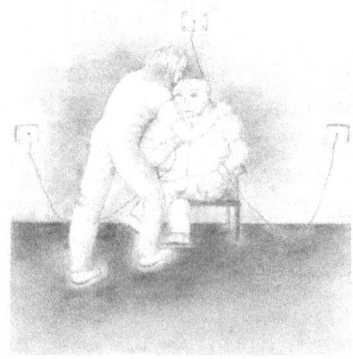

George and Toby

60

***

I checked with Federal Prison Records and there is, indeed, no record of his birth, nor of any relations. They have the transfer papers from the North Carolina asylum but those are fairly sparse in detail. He was arrested in the small church cemetery of Galingwood Baptist Church in Galingwood, North Carolina for the crime of desecration. He was tried by the Supreme Court of that state and convicted of the same crime, but easily convinced of his insanity the judge sentenced him to permanent confinement at the North Carolina Asylum for the Chronically Incurable. He escaped twice and in the fall of 1943 he was committed to the present facility, being considered dangerous and too abhorrent in his behavior toward decent society to be allowed freedom of any degree.

I will likely have to do a considerable amount of research, utilizing other sources to obtain further substantiation or refutation of the claims of the patient/inmate, Toby.

On an informal aside note, curiosity about Toby's claim to having existed for thousands of years, and to have "crawled out from under a rock" in the year 3112B.C to be exact, led me to do some very informal research regarding any particular significance to that time period. There is a popular group, putting up a lot of information on the internet, stating that a 7th century Mayan prophet, Pacal Votan, saw the evolution of the world as divided into 26,000 year cycles. According to the prophet, the age we are living in now, variously referred to as "The Time of Great Purification," "The Shift of the Ages," "The Age of the Fifth Sun," etc., began in the year 3113 B.C. and will end in the year 2012 A.D. The group also claims that certain other cultures, including the "Sumerians, Tibetans, Egyptians, Cherokees, and Hopi refer to this same 26,000 year cycle in their mystical belief systems and each have developed calendars based on this great cycle."

Don't You Pity the Critic?
a song

Don't you pity the Critic, whose work is so important
Who in the space of a minute is creating our good fortune,
and suffering hell ...

Did we not dwell in the waters of the deepest dark ocean
Our sons and our daughters in the darkest devotion
And did we not with the passing of ages, consider our leaving
With the turning of pages as the world was conceiving

Don't you pity the Critic, whose work is so important
Who in the space of a minute is creating our good fortune,
and suffering hell ...

Did we not, with our innocent eyes, discover our burden
With our innocent lies was a fate that was certain
Coming and going and coming and going and coming and going
Meeting and knowing, separating and going

Haven't we come now to sit at Your feet, the weary and broken
where the stories repeating and the love is what's spoken
    where the stories completing and the love is unbroken

Don't you pity the Critic, whose work is so important

dead man

"I never had so many fears till I died. You think maybe, 'What's to fear? You're already dead,' but that's not how it is. That Punkin Head that they got chained to the wall, he eats death. He wants to. They got him trussed up pretty good, but he's goddamn fearful, I tell ya. He's a damned abortion that shoulda happened. How in hell those sorry suckers can believe in God with ones like Punkin Head around? Of course they keep 'im in here so as to protect the dainty."

Ansel says, "So he's a source of fear to you. Do you have other fears as a dead person?"

"There's only the fear of life. There's nothing else to fear."

NINE: George with his friends & the message that is later referred to as "The Expectations of Love"

There is no moment in eternity more important than this moment.
—Emerson

the boys come into the hall
Ansel

Just then the boys come in to the hall. They meander about casually for a couple of minutes before settling down as a group on a pair of flimsy metal-framed, lightly upholstered benches near the south end, and some folding chairs they gather from locations around the room. They're reminiscent of a troupe of high schoolers, with the crazy names they've adopted, their joking and laughing, and poking light fun at almost everything around them, including each other. Carefree in first impression, but wary and weighing in upon closer inspection. Without that closer inspection, it is not obvious there is even a hierarchy. For they're not cruel, these boys, some of them in their thirties, some as old as their sixties. Not cruel as a group, anyway. No one is singled out and picked on. That is not their game.

This bunch has more freedom than most. Within certain blocks of time, and without the presence of any current, exceptionally exasperating circumstances, they are allowed limited, monitored movement between a few designated floors. They've proven themselves. They don't get into trouble. They don't threaten or harass anyone. The staff, who will on the one hand not hesitate to severely punish any individual inmate, including the members of this band of jollies, also seem to find these fellows somehow entertaining. Besides, the powers that be within the levels of the prison authority, have inexplicably sanctioned their special privileges.

It is strange and surprising to me that I should say they are reminiscent of high school boys at all, when I am conscious of their actual physical characteristics. Half of them are much closer in physical resemblance to some of the down and out bums residing on our inner city streets. Some with long scraggly hair and beards, some bald and scruffy. Others are clean cut, meticulous, even obsessive in grooming, a strange contrast with the almost invariably ill-fitting drab blue jumpsuit.

There are many striking features among them, some of natural inheritance, like Horatio and his huge forehead. Horatio is a big man. A man of much muscle and substance. Great biceps. And he has the largest forehead I've ever seen. It is like a mighty muscle of its own. Horatio is a very gentle man. Bascomb, his given name is Jesús, is one of the clean cut ones, of Spanish descent, but with his intense, New Mexico sky blue eyes. His eyes are literally like looking at the blue of the sky, partly cloudy. There's no describing them.

Lao Tse is a Native American, Apache. His real name is Thomas Small. He took the name Lao Tse, his friends say, because he's heard people claim that Taoism is like Native American philosophy. But Lao Tse has told me there is no Native American philosophy to his knowledge, and that that's all a crock of shit, but he likes the name. His gaunt, round face with scarce beard stubble and head banded hair that stops short of his shoulders, brings to mind the legends of the desert, like Geronimo, Cochise, and Cochise's son Naiche.

Some have striking history related features. Milton, for instance. Milton is an Indian. His ancestors are from South India, although he's American born and American minded, no doubt, no trace of an Indian accent. Anyway, Milton has a horrific knife scar from the middle top of his head, down the left side of his face, right through the ear and down past his neck. He won't say how much farther it goes. It's like two inches wide at its widest, on the neck. No hair grows on it on his head. It is multicolored and sensitive looking, although Milton says it causes him no suffering. Says it's an attention getter. Milton wears dreadlocks and is charming and articulate. Handsome man. Very crazy.

Jean-Paul's problem is a lacking of one arm altogether and the lacking of a hand on the existing arm. His crime was an act of violence with the handless arm, but his nature is as sweet and friendly as any man you would care to meet. He lost his arms in his native China in an act of civil disobedience. His friends contend that Jean-Paul's crime in the U.S. was an act of self-defense. Usually he is wearing long hair and two or three days worth of beard, most likely attributable to the difficulty of more attentive grooming. He seems to have a close relationship with George, and George appears often to be the first to assist Jean-Paul with any physical task or difficulty.

Just now, George has sought out and found, on the floor near the wall, a battered pillow which he fluffs and arranges on one end of a bench for Jean-Paul, to cushion him against the benches cold aluminum arm. Jean-Paul graciously accepts this special act of kindness, but with obvious wonder and unconcealed reverence.

Then George walks off a little distance from his companions. He stands with one leg locked and the other relaxed. He is looking around the room, seemingly taking it all in. He is an average looking American man, of average build, neither thin nor heavy, although he appears to possess physical strength. There is a developing belly for a man of his young age of thirty-four years. He has fine, straight, shoulder length, prematurely salt and pepper, formerly dark hair. His beard is trimmed, medium short, with less grey than the head hair. His height is 5'9" to 5" 11" I would say.

In his eyes is a notable sadness, and when his gaze momentarily falls on me, it is difficult to bear and I look away, though in doing so I am overcome with a sudden forlorn feeling I do not understand. I was not conscious of any truly profound current emotion within myself until this moment. And so I watch him as the others are watching him, those that are able to. Some of the inmates are scarcely able to focus on anything at all, other than themselves. I tell myself I will not look away again. I will not miss another opportunity.

Finally he begins to speak. The room, a normal din of cacophony, falls silent. He speaks in a voice raised enough to extend to the distances of the large room.

message of George – VI
~ The Expectations of Love ~

"The expectations of Love," he says, almost as if to himself. I am only able to hear these first soft words because of my relatively close proximity to George and because of the focus I have just committed to. He pauses for a few seconds, as if to allow for the effect of the words, before he continues.

"Love doesn't come down from the heavens, fall like rain from on high.

"Love comes from the lowly, the pure manifestation of humility, the poor and innocent childlike, the lesser children of the Creator. The trodden under, the written off, the unremembered, the unknown,—these are the tenders, the keepers of the sacred flame of Love.

"Deep within the coarse cracks of the daily trampled walks there are the vaults and the formidable places wherein the locked safes of Love are maintained.

"For it is always the case that there are two streets really, layers if you must, in the towns and cities. There are two paths and two roads across the land o'er the back roads and the byways and also of the open highways of the country.

"For those of means and ambition, of desire and position, there are the ways above.

"And down beneath the cracks and dissolved back into the earth are the low ways and the low places. Those who live in the low places are called the lowly. Only Love is expected of the citizens there. Love is the currency of that place. Love is the mark of success. Love is the language. There are other languages spoken, but Love is the only universal language. All transportation is by the power of, on the feet of, the back of, the wheels of, the wings of Love. Passport

and visa are given with Love. The homes are inspired, designed, blueprinted by and erected with and constructed out of Love. The most Lovely homes are more costly, the price of Love is higher. And the pastimes that are enjoyed are enjoyments of Love. No knowledge of lust exists there. There is no fruit of such knowledge available. The serpent is quite innocent. The serpent is family.

"And when the dirt rains down through the cracks from above, it nourishes the fields and the forests and the farms of Love. It replenishes the wells and the ponds and the great lakes and seas and the mighty ocean of Love.

"The technology and the industry of that land is conversion. Conversion of resources. For upon the land rains the dirt and the filth, the waste products of corruption and abuse and violence and the terror of violence. The seed of men. And their spit. Their waste. Their bodily fluids. And the blood of beasts and the hair and the bile and scraps of their entrails. All the sins and the hatred and fears and the despair of the streets and the dark alleys and the lonely and dark country roads and the deep places of horror in the forests and in the private rooms and in the hidden mountains, where evil deeds are conceived. The resources. The collection. The processing. The refining. The knowledge. The greatest of these is knowledge. Only Love can recognize the essence of Love in all things.

"Love is. There is no explanation for it, no (two or three unclear words) *accounting for it.*

"The people have no place to get to. No place to go. There is no one to avoid. No one to know.

"History is forbidden below. But it is not remembered anyway, and the souls who live there are not remembered either, and there is no concept of the future."

***

George walks back to his comrades in silence. And out of that silence comes a sound, an enchanting subtle musical sound, coming from I don't know where. In his talk, I have no idea what he was getting at, whether it was parable or truth or what, and I know nothing of what happened. But for reasons I can't explain or understand, I now count those moments, among the most memorable of my life. Scholars, teachers, friends, philosophers and critics, I may choose to cherish or to relinquish your opinions. I assume I will be judged the victim of charisma, of a deceptive melodrama. But I can't be concerned. I know I have been given a glimpse of some part of the great drama of creation and I will never relinquish the value of the experience.

TEN: A benefactor

Saints never look at our failings. If they did, who would come to them?
—Baba Sawan Singh Ji

a benefactor

He is walking home through the park, from a late meeting at the center, when he finds the man. "What's this?" he says. He hears the difficult breathing and the rustling about, investigates and finds him backed up to the concrete gazebo foundation behind some shrubs of yew. "Oh, here you are, then." The man he finds is poorly dressed and has such a threadbare coat as to be all but useless against the cold night air. The man is shivering violently with hypothermia. He is awake but disoriented and trance-like in his distress.

Taking off his greatcoat, he lays it on the ground and then picking the man up, he lays him down on the coat and wraps him in it. Although the man's arms are not in the sleeves, he buttons the front of the coat. Then from his knees he picks the bundle up and lays it across his shoulder, gets to his feet and continues to his home.

Later, when the rescued man awakens, he hears voices, and finding them comforting he lays still and listens.

***

"The physical body is just like a raiment which has to be cast off both by the disciple and the Master, the moment this spiritual journey begins; as it is the untrammeled spirit that has to tread the spiritual path. But so long as he works on the physical plane as a teacher to the stray brethren, blessed indeed is his form full of Godly Grace, shedding Godly Light around him and charging all and sundry with powerful rays of spirituality. Man is the teacher of man and ideal man has ever been the ideal of man." [1]

***

There is a period of silence and he lays on his back, warm, comfortable. Rough wooden beams overhead. Subtle scent of

---

[1] Godman, by Kirpal Singh p.73

sandalwood in the room. Then a different voice continues in the same vein as if they are taking turns reading.

***

"Those who regard it as idolatry do not know the secret of the Master's greatness. This 'man worship' as they call it, is much better than 'book worship' or 'idol worship,' because it is a worship of Higher Consciousness by lower consciousness. Life can come from Life, not from inert matter. Hazrat Khusro, a great Sufi poet in his well-known couplet, tells us:

***

"People allege that Khusro has become an idol worshiper,
Verily do I admit it, for the world has nothing to do with me."

***

Again, another Persian poet from his sick bed said:

***

"O ignorant physician! take thy leave, for thou knowest not
that for the love-sick there is no other remedy
except the sight of his Beloved." [2]

***

So absorbed in the words and the mood as he is, he doesn't notice the man standing next to his bed, though his eyes are open. But when the man lays his hand upon his forehead, he is not startled, rather he is further comforted.
"Are you a doctor?"
"Yes."
"What is this place? It's not a hospital, is it?"
"Not in the usual sense. It is my house."

---

[2] Godman, by Kirpal Singh p.73

They look at each other. In the look there is a painful joy that each recognizes in the others eyes, but after a moment George looks away, confused, afraid.

"You found me, out there." he says.

"Yes, you were …," the man hesitates.

"I think I was dying."

"It was not meant to be."

"Not yet. I suppose it must be prolonged."

"Please allow yourself to rest. You can rest here without worry."

As the man leaves his side he becomes conscious of yet another voice from the other room

***

"Long and dreary has been the struggle of the mind but all in vain,
All potent art Thou and can do aught, then why this delay?
Wandering up and down in the wheel of life, I have never had a success" [3]

***

He is stunned by the words, and in his brain, electrical charges sputter and spark, frightening and painful, as if his mind is short-circuiting.

***

"Entangled in evil thoughts, I am an utter stranger in a strange land,
Reform me this time and I shall lovingly think of Thee all the time.
I feel repentant and sad as I know not how to contact my Beloved
He lives in the High Heavens while I am a creature of the earth and miserable without Him." [4]

***

George is overwhelmed by tiredness now, the head pains having subsided. They are singing in a language he cannot understand, but the

---

[3] Prayer, by Kirpal Singh p.102
[4] Prayer, by Kirpal Singh p.103

voices are sweet and full of melancholy, the sandalwood is soothing, and he falls asleep, much calmed and he dreams.

In his dream, there is a man standing on a high ledge overhanging a great body of water. George can see the man, a small figure leaning into the fierce wind that is coming off the water. He can see him from where he lays in the rocks. The man's clothes and his beard are flapping wildly, his jacket bubbled out behind him, as he is pointing frantically at something below. Then George sees the ship. It is close in and nearly hidden in the mist created by the breakers striking the cliffs. The vessel is an ancient sailing ship and it is bobbing wildly in the frenetic condition of the water, which it occupies in a precarious position.

The man on the ledge seems to be doing his pointing for the benefit of the inhabitants of the ship. And indeed the ship raises its sails and acts by his bidding as it moves, phantom-like through the mist, though it should only be dashed against the rocks. At long last it comes to a position directly offshore from where George is lying and again lowers its sails, and he can see from that distance that the tiny men are lowering the anchor.

He thinks he hears a small voice, carried swiftly on a gust of wind and gone as swiftly. "Hold fast."

"Hold fast, good fellow!" he hears again, this time louder.

A small boat is being lowered over the starboard side. And then there are men, rowing through the impossible waves of the now even more tempestuous storm. Strangely, it is not a boat but a great bird that arrives on the shore. He hears sweet voices singing. As its passengers approach him with their singing, he sees they are not earthly men but beautiful, tall elven-like beings, each equally possessing both feminine and masculine qualities. They do not speak or interrupt their song as they lift his broken body effortlessly out of the rocks. And looking back down at the ground where he had lain, he sees the red blood that runs freely from him onto the sand.

A strange calm has come over the waters that he is only now aware of. As they walk into the shallow waves with him and continue into the gentle blue sea, the bird comes up under them and lifts them up and they ride in perfect serenity to the waiting ship.

He hears a voice. Has he has fallen asleep and been taken aboard the great ship? He opens his eyes, tentatively. It is the man from the ledge.

"I was looking for you—for a long time," the man is telling him.

"I didn't know."

"I know. But I have something to give you."

"I'm only a lost soul," George says.

"But I found you," says the man. "So how can you be lost?" The man places his hand on George's forehead. His hand is cool and comforting.

"Now, for a time, you must forget. You have to go back," the man is saying.

Hearing that, George cries out in a panic. He tries to sit up in his alarm. "But I have no place to go. I've made a bad mess of my life. And I thought, I'm sorry, but I couldn't help it. I hoped—like a stray dog—maybe you could keep me?"

So the man comforts him, puts his hand under his head and helps him to lie back down, "It will be, George. I promise to you that it will be. I will never leave you. Only for a little while, now …"

But George falls back to an oblivion of sleep. He doesn't hear any more of the man's words.

ELEVEN: The Ghost Poet

A man finds happiness so fleetingly, like the petals melting off a prairie rose. Even as you touch that feeling it dries up, leaving only the dust of that emotion, a powder of hope.

—*Louise Erdrich (Nanapush) in* Four Souls

Lao Tse
-the ghost poet-
Ozwald

When I asked Lao Tse if he would talk about himself and or George, he told me he'd have to think about it. He said there might be something.

It was a week later that he came up to me and told me that there was something he'd like to tell. Something from the old days, he said. He asked me to come to his cell so he could tell it in private.

***

"It was a funny thing about drugs in those days. You didn't so much make a conscious decision to take some drug, you know. It would just be available and like you'd heard of it, but, then there it is—and maybe you'd hesitate for a second—but you don't know nothin' about a drug till you take it. Hell, that's basically the way people smoke their first cigarette, take their first drink, whatever. And you're never quite the same after. You gain somethin', you lose somethin'. It's just that with some things, it seems like a bigger deal. You take acid, eat peyote, your whole perspective can sure as shit change. A lot of drugs feed on your lower tendencies, work on your will power, make you addicted. But acid, peyote, hallucinogens, they blow your mind. You figure out quick that you've had everything wrong all your life. Only thing is any new conclusions you come to when you're on the stuff—oops, wrong again. You know that what you knew, you don't know, but you get in deeper when you knew you don't know and can't know any damn thing at all. You could be wrong about that too, but who the hell knows? You know what I mean, Ozwald?"

He puts his hands up, shrugs his shoulders. Smiles an unknowing smile at me, goes on."In those days I wanted to be a poet. I wanted to express truth and I wanted the life of a poet. Be careful what you want, man. If we ever see any truth in this life, we tend to wish we hadn't. Life's a ghost story, I'm afraid.

"In those days I wanted to be a poet but I became a ghost. You might find something romantic in that. Some fools do. That's 'cause they're still babies, suckin' at the world's tit. Don't know to be afraid a nuthin. It's hard to swallow the pill, the idea of things bein' bad and not good. All the fools are happy. Happy,sad. Happy,sad.

"I'd been hanging out on the street just getting to know everybody, sort of. The musicians, the poets and writers, all the artists and the crafts people. The winos and the addicts too. And the bag ladies, everybody. It was a scene. I was livin the life I figured I'd been born for. Hell, I'm an Indian, what else should I do.

"He come up to me after a little gig I did at a health food buffet place. They let you sit up on a little stool in the corner and do your thing. Folksingers and poets. People'd eat, talk, maybe somebody'd pay attention. Maybe somebody'd give ya a tip. Musicians could do pretty good out on the street, but people mostly think you're crazy if you stand on the corner reciting poetry.

"I'd seen 'im around. Seen 'im walkin with this way pretty maid. Some of the vendors holler'n' 'Hey Bobby' at him, like old pals. Like he knew everybody. Never had no personal communication with him before this time though. He said, 'You're pretty good.' He said 'You just need ta learn how to talk.'

"I wasn't quite sure what to make of that. He tore off on a rant that sounded pretty much like gibberish to me. I guess it was supposed to be an example of *how to talk.* At that point another guy I'd met came up and, after a minute, he asked us if we wanted to go smoke a joint. We said, 'Okay'

"The whole arrangement of the market was built on the edge of the cliff, following the curve of the bay, behind. Every hundred yards or maybe a little less, there were long wooden flights of stairs going down to the street below.

"About halfway down the hill we left the stairs to the right and made our way along the hillside to a place between the supports for the railroad bridge that went over the crescent concave of the bay. It was a common place to go for smoking dope I guess, and the winos and others used it for passing a bottle around, too. But it was just us there at that time. We smoked the dooby as a train went over, which Bobby and I agreed was a kind of rare occurrence, but Kim, our Vietnamese friend with the weed, said he'd seen them every now and then.

"About two thirds of the way through the doob, Bobby started off on a poem without any introduction or request from us to hear one or any request from him if we wanted to hear one. He took off out of the gate fast, firing out streams of images and animating with hands and arms and legs. He hit full stride within moments and he would look at you and then turn away or look up at the bridges, or out to the bay. When he'd look at you it was intense and every word burned your conscious and triggered your memory. I looked at Kim and he was right there, too. And some of the words burned like little flicks of a knife that cut the skin and make it bleed and other words hit like hammers of fists that knock you back and take the wind out of you, confuse you and rattle your mind. I think now that he was not doing anything different than the rant he'd started outside the café, but it took the either the drug or the situation to open my mind to it.

"After a timeless period in the hazy vacuum of that space, the *poem* stopped. We stood there, Bobby sat down on the massive length of concrete that the big steel frame was bolted to. We looked at the bay. We looked around. Silent. The pigeons burbling above. The cars motoring below. Ferry coming in and a big cargo ship just sitting out there. Almost distinguishable voices drifting up from the open restaurants on the street.

"Bobby said he had to go meet his girlfriend so he left.

"After he was gone I realized I was overcome, not only with awareness of the realities of Bobby's words, but sadly, depressingly, I was green jealous.

"'How can I even think about being a poet?' I blurted out to Kim.

"'What do you mean?'

"'I mean, I see now what a poet is. I mean, that wasn't a poem; I'd say that was just straight from his soul. It just poured out of him like out of a freaking prophet or something.'

"'It was amazing,' Kim agreed.

"'And me, I agonize over these lines, spend hours, days trying to come up with just the right thing. Maybe come up with a dozen lines. What the hell am I doing. Who am I kidding, that I pretend to be a poet.'

"'Don't be so hard on yourself man.' Kim says to me. ' I guess he's been doing it for a long time.' Then he adds, 'I've even been writing a few lines myself these days.'

"'Thanks, I appreciate it. But I still feel discouraged.'

"I was on an ego thing, you know. And I saw that Bobby, who acted all flamboyant and loud and got the girls and got everybody's attention probably brought no more ego tripping to *it*," Lao Tse makes the sign of quotation marks with his fingers when he says the word *it*, "than I did."

***

"A couple of days later I saw Kim and we went down and burned another one. He was a dope dealer you know, though he looked like a kid, and he was on acid but he was one of those personalities who could function outwardly like normal. I never could understand that. But Kim is telling me how he feels that LSD is a gift from God and how he wants to spread it around and open people's eyes and stuff. That sounded pretty good, as I hadn't really gotten that impression with my limited experience with the stuff.

"As it went, he gave me a few hits to take with me and *spread the word* and so I had an opportunity to broaden my horizons once again."

Here Lao Tse gives me another unknowing look with a little unknowing wink. He asks me to get him a drink, since he doesn't go near the fountain, for some reason that he doesn't explain, so I get him one from the fountain in a plastic glass that he keeps on his person. He drinks slowly, long and noisy. Then he's ready to talk again.

"We ate the acid on the bus ride to Bobby's apartment. There were five of us, including Bobby's girlfriend who didn't take any. There was also my friend Garland, who was a transient, originally from Philadelphia, and his friend, Rick Littlefoot, who I didn't really like. The guy was friendly but he was like into black arts crap and he sure wasn't somebody I could see chumming up with. I'd met the guy's ol' lady once and she gave me the creeps too.

"About an hour after we got to the apartment, I was so blasted. We were drinking beer and rolling cigarettes and listening to Leonard Cohen but that got old as we'd started trippin' so we put on some old blues that was working for us better.

"It seems like something comes out about a person's true colors. Well, maybe the truth comes out and maybe it don't. Maybe it's all imagination, who the hell knows? After awhile, to me, people start lookin' like Gumby and Pokey only not cute. But them black arts people I mentioned, their hard edges and their hard words just seemed to get harder. I was becoming a little overly aware of everybody's hard edges, I'd say. But you can't turn back, you know. So as I'd feel ever more sensitive to life and cognizant, I guess you could say, of a miracle of life, at the same time other folks are sharpenin' their blades and flexing muscles, wielding their bludgeons. I mean I'm tryin to be a flower child here, and they with their canines dripping as they lift their faces from the belly of the beast.

"Later, I remember Bobby talking to me and Garland and then Garland is gone and it's just Bobby and me and it's like he's giving me some kind of class or something. But he goes on like explaining to me how the true nature of things are like ghosts and spirits and he's telling me, *'This is spiritual'*, cause he knows I'm looking for the spiritual. And as things get crazier, it seems like he's mocking me, *'This is spiritual'*, *'This is spiritual'*. And he's showing me these scars on his chest and saying how he used to get down when he was into Satanism but now he's gone back to the Sundance and the old ways, somethin' like that. And he's got this impression of himself, it seems as a poet, as an agent from the dark, come to warn folks, come to show 'em the reality. Anyway, it must have got to be the middle of the night somehow and everybody seemed to be asleep, but me and Bobby. Or they left, I don't even remember.

"Bobby looks like anybody's incarnation of some beast from hell. He has buffalo horns, huge saber tooth fangs and a face all perverted that you can't even look at. I figure he'll probly eat me or worse, but we decide to go out walking around and so we do that. Me and the 'many colored Beast', walking downstairs out of a dive apartment in the slums. It's not just me. It may be acid inspired, but he knows what he is. Lets me know he knows. As morning comes closer, his horns are getting shorter as well as his fangs. His long shaggy hair and mane, gradually turning back into Bobby's long black hair.

"But he's one who rarely ever shuts up. You just want some peace, after being up all night, and you think you've had more than enough, but he goes on and on. Bragging about his homemade hooch, harassing his girlfriend, harassing me. After breakfast we hop the bus and go back downtown. He's got the idea we're soul mates. Of one mind. I know we're not, but it feels good somehow, in my delirium, to have a soul mate, though I had never expected it to be the devil, if I did have one.

"It's nine o'clock in the morning and there's drunks stumbling out of the bars, red men, yellow men, white man, black men, whatever color. They get off to a good start down there. And he's raving away and they're all in perfect tune and they seem to get every word he says and everybody's dancin' around like their ship just come in. The dance of the winos. Bobby's the music, he's in his element."

Lao Tse seems tired now. I ask him if he is. He says he is.

I say, "We can continue later."

He says, "I ain't told ya nothing good yet."

I say, "That's a very promising prospect, hearing something good."

"Well, I wanna tell ya somethin' good."

"Good."

***

Two days later, Lao Tse approaches me that he wants to go on with his story. I'm glad to hear it. He wants to go into the big room this time, which we do and he leads me to a bench near the back wall.

"There probly ain't so much more to tell," he starts out.

I find it interesting that someone who spent at least a portion of his life, living the life of a poet, is in the habit of using such poor grammar.

At one point I think it made me question the authenticity of his story, but I got over it.

He's looking around, like he's looking for the words. "There probly ain't that much more," he repeats, "but maybe there's some more."

I don't say anything.

"I didn't want anything to do with Bobby after that. I didn't decide that he was flat out evil or anything. I guess I was convinced that he did see himself as some kind of messenger from hell. That he was serving the people in that capacity, as perverted as it was.

"But I couldn't be around him. I sure as hell couldn't handle it. Somehow, someway, he'd got to me though, and I found his *way* to have a certain romance. I think now that it's in league with, it's a similar romance that gullible people have found down through time in hero worshiping crime figures and cutthroats, like Robin Hood, Jesse James, etc. Bobby wasn't a criminal, don't get me wrong on that. He wasn't out to hurt people. But he took his energy, his zest for his poetry, from the darkness. I do think his intentions were good. But he had nothing to offer. Isn't that the way? Everybody's carryin' some warning, ain't they? Don't go down this road. Don't do what I done. But they ain't none of 'em can tell you what road *to* go down.

"I killed a man. He was goin' ta rob me and he threatened me and I felt threatened and I shot him and I stabbed him over and over. I was pretty freaked out. Self defense, but the law didn' care. Illegal weapons and excessive use of violence. Also, possession of an illegal substance, namely amphetamines. I'd gone pretty far down the road by that time. I guess my poetry'd taken a pretty dark turn as well.

"But that was the beginning for me. What seemed like it could be the end was the beginning. Some folks would have us believe that all roads lead to hell. Some would go the other way and say they all lead us home. I don't know as one's more true than the other. I was bounced around within the prison system a bit before I got here. Here I met George and all the stuff that went before is only water under the bridge now. I guess George is the real poet. Bobby only seems like a poor troubled kid with a huge ego to me now. I asked George about him. George said to forget about him. I'm okay with that. George has to remember everybody, why should I worry?"

"Earlier, you referred to yourself as a ghost," I remind him.

"No, no, no, ya got me wrong. I didn't say I was *well*. No, I'm a ghost alright. I've never got back and I ain't comin' back. So don't think you pinned one on me, Ozwald." He hasn't raised his voice but his demeanor has suddenly become severe.

I tell him I didn't mean to pin one on him.

He says, "The hell you didn't."

I say, "Okay, maybe I had some small motivation like that for saying it."

He says, "Damn sure you did. But I forgive you for it." With that forgiveness given, he walks away. I am left to my own conclusions.

Ultimately I concluded, or rather I came to the personal theory, that Lao Tse was convinced that George didn't care whether he was a ghost or a man.

wild Indians
a poem

we've run from the old world
we've show'd no respect for it
their god of work
their broken spirits
their fear of law
their stiff upper lips
we gave back the poison
we had no taste for it
the dead food
the fine spirits
the man made materials
the medicine cabinet
to the hills we've escaped
to the stars we've flown
to the sea
from their precious idol, tax and spend
from their beloved deity, on vacation
from their holy scripture, fire and brimstone
from their sacred pilgrimage to vault and casket
we've turned back the clocks
we've thrown the clocks to hell
it's all start to finish
it's all live and die
it's all lie to live
where all stand to fall
we've run from the old world
we've show'd no respect for it
their guns and drums
their blood and thirst
their right to might
their going forward curse
when the gate was left open

we turned and fled
oh sun and stone
oh flesh and bone
oh curse and wailing
oh revenge and failing

we've run on off roads, so deep and rutted
we've run barefoot and pregnant and crying and mudded
we've stopped when the old ones are too sick and coughing
we've stopped when the young ones are vomiting from drinking
we've stopped to catch our breath when it is bleeding
we've stopped to bury those who no longer needed breathing
we've stopped to try and remember our languages and speaking
we've stopped to try and forget our world that we loved ...
we've stopped to try and see where we were going
we've stopped to pray for help and showing ...
we've run on blind and unknowing.

TWELVE: Jeff gains new insights from Stephen and Fyodor

When the Lord wants to make a great poem of a man's life, He sends him or her to the school of privations, worries and difficulties, and all the time He keeps extending His protective hand over him or her to pass through unscathed.
—Kirpal Singh from the book Spiritual Elixer

to the river
a poem

We went to the river every morning and we bathed. The river is known the world over as a holy place of pilgrimage. We didn't go there for that. Our place of pilgrimage was at your feet. We only bathed in the river to be presentable to you. The way we saw it was that if it wasn't available at your store, we didn't need it.

***

And You gave us a hard time. You broke our fragile certainties about life. You took your sword and you divided us—from our families, our parents, our siblings, our children, from our friends, even from our wives and our husbands, and from our countries, our homes. You took our wealth and our positions from us. You took our entertainment. You took our aspirations, our retirement. Our rites and our rituals. You didn't leave us much.

***

What did you leave with us? What did you leave with us? Stripped down models, we became. You left us with nothing in between us. Between us and you.

***

Nothing to protect us from your love. Your love that consumes us. We thought of us, we used to think of us as something—something to fight for, something to guard. But what you left to us was invisible, untraceable. We were apparently made of stuff. Only stuff.

***

Oh, I ran away. Unable to bear the pain of my losses I ran away. Yes I ran away for a thousand, for a million years and more. I ran to the stars and to the mountains and the plains. To the burning hot places under the sun and to the frozen 'land of the midnight sun'. I took to the sea, to the heavens and suffered all the hells. I went to the books, I went to the movies. I went to the dogs and I went to the drugs, and I even went over the edge into the insanity. A train came by and I went aboard. On board there was music playing and I rode the train and the music spoke to me and lifted me and carried me for an eternity until it squandered me and buried me.

***

And they stopped the train and carried me off and held a fine ceremony and erected a memorial and a testimony to me was spoken. And they proclaimed that I was a great actor. That I had lived a life. That I had lived lives, upon lives, upon lives and that I was a great actor. I could play most any part, and had. And a great body of work was my legacy. And there was an inscription at the bottom of a stone that was set over my eternal resting place. The inscription was a cryptic message. 'Who is the actor?'

***

As I bathe in the river with the others, I think of these things. Who is the actor? And I have a sense that I don't need to know anything of actors. I don't need to have anything left. That me, I, words of self, they have no more reality than tomorrow or yesterday.

***

Look at me and give me a life. Talk to me and give me a voice. I will walk off into the sunset of your glance. I will follow the melody of your words, the harmony of your thoughts. I have nowhere else to go, what else can I do?

ordinary blues

"There's little to discover about me. But I want to know about you. Do you feel safe here? Don't you know the possibilities?"

Jeff is holding back these days. He's lost some of the bravado, some of the impulsiveness, with which he started the project. It's precisely because of a hard earned awareness of *possibilities*. So Stephen's counsel is ironic. Still it is not received grudgingly.

He replies, "I don't know the possibilities. I appreciate your concern, Stephen, because I have just begun to learn that very lesson, the lesson of how little I know."

"Well, you're young, it's common for the young to be certain."

"Are you sure that is it?"

"No, I'm not."

Now Jeff sits without speaking, quite lost in the realm of possibility. Another byproduct of the work here, for him, is that he is developing an ability to be silent in the presence of others. And neither does he take note of this silence nor of the brief time that passes. In time he speaks and Stephen listens. "Something seems to be missing from the world, does it not, Stephen? There is no definition to it."

"The Creator may have left that for us—the definition," Stephen says.

"Left it for us, or left it up to us?"

"I agree, it makes a big difference. But I don't know the answer. I can not easily accept it either way, but I pray that he didn't leave it up to us."

"Stephen, I appreciate your humility, but I feel there is much to discover about you."

"Perhaps. But," Jeff does not pressure him, "it's just too big for us, Jeffrey. It's too big for me, anyway. Every answer has a question. All I have ever seen is danger, and the dread of danger, and the fulfillment of danger."

"I'm sorry, Stephen. I didn't mean to upset you."

"You haven't. I am what I am."

"They have not been good to you, the authorities."

"They are not the authorities. They never have been. They are small terrorists. Some have this agenda and some have that. They have the desire for authority but it will never be. George has authority—is authority."

"He seems so troubled, himself though, if you will forgive me for saying."

"Why not? He has my trouble." Stephen makes a motion with his head over his shoulder. "He has their troubles."

"I could use some help with my trouble, as well," Jeff admits.

Stephen only shrugs his shoulders.

Now these jivas

Fyodor pulls hard on the cigarette that Jeff has offered and lit for him. He's ready to talk.

"George is many things to us. Besides bein' a somewhat unwillin' spiritual leader, he's our only real counselor and confidant, I'd say. And on top a all a that, he's kind of a educator. He's taught us a lot about other cultures, for instance. I don't even know how he got all this information. But I guess he's been around some."

"He doesn't tell you about his personal life?"

"No, not that. He never has. But I expect he's been through some of it like the rest of us.

"But back to the culture, stuff, I was goin' ta say that he uses some very interesting terms." The sly Fyodor raises his eyebrows and gives Jeff a 'knowing look.

Jeff just waits.

"He's told us about how the world was created you know. Did you know that?"

"How the world was created" Jeff asks.

"No, I mean that he told us about it."

"No I didn't."

"Well he did."

Jeff waits.

"He told us that God had created his family, like. Like sons and daughters and he gave them all special powers and special knowledge and like that. They were all beautiful and wise and everythin'. But I guess after awhile, one of his sons, the most beautiful one, in many ways.

"George said it that way. 'In many ways'.

"Well this one son, somehow got greedy and he wanted his own world. So he devoted hisself to God for a long, long time, longer than we can even imagine with our limited intellect. And when God was pleased with him, he asked his son if he could do something for him, as a gift for that devotion. Well this son, he told God right then that he wanted his own world. That hit God kinda hard, I suppose, seein' that his son wasn't happy with the world he already was a part of, but anyway he went along with it because he loved him and he gave him his own world.

"Meanwhile, God created the jivas. George told us that God had created the jivas from hisself. Jiva is a name for a soul in a body. I guess God was just so full of creativity that he went on creatin' and creatin' and fillin' up his beautiful world. And these jivas, although they was part of God, they were enough apart from God so as to be able to move around and live all kind of perfect and peaceful lives, full of grace and beauty and love, according to George.

"But his son, the one with his own new world was busy creatin' his place as well. And after awhile, and I guess it was another of those really long whiles again, but after awhile he decided he needed some life in his world. So what does he do?"

After a bit, Jeff realizes that Fyodor seems to be waiting for him to reply.

"Uh, I don' know."

"Well, he starts up devotin' himself to God again. Are you payin' attention, son?"

"Yeah, sorry. I just didn't know it was a question."

"Okay," Fyodor says, shrugging his shoulders.

"Well after a long time he gets up the nerve I guess and he asks God for the jivas. You can about imagine how that made God feel. Well maybe you cain't, but I cain't."

This time it's Jeff's turn to raise his eyebrows.

"But anyway, God gets talked into it because he loves his son so much. I never could figure out about how much God loved the jivas as to give 'em up to that greedy son, but that's what he done. He done it on a condition though." Fyodor looks Jeff right in the eye. "The condition was that whenever any of the jivas was to get tired of the place of the greedy son, that he, God himself, was a goin' to come and take 'em home. He was a goin' to come in the form of a man. What you think about that?"

Jeff hesitates for a moment, then offers, "I don't know what to think about it."

"Well, it's a little like the Bible story, ain't it?"

"Yeah, I can see a similarity."

"Thass good," he says, and he sits back into the chair and says again, nodding his head, "Thass good." Then he sits back up and goes on.

"Now these jivas seem to have got here with only a small part of their knowledge intact. For one thing, they forgot their manners completely. The way they treat each other. It's just Godawful. Behind most everry smile, most everry handshake, most every low bow, there's a distrust—a fear at best. Opportunism and design are the rule, you know. Anybody with a half a brain can see that.

"Ain't nobody knows how to act right. And them that thinks they do, most often they acts the worst. Walk down the street with you head up or walk up the street with you head down. It's all wrong. We're all wrong.

"But in another way, it's alright. It's alright. I want to tell you about a incident what set me free, Jeff—Jeff, you said it was, didn' ya?"

"Yes"

"I guess you got the time, huh Jeff?"

"I'd love to hear it."

"Hell of a way to make a living, listening to psychos and weirdo's tell stories."

"I'm not making much of living at it, Fyodor. It might be a kind of investment, but not necessarily one that will pay off as a living."

"Well, time'll be the judge a that. You boys just keep plyin' us with cigarettes and we'll make up this shit till the cows come home." At that he laughs a good, loud, but also good natured laugh, slapping Jeff on the knee so hard it hurts.

"Just kiddin'. Aw, I'm just messin' with ya. Don't look so worried."

"I'm not worried, just my knee hurts."

"Oh well, I guess you'll get over it." He breaks out laughing again. Jeff slides his chair back out of reach.

"Okay, okay, I get the message. Well, I'll just get on with it, then. But, ah, wonder if I could pry another one a them smokes from you? To sort of help keep my mind engaged."

Jeff gives him one.

"Started out, I was working for the city. I had been on that esteemed payroll for fifteen years. Mechanical maintenance. Jack of all trades, if you know what I mean. The job was alright, I'll say. Had a certain pride in it. If it didn't work or it was broke, didn' matter what it was, they'd bring it to our department. I worked with four, five other guys, depending. If it couldn't be brought, we'd go out with a truck. Honest work, no problem with that. It was the macho aspect of it that I didn' care for. And the complaining. Man, they harass you to death if you don't put on the same ol' big act, like a tough guy. Same guys that're cryin' like babies from morning to night about how tough it is. If it's not complaining about one thing it's another. Whinin' about their father-in-laws or their son-in-laws or bitchin' about their wives' spending habits or their kids bein' lazy. It's all games, that's all it is. All splutter and bravado.

"So one night me and this fella, Jesse, are out on a call for a busted up street light, which was located in a kind of dark area below another street that passed over. The electricians had already cut the power to it but it was our job to remove the broken light pole and replace it if we had a replacement for it. When we got there I was pretty sure, right away, we didn't have that particular light pole on hand, but I sent Jesse to the warehouse to look while I worked at getting the old one out.

"The fella that hit the thing got messed up bad, which I confirmed later, but I was already convinced of it because, not only was the pole completely mangled but it was obvious the vehicle had been thrown to the right of the pole and hit the concrete bridge abutment on that side hard. There were pieces of plastic still layin' around a lot of glass. The worst of it though, that bothered me was, on the pole there was these long human hairs stuck to it in a mass of clotted blood and skin. So somebody must have come out or at least part way out of the vehicle at the pole before the vehicle hit the abutment. I ain't no detective, but my thinking was fairly confirmed in the local paper the next day.

"Jesse came back and he said we didn' have no light like that but he had brought a temporary light that we used sometimes in such a circumstance and after we finished getting the original light out and into the truck, we got that set up and called the electrician to come and wire it in temporary.

"I guess I really wasn't cut out for that macho stuff, because it weren't long after that that things started to slide out from under me. It wasn't that the accident itself bothered me so much. I mean it bothered me but not to where I couldn't work or nothin'. It's just that I couldn't play the game no more. I'd go to work and the boys'd start in with their shit and I just couldn't put up with it. I found myself getting angry regular and then I just got angry more and more regular. Them guys could only put up with that for so long and then when they got tired a complainin' to each other, they started complainin' to the boss.

"'Bout then I started in drinkin'. I swear I never was a drinkin' man before that. Well, as you can easily guess, that didn' go over well with the little woman. I feel stupid now even usin' that damn macho word, 'little woman' as I never could abide that kinda chauvinist talk but it rubs off on ya and these things get stuck in places inside of us, we don't even know where they're at. But my wife didn' like my drinkin'. I'll just say that.

"But I didn' stop and, soon enough, sure enough, I was getting in trouble. My employers, at my boss's recommendation got me into a treatment center, which was paid for by the city. It got me to stop drinking temporary, but it didn' get down to what was botherin' me, makin' me so angry and all kind of other feelings started comin' up as well then, without the booze. I started getting all mixed up about differn't things. She'd come in with the kids, for one thing, and I'll be damned if I didn' remember their names right. It was kind of embarrassing. I couldn' get 'em straight. And sometimes she'd be telling me somethin' about somethin' that happened with some of our church friends or somethin' like that and I couldn' figure out what she was talking about."

He stops suddenly and says, "Jeff, my man, how ya doin? Ya hangin' in there with this little ramble?"

Jeff says, "No problem, Fyodor. I'm quite fascinated, actually."

"Okay, that's it. I'm gonna have to recommend they put you on full time now. Nobody else around here would've stayed with me for the first two minutes."

Jeff laughs at that and asks him to please go on.

So he does. "Well, I get out of there after awhile, mostly 'cause I don' cause no real trouble, I guess. I go home with the wife and try to settle in to some kind of routine at home since I'm not ready to go to work yet. The doc wrote me out the papers sayin' that. Says I'm showing signs of delusional hypochondria, but that I'm also having memory problems. He was sure nuff right on the second part of it, I'll tell ya that.

"The short of it is that pretty soon I started in drinkin' again. We were starting to have to watch our budget pretty close so I took to some of that cheap vino, ya know and that rot gut stuff's hard on a person, physically, not to mention the mental part.

"After that I entered a new phase of the process of what I like to call my emancipation. Oh, my great-great-grandparents, they were slaves, ya know. Their's was a different kind of emancipation."

At this point, Jeff notices Fyodor make a slight gesture with his fingers like he's getting ready to ask for another cigarette. He offers him one unasked.

"That's right kind of you, my man. Got to say I 'preciate that." He accepts the light that Jeff offers as well, and then takes a long drag off of the cigarette.

"What I was getting to was, that the nature of that new phase was the beginning of my hallucinations. At least that's what they call 'em. I ain't hunnerd percent convinced that it's all in my head, you know. For one thing I'm not exactly the brightest ornament on the Christmas Tree, you know what I'm sayin', Jeff? But I see, I mean, well hell, I talk with folks I'm not really capable of imagining, I'd say. And in places that dify discription." He sits back smoking for a couple of long minutes while Jeff patiently waits, assuming he'll go on. Which he does.

"My crimes is not much," he says, shaking his head. "My crimes is not much."

"What are your crimes, Fyodor, if you don't mind my asking?"

"It's alright," and he sits back in his chair, smoking. "That's 'bout what I was getting to anyhow."

He reaches his arm out and makes a broad arc as if to signify a large area or a large idea.

"All over the world, there's blood. It's an old world, now. It smells bad from the bad blood and the long history of violence upon it. The autumn come and it falls back and tries to hide the world. The winter come and it tries to preserve the world. The spring come and it tries to refresh the world. But the smell of it all cain't be covered or cleaned away, and when the summer time comes and the world heats up it gets mighty potent. Don' know how folks can stand it. Don' know how they ignore it.

"They say I'm a killer but I don' zactly see it thataway. All's I remember is the dreams or the hallucinations or whatever you want ta call 'em. Folks that was so hard up, all they knew was bad. Ol' guys." He's running the fingers of his right hand back and forth across his mouth and chin whiskers. "Older than you could ever know." A bit of water spills out of Fyodor's wet eyes and rolls slowly down his face, and he looks away.

"What happened, Fyodor?"

"We were in the same place, Jeff. They was worse off'n I was, even. Who in the hell wants to go on? Been goin' on and on forever. God don' help. Booze don' help. Family cain't help. Who's gonna help? Goddamit—who's gonna help?"

"You helped them?"

"I don' know." His body is shaking a little bit, speaking very softly now. "Maybe not. I just done what they asked me ta do. But we were in the same place."

"This was all one event?" Jeff asks.

"Oh, no. Oh no, it was more'n one event."

"You were hallucinating?"

"We were in the same place."

"Oh"

"Had you known these men before?"

"I'd known one of 'em."

Jeff asks how many there were.

"There was two."

"Oh," Jeff said, sighing, somewhat relieved.

"They were not bad men, Jeff. I don' *want* you to get the wrong idea."

"Were they good men?"

"They were men."

After a pause, Jeff asks, "What now for you, Fyodor?"

Fyodor looks at him, looks down the hall, looks back. "It's differ'n't now." He looks down, looks up at Jeff. "I don' wanna talk no more."

THIRTEEN: The nature of George

All things were made by him
and without him was not anything made that was made
In him was life; and the life was the light of men
And the light shineth in darkness;
and the darkness comprehended it not.
—*The Gospel of John 1: 2-5*

the lake and the pool

George is walking alone through an Aspen forest trail full of golden, green-filtered sunlight. It is not quiet because the birds are singing, the late season Aspen leaves are rattling, chipmunks are occasionally darting this way and that on forest floor, squirrels are squabbling in the trees. As he walks on he also begins to hear the sound of water. When the trail opens into full sunlight he finds himself at the lip of a blue mountain lake. There is a clearing and a meadow on the far side with small grey mountains rising up behind and to the north. The sound, he discovers after a short walk, is coming from a small fall at the southern rim where the nearly round lake drains into a pool, which is surrounded by huge stones of strange and beautiful appearance.

He climbs down the twenty-five feet of embankment for a closer scrutiny. From below, the stones are even more remarkable, the pool more beautiful, and George is soon feeling a sense of tranquility outside of his remembered experience. The enchanting waterfall sounds so sweet and natural that he feels hypnotized by the increasing musical sensation of it. The birds of the forest are also still audible and they provide a perfect background accompaniment. Sparkling jewels of color and light reflecting and refracting in the air and in the pool are dancing to the grand and delightful music of this natural phenomenon.

As he sits helplessly, but willingly, in absolute stillness he notices for the first time that the stones are undoubtedly familiar forms. Human like, they are, but although some are nearly recognizable to him, others only evoke a strong sense of familiarity. Some have an elf-like quality while some are more reminiscent of innocent indigenous and primitive people of a variety of races and nations. There are also beings of an angelic nature, cherubim, seraphim, gandharvas, apsaras, and fairies.

As George sits in perfect peace and wonder, the shy beings display their delight in his presence with obeisances and offerings of incense, sage, precious jewels and golden jewelry. Maidens bring him cups full of water of the falls and it is heavenly nectar. He in turn serves them all prasäd of His own manifestation and He bestows loving glances upon them and their love for Him is great and good.

He speaks to them then, this assembly of beautiful people, and He tells them stories of ancient and glorious things, and He tells them how He loves them.

But after a time He shows them His tears and His great sorrow. He tells them of the miseries in the world, the great suffering of His disciples, and as He speaks to them, their hearts are broken; they cannot bear it. And though they love Him so and desire His company and His darshan, they cannot bear the knowledge of His burden. So they return to their forms of stone and then the pool becomes a pitiful little fountain in the dirty city and the lake is seen to be the dirty plaza where the people carelessly throw their litter, where George is a homeless relic of his own dismal and distorted fate. And as the sun is going down, George is left without an opportunity to secure a bed in one of the shelters for the night.

The nature of George

the misty swirls
a poem

Where have you gone?
You've forgotten me.
Like an orphaned fawn
I live dangerously.
I looked out on the road
but no dust was stirring
until my back was bowed

and my vision was blurring.
When my house burned down
I sought your shelter
But when you couldn't be found
I ran helter-skelter.
I went out on the land
begging food so poor.
Is this what you had planned
when you left before,
to leave my world so dry
bereft and broken
to leave without saying why
when it had all been spoken,
fallen on deaf ears
to lay among the pearls
among the swine my dears?
Into the misty swirls
have a look, have a look
You can go your own way
but I'm an open book
and you're a breath away.
Yes, you're old and weak
yet you have the charms
mild and meek,
hold you in my arms.

FOURTEEN: An interview with Clancy

From the things He created, Allah has given you a covering shade, and He has made for you refuges in the mountains. He has given you garments to protect you from the heat, and garments to protect you from your own violence. As such it is that He perfects His favors upon you, in order that you submit.
—Qur'an, 16.81

interview with Clancy
Ansel

George doesn't let us interview him. In fact he genuinely seems to avoid us. If we approach him, any one of us, he walks away. If we meet him by coincidence in the hallway, for instance, or in the elevator he is aloof. It's not that he is rude, on the contrary, he seems afraid of us. He seems painfully shy. That, however, doesn't really jibe with his behavior with his friends. In that environment he is most definitely, and obviously, their charismatic leader.

So I talked to Horatio about it, asked him if he could have a word with George, maybe smooth the way for me, or for one of the others. Horatio is always approachable. But he clams up on me as soon as he realizes what I want. Clams up solid. Won't even talk about it. Strange, it seems to me. Very strange. In a world of strange. I tell him so. He's unmoved. I plead with him. He's unmovable.

I try Milton. Milton pretends he's crazy as soon as he gets my drift. Milton is crazy. But he pretends he is crazy in a way that he is not. Very strange. Again, I plead. Milton hides behind his game of craziness.

We question the staff. "Does he speak to any of them?"

"Not a word, ever. Not even upon threat of punishment. Not even under punishment. Except for Clancy."

"Who's Clancy," we ask.

"He's a night guard. George is known to speak to him". So we, Jeff and I, get night passes. Ozwald is out sick for a few days. Has some horrible kind of flu that's landed him an overnighter in the hospital. We visited him and he was so out of it he was delusional, hallucinating. The doctors say it's a bad virus that's going around, but Ozwald thinks it's something Toby did to him. Makes us wonder a little bit too, though, with that Toby. He's a heavy-duty case. I'm personally glad to leave him to Ozwald.

But back to Clancy. Clancy turns out to be an exception to the stereotypical guard. I know, it's a prejudice. It's hard to shake, though.

The guards are so hard and most of them come off with so much arrogance that, I admit, I've begun to develop that prejudice. It's a seed that grows and, like a weed, it's hard to kill. But Clancy is a definite exception.

***

He isn't on the floor when we get there, but another guard informs us that he'll be up shortly as he's *riding shotgun* with the meds cart. After twenty minutes he and the nurse exit the elevator and the guard confirms that it's him. He accompanies the nurse to the station where he unlocks the door for her and then moves out onto the floor and then over to a position by one of the windows on the far wall. Jeff and I look at each other, shrug our shoulders and then we go over to him. First thing that surprises is his physical appearance. He's like six foot five, and string bean thin, a little bit slouched like some very tall folks are. He doesn't look like he could handle himself in a physical confrontation, which is the opposite of the first impressions you get from most of the guards. Their very presence, their appearance, is intimidating. The women as much as the men. Later on we find out how deceiving looks can be. Clancy is no slouch. I mean he slouches, but he's no slouch.

I introduce Jeff and myself and Clancy responds personably. That's the second surprise. He tells us he's been made aware of the work we have been doing and that he was informed we were coming to see him. As we talk his eyes are steadily moving around the area but, somehow, it doesn't make him appear distracted. Rather he seems competently focused on his job as well as aware of every aspect of our conversation. Later on we will also get some idea of just how intelligent this long tall prison guard is.

"As you know, Clancy, we have come to speak to you about George and about what we have come to view as the phenomena of George, or should I say, the phenomena surrounding George," I say.

Clancy nods, "Yes that's what I'm expecting from you."

"So you're agreeable to an interview?"

"Up to a point, I am," he says, matter of fact, but still not threatening or intimidating. I'm beginning to gain some confidence in the possibilities here.

"Maybe we could begin by asking you some questions about yourself?" Again I'm bracing myself for the negative reaction which doesn't come.

"How long have you worked here?" I say.

"I'm in my third year."

"Are you local to the area?"

"No, I'm from New England. New Hampshire and southwestern Massachusetts. I kind of have roots from both."

"I don't hear it in your accent," Jeff tells him.

"People tell me that. I suppose it's because my parents were originally Midwesterners. They hung onto *their* roots, I guess."

Then Jeff goes where I certainly wouldn't have gone quite yet. "Excuse me for saying so, Clancy, but you don't seem to quite fit the mold here on first impression."

Clancy is looking at him pretty intently at this point. "How did you get into this line of work?"

"Maybe we should get onto talking about George and his pals," he says. I don't know what Jeff's thinking, but I don't need for Clancy to draw a picture and I'm hoping Jeff will slow down a little bit.

Jeff says, "I'm sorry, Clancy, but it might be all kind of related. We've been observing George and his *pals*, as you call them, for a while now and one thing has come out. George doesn't relate to everybody. At least not that it shows. He doesn't talk to any of the other guards, even under heavy pressure to do so, and he won't talk to Ansel or I or Ozwald, who's the other associate involved in our project."

Clancy is looking kind of fierce to me at this point, but he lets Jeff go on. "And as far as the inmates go, it's not clear to us whatsoever. He pays very special, I would even say a very loving, type of attention to some pretty hard core individuals. But, surprisingly, there does seem to be reciprocation from those people. Some of them don't seem to give a damn about anyone but themselves, but ask 'em about George and they get all teary eyed—and what we've been told is that he talks to you, Clancy. So it makes me think, and I'm pretty sure Ansel feels the same," *Drag me into it*, I'm thinking, "that there must be something special about you." Clancy is looking around the room. The tension I was sensing seems to have dissipated. But he doesn't say anything. I look at Jeff trying to telepathically convince him to just wait now. I don't know if it is my telepathy, really, but he waits.

In time, Clancy informs us he has to make his rounds but says we can walk with him if we like. I look at my watch and it's a quarter to eight. We walk around the perimeter of the large room, past Toby, who doesn't look at us, and past Walt, who does. We go past the other guard and past the nurses station and enter the hallway. There we go by Eugene and continue on down the hallway. There's been no sign of George or his *pals* up to this point. But as we pass Milton and Jean-Paul's cell we find them hanging out in there. George is sitting on the floor along with Jean-Paul, Ahmed and Bascomb, and Milton and Horatio are draped sideways across the beds. We continue down the hall and around the end, Clancy looking methodically and carefully into all the cells. Although the lavatory has a large, unbreakable glass window through which one can see the two urinals and even the two stalls, Clancy goes in and gives it a thorough looking over. There are a few cells not occupied and they are locked shut, but all the ones being lived in are locked open. George's cell that he shares with Anthony is in the back end of the corridor. Anthony is in there and he is muttering to himself. He curses at us as we go by, although I don't remember the exact nature of the curse, even if I did actually hear the exact nature of it. But it was unmistakably that.

It occurs to me that there are some things that crazy people, even in prison, can get away with that would be likely cause for severe confrontation and/or consequences for anyone else.

Around the far side hall we are witness to a man sexually abusing himself. He's in his cell, with his sex organ exposed and aroused as he raps his head along the bars in the manner that prisoners in the movies would rap their metal cups along the bars to draw the attention of the guards. Clancy walks crisply into the cell, throws the man on his bed and gives him a judicious little rap on his testicles, which sets the man to howling, but succeeds in curtailing the aforementioned offensive behavior. But I have to wonder if this was only a punishing deterrent or if perhaps the man had thus achieved the desired result of his abuse. In any case, we went on.

As we come out of the hall into big room, we see that there are three prisoners playing cards at the first table. As we approach, one of the men, without looking up from his cards, asks Clancy if the sex was as good for him as it was for Jaiden back there in the cell. Clancy instantly jerks the chair out from under the man, but before he reaches the floor, has him by one large hand from the back of the neck and by the other at the waist of his jumpsuit. He flings the man into the air over his head and as the fellow is coming down, he gives him a horrible upward blow to the abdomen with his nightstick.

He then pounces on his victim where he falls onto the floor and again strikes him with the stick, this time across the back. I'm convinced that I hear a rib crack with the hit.

As he raises his arm to strike again, he also raises his eyes. Those eyes that are fixed in violent focus. A focus, now beyond the initial rage, even beyond anger. Like a great predator bird he appears, with mighty wing and powerful talon, and dark mindless eyes over the sharp pointed beak of his nose set in that terrible narrow face. But those eyes, blind to all else as they are in the white heat of their cruel and sad purpose, cross another gaze inadvertently, as they are momentarily uplifted. George is sitting on a bench, back against the wall, looking at him. Clancy's purpose disappears in that instant. The features of his face lose the suspension of their fierce intention. His entire body is now speaking another language.

He gently lays down the nightstick. His shoulders come down. His head falls forward. Then he puts his hands gently under the head of the beaten man and makes a request in a soft voice, of no one in particular, since a small crowd has gathered round, for a glass of water for the man.

After helping him drink from the glass that Bascomb brings, Clancy picks him up and carries him in silence to his cell with the rest of us following like curious bumpkins, cowed by the display of vicious terror, and yet awed by the spectacle, as well as dismayed by the sudden tranquil turn of temper. And the now gentle guard lays him in his bed with the grace and concern of an older brother for his wounded or exhausted younger, then goes out to the nurse and instructs the young associate to go in and attend to the poor man.

After that, Clancy isn't in the mood to continue with the interview, but when Jeff asks, now in a tone that has a much more polite character to it than that of his earlier questioning, if we can come back tomorrow night, the distracted man agrees.

***

At the apartment, as Jeff and I go over our rather fragmented and somewhat inconsistent notes, the evening in the ward strikes us as somehow extremely valuable. Not that we understand anything or could explain it if we did. Clancy, who is obviously some version of a bipolar personality, we reason, seems to be a rare individual who has been fortunate to find employment that suits his otherwise self-destructive behavior. That part is easy. At the risk of great generalization, it is possible that it is not at all inconsistent with some very common prison guard attributes.

What seems valuable, in terms of our work here, is our fortune in witnessing first hand, what appeared to be an example of George's influence. I know that conclusion could be dismissed as the result of a sort of predisposed imagination, but both of us observed the connection, the visual communication between the two men. It was something tangible; I would go so far as to say, unmistakable. It was the sort of thing people had been relating to us, to *our* general sense of cynicism, in the interviews.

***

The next night, Clancy is on the floor when we arrive. He is calm and seems open to our questioning, as we sit at one of the tables in the big hall.

"Did you know George or did you ever meet him outside of this institution," I ask as we begin. There seems no need for any small talk or lead up questions.

"No, I didn't."

"When did you meet him here?" Jeff asks.

"I became aware of him as soon as I came to the mental ward, which was over two years ago. I wouldn't call it meeting him in the usual sense. He's an inmate. I'm his authority."

"Do you, yourself, consider George to be some type of holy man?" This is my question. The one I very much want to ask.

Clancy looks at me with penetrating intent, as if trying to read something about me, but not in a threatening manner. "George is a unique individual. He has some *quality* that I do not understand. Many men have qualities I don't understand. That's not my job. However, I think he helps some of the men. He gives them hope. He seems to be a positive influence on them."

"But does he have an effect on you personally?"

"As I said, I am his authority, his superior. He is a prisoner. I am a prison guard. I do not get involved with the prisoners on personal levels."

I try a new tack. "If you met George on the street, outside of work, would that make a difference?"

"I can't say."

"Does he talk to you, personally? Have you ever had a conversation with him?" Jeff asks exactly what I would have said at exactly the same place.

"Yes I have. It's not prohibited to have conversations with the prisoners."

"Would you be willing to share any of the content of such a conversation with George?" Jeff continues.

This time Jeff gets the look, but again it is not threatening. Clancy has obviously prepared himself for this type of questioning.

"Look, I'm going to tell you guys right now, whatever I am at liberty to tell you. You want to know what I think about George, who he is, what my relationship is with him. Alright, but no more questions after this."

We tell him we agree to that. He tells us he doesn't care whether we agree or not. "No more questions after that."

We nod our heads.

Clancy says, "George is a man of God. You might, understandably, wonder how I can make a determination like that. Well, I don't know. But still I have no doubt about it. It's not anything he has said to me. Our conversations are light hearted and good natured at best. However, I've never heard him say anything I would not agree with, or that I would consider to be demeaning to another human being.

"But it's not what he says. What *it* is I will not attempt to explain to you two gentlemen or to anyone, because it is not something that is explainable.

"Now I have a job to do," and he gets up.

So we get up too. We take the hint, you know. I had had an urge when we were talking with him to ask after the health of the inmate that he had the altercation with last night, since we were all getting along so well, but I know that would have been pushing my luck. I also am pretty sure I can get that information from other sources on the day shift. Maybe I will be able to visit the man myself, even if he's in the infirmary.

***

We ask to take a stroll through the corridors after our talk with Clancy. We're curious as to what it's like at night, when the prisoners are locked in their cells. The other night guard, a huge man named Ed, tells us that we can walk with him when he makes his rounds. So, that's no problem, we just sit at one of the tables, discussing our experiences with Clancy until Ed can take us around. We feel quite fortunate that we will be getting the opportunity.

"Really got to admit the institution has really treated us fairly," Jeff remarks, at one point.

"Very much so," I agree.

"I expected less. I expected them to be much more closed, more paranoid of our prying eyes."

"That's just what I'm saying, Ans."

But it begins to feel that quite a bit of time has gone by since we talked to Ed, and we start glancing at our watches. "Only a half hour; no big deal." But another half hour goes by, and still no Ed for us. He's made a couple of trips around the room, and each time returned to his position by the nurse's station. We have by then begun to keep an eye on his doings, not staring, exactly, but out of our peripheral vision.

"You know Jeff, I was doing a little digging around on the internet the other night and I found that a lot of the modern prisons don't use bars on the cells at all. Some have these shatterproof glass doors and some had solid doors, with just little windows in them."

"Yeah I had wondered about that myself," Jeff says.

"The other day, I asked that guard, Zeke, about it."

"Oh yeah, whu'd he say?"

"Said, 'We got bars'."

"Oh. Okay, I can see that now."

Another half hour goes by. We're wondering if Ed forgot about us. We're tired and want to go home. We are wondering if he lied to us. Wondering if he doesn't like us.

Finally, Jeff says, "Alright, we've been more than patient. I'm going to go talk to him."

"Okay, guess I'll go with you," I say, my heart not in it, but not knowing what else to do.

"Hey, Ed, how's it goin?" Jeff begins, with a smile.

"Alright," says Ed.

"Just checking to see, you didn't forget about our trip around the cells, we talked about," Jeff says, good-naturedly.

"I didn't forget."

"Just hasn't come time for your rounds yet, huh?"

"Yeah," is all Ed says.

If it was me, I would have let it go for sure, but Jeff isn't me.

"So what time do those rounds come up, anyway?" he asks.

"They come up toward morning," Ed says.

***

Our tiredness and desire to get home is finally trumped by our desire to go around the cells, after a lengthy discussion back at our table. We start hitting the nurses' coffee and settle in. It's like a ghost town in the hall. We're used to seeing a lot of activity during the day. A ghost town, quite literally, because the energy of the place is so powerful, and so disturbing.

The minutes go by like quarter hours, the hours, like entire evenings. There is the occasional shriek from the corridors, the occasional rattling of steel doors. Jeff and I try to make a game of it, guessing who are the noisemakers. It's kind of pathetic, I know, making a game of people's anxieties, but these are desperate times. We even speculate that some anxieties may well be the products of sheer boredom. At six fifteen Ed walks over and invites us to walk the floor with him. "Sure, we'll pitch in, if you need the help," Jeff quips, smiling. Ed ignores the comment— thank God I'm thinking—or at least he doesn't react to it. I guess Jeff just can't hold it in sometimes.

We start down the right side corridor past Ahmed and Carol J.'s cell, which is on the right, the restrooms on the left. The walkway is dimly lit and the cells are unlit save what washes in from the track lighting in the walkway. There is silence on the floor, save for the creak of Ed's leather pistol holster in concert with the clink and clatter of various other items attached to our otherwise reticent guide. I feel myself a part of a troupe of ghostly visitants upon the already tormented souls of this ward.

We pass the *dead man's* cell, which is the only cell on the left in this portion of the corridor. On the right is Toby's nighttime station of confinement. He is sitting on his bed, watching silently as we approach. It occurs to me at that moment, the irony, perhaps the cruelty, of his location directly across from a man who is all but dead, given Toby's predilection. Was the placement intentional? I can't help but wonder. But it's the type of question of which I suspect I will never learn the answer.

I continue to be aware of the stillness of the inmates. I would have certainly expected more activity from a group, comprised in part by men prone to a nightmarish quality of life, even during the daylight hours. I am also impressed with Jeff's self-containment. I am thinking these thoughts, somewhat distractedly, going by Milton and Jean Paul's shared cell without hardly noticing. But then we near the end of the corridor and I realize we will be passing George and Anthony's cell next. We find George standing at the foot of his bed, with Anthony apparently asleep in his. Ed stops, perhaps aware of our curiosity, maybe having some reason of his own. It is quite dark in the cell, but I am aware of George's absolute stillness. We are seeing only his right side profile but I am able to determine that his eye is definitely closed. I cannot perceive any sign of his breathing. I am fairly entranced by the sight of him, yet keenly embarrassed at the seeming voyeurism in our watching him.

Because of my embarrassment I turn away, but then it occurs to me to go back and take a look into Milton and Jean Paul's cell, since I missed the opportunity as we went by moments ago. The cells are divided by solid walls, rather than by bars, and when I get past the divider I am shocked to find both of them sitting on the floor, each in a cross-legged posture, also with eyes closed, and to all appearances, deeply absorbed in some form of meditation. But I soon find myself embarrassed, just as I was in looking at George, so I return to the others, who are waiting for me, and we go on.

We walk the rear and left side corridors, without incident, the entire floor of inmates alike, passively presenting an impression of being at rest, which is so contrary to my expectations that, to this day, it remains a source of bewilderment to me.

We exit the corridor and walk to the guard's station with Ed. We thank him sincerely. But Ed is not interested in our thanks.

"I hope you boys learned something from this business," he begins. "There's a differ'nt view that y'all got now, I expect, than yuh've seen before.

"We acknowledge to him that we were quite impressed with what we saw, not sure where he's taking us with this.

"As you can plainly see, the devil's got a holt in there pretty damn strong, with that George bein' the representative of his evil choice. Them poor goddamned other boys is just gullible statistics is all they are. I was glad ta take ya through because I wanted you to git a chance ta see things in their proper light. That light bein' darkness, if ya take my meanin'."

We wait, not sure if he's done. He isn't.

"'I admit I had my motive. Now that yuh've seen, and knowin' that you fellas got some pull, somehow or t'other, I'as thinkin' that mebee yuh'd help me convince the higher ups of the truth." He hesitates, thinking how to say it. "Cuz that George has slyly got 'em thinkin' he's harmless. But we know better, huh? Him standin there dead-like in the middle of the night, got the rest of 'em so spooked they don't dare put out a whimper till daylight. Hell, he ain't even breathin'—you seen it; the son of a bitch ain't even breathin'."

Ed kind of put us on the spot there with that little lecture. I didn't have a clue how to react. Neither did Jeff, I would venture, but of course, that rarely ever stops Jeff. He politely tells Ed that we'd do what we could, "But don't count on us too heavily," he says, putting his hand on Ed's shoulder, "'cause whatever pull we have, well it may not be enough, in a case like this." We leave then, the events of the last hour having awakened us more than we've been all night.

"In a case like this?" I say to Jeff, in the elevator, looking at him, incredulous.

"It's a rare case," Jeff answers soberly, not looking up.

"Well, you're right about that," I say back to him.

***

That night I dream. I remember it fairly well — for a dream.

I am watching a bullfrog. He's sitting in a big puddle, with the brown dirty water up almost to his knees. I am sitting on the ground before the puddle. The ground is wet and cold, and I am not sure how long we've been there but I feel somehow responsible for him. He just looks at me, big eyes with big dark pupils, Mona Lisa smile, his vocal sac undulating slightly.

"This doesn't look right for you," I have said to him.

"It doesn't matter; it's not in my will," he says.

I hear a blast of some horn and then a loud roaring noise and I leap at the last moment, realizing for the first time that I have frog legs. Frog legs that have saved my life as a car comes barreling through the puddle, throwing water high into the air so that I am thoroughly soaked and flustered. I fall about in some confusion as I come to understand that it is a road. We're sitting on a road. Finally I remember the frog.

He's covered with mud and looking more miserable than before.

"It's a road!" I inform him in my anxiety. "Why don't we go?"

"It's not my will," he replies, calm and resigned.

"What *is* your will," I ask.

"No," he tells me, "please understand, I am not here by my will."

I look at him, pleading in my expression and voice. "By whose, then?"

But you know how dreams are; I don't get the answer, at least not at that point, because another car comes along. As it is about to splash through the puddle, a door opens and a hand, connected to an arm reaches out and grabs me. I don't understand because I think, I'm big, like a person, but somehow this hand grabs me and pulls me into the car and I'm yelling, "Watch out for …," but I don't know the bullfrogs name. But the boy—it turns out to be a boy who had grabbed me—says, "He's alright, don't worry."

"Who's alright?" I say, suspicious.

"It's only a puddle."

"But the wheels. The wheels could hit him. I don't think he's very aware."

"Oh, he's been hit by so many wheels. Don't you know who he is?" the boy says.

"He's my friend. But it doesn't seem right for him."

"Well, he's not right, of course," says a deep man's voice, like a big bullfrog voice from the front of the car. I look up and the man, who seems to be the driver, is turned around, looking at me from between the front seats.

The man continues to look back, ignoring his driving as the car speeds along and I sort of panic, thinking he should be watching where we're going. I shriek to the boy, "He could hit him—he could hit another car!" I shriek to the boy.

"There's nothing to hit," says my young capturer. "We're not there."

I don't have a clue what he means by that. I look out the windows. It occurs to me that I'm glad I have human vision. I can't figure out if I'm a frog or a human, or what I am. But the sky is the sky and the clouds are going by.

"Can't you please take me back to him? He's kind of innocent, and foolish."

A woman's voice, also in the front seat, says, "You're very attached to that puddle, my dear."

I gasp in exasperation. "Not the puddle. He's my friend. It's not right. He's not right for the puddle."

"Who is, then?" says the boy.

"Well—," I start to say, but we have arrived. The door opens and the boy gives me a bit of a push from behind, and I leap, landing right next to my friend, in the puddle.

I don't think it registered with me in the dream, but now it seems strange that it didn't, because my friend is no frog at all now. He is a man. I couldn't get a real good look at him, all wet and covered with the soupy mud.

"They brought me back," I say to him.

He looks sad for me. "I'm sorry," he replies.

And then we're walking and we're outside of the prison, but I say, "You're sorry I came back?"

"I requested your release."

"I asked to come back for you," I tell him, feeling like I'm not really knowing what I'm talking about. But I'm beginning to think that I've had it wrong—about who's looking after who, that is. Do you know what I mean?

He responds by holding open a spot in the fence. I don't know how he does that.

"It didn't seem right for you," I say as we walk across the wet grass on our bare frogs feet. I know I've said that to him already, but it's the thing that keeps coming back to me.

"You are living in a dream world, Ansel," he says, and it's the first time I know who I am in the dream.

"Who is Ansel," I ask him for some reason, and then we're moving through the bricks and we are the stuff of the bricks and then we are the stuff of steel and of the other materials of the walls and the floors and we are invisible in the open air of the rooms. The prisoners of the various floors cannot see us, nor can I see my companion, but when we go through the walls and the floors we have form, but it is the form of materials.

When we come out from one of the walls, he is again visible, but he is covered with dust and some kind of powder, and he is very disheveled looking. He turns to me and puts his hands on my shoulders. "It is right for me. You are not right."

"Can I help you?" I ask him, again not sure what I mean, looking out the window.

When I looked back he was gone. "Hey," I called out, not knowing what else to call him.

Then I woke up. It was the telephone ringing.

"Yes? What? It's a cliché? You don't like the cliché, 'Then I woke up'? Well, we have to wake up at some point."

FIFTEEN: The tragic fate of an unlikely hero

The desert was a cold-blooded creature, entirely dependent on the sun for its warmth.
　　　　　　　—Kirk Mitchell from the novel Cry Dancer

junk yard dog

The first time he hears it, he doesn't know what to make of it, so he doesn't make much of it. Probably just some dogs rummaging around. His first impression upon being roused from sleep is that a woman had screamed and one of the car doors had slammed. But the mind plays tricks from that state of half wakefulness. Fabricates. Draws from the near death experience of sleep, the stuff of it's creations. Adds drama, inappropriate. Enhances the simple musical phrase with the spirit of, the grandeur of, the cosmos. Magnifies the little cry of surprise, or the scuffling and yelping of dogs, through the distorted lens of terror.

But drifting back down from the junkyard dark of night into that other darkness he hears it again. Someone definitely screamed. His eyes are open now. There's almost no starlight, there's no moonlight, and the minimal lighting of the yard does not reach him in his chosen dwelling, so he can scarcely see a thing as he sits up. The big back seat of the Caddy is comfortable and he doesn't relish going out into the cold night, but he knows he will.

Climbing out of the big old bag, he slips on the boots, pulls up the plastic twine laces and opens the door in silence. And in silence he comes down over the stacked assortment of wrecks to the hard packed dirt of the aisle between. From there he listens and soon he hears. The low talking of men, the stifled sobbing, and hard nervous breathing of a woman. Following these sounds he comes around the corner. He needs no light. In these bleak tunnels, he is home.

They're in a new addition, brought in at day's end and left on the ground in the aisle. He goes and sits below the grille of the car and they have no idea. They are speaking badly to her and to each other. He can smell the alcohol and the sweat of the men, the blood and the fear of the woman.

He is turning the stones in his hand. He is standing outside of the broken side window. When the blood bursts from the back of the man's head and he collapses onto the floor of the back seat, the man in the front seat stares, and when he turns his face to the window in fear the small rock embeds itself in his skull like a third eye turned to stone. He pockets the big iron slingshot and opens the rear door, drags the dead man out and drops him on the hard dirt. Then he goes around to the other side of the vehicle.

She is delirious and strikes blindly at him but he lifts her shoulders with a careful, firm grip and takes her out of the car. As he carries her she stops struggling and goes unconscious. At a certain place he squats down, holding her on his lap with one arm and reaches into a nearly flattened car and extracts a thing of thick, soft rubber, wrapped around two metal poles. He unrolls it on the ground and lays her on the rubber, picks up the poles at her head and walks. But when he looks back, her feet are too low and in danger of bumping on the hardened wheel ruts and so he lays the travois down and lifts her to a higher position.

At the fence he lifts the wire where it is cut to one foot vertically from the ground on either end, clips the loose wire ends back into the fence above, crawls under, turns and pulls her through the narrow opening, a place known only to him and the dogs. He doesn't close the opening but picks up the poles and walks quickly across the empty lot and beyond into the black alley. Some dog barks but he makes a sound and the dog is quiet. He hears her moaning and then crying softly but anxiously like before and he begins to run with the contraption following efficient and smooth behind.

Across the street from the hospital he goes into the phone booth and dials 911. "There's a bad hurt lady out here."

"Where?"

"On Seventy Fifth in front of yer hospital."

He lays her in the grass, rolls up the travois and runs. But he watches in the shadow of a large stone piece of some art in the plaza across the street.

When he gets back to the salvage yard and the two dead bodies, he drags the one out of the front seat and puts him onto the travois. At a spot far down through the aisles he ascends a large wooden ramp. At the top he stops, opens a car adjacent to the ramp, from the drivers side and opens the trunk. He puts the man in the trunk and goes back down for the man in the aisle. He puts the second man in a second car at the top of the ramp.

"You'll get squished up in little boxes tomorrah, fellas. Squished up lidl' devils."

When he finishes cleaning up the car down below, there is a slight glow of first light coming over the horizon of junk metal at the east end of the yard. He's sleeping comfortably in the Cadillac when the gate creaks open an hour later. He should be out during the day but he's slept daytime before. In fifteen years there's never been a lick of trouble And there isn't any that day, either.

***

Due to the blinding light in his eyes and the sense of shock, he stumbles after knocking the man down when he bolts from the backseat of the late model Chrysler at the back of the heap. He's still up and running across the cars before the other man with the another light can get to him. But the stumble gave the men below time to get into position. When he comes flying, nimble as a goat down the stack, the Taser stun gun finds him. He falls like a bird, shot down from the sky into the aisle below.

"Jeez, Tony, ya could'n let 'im get a little closer to the ground?"

"Yeah? Well the wiry little son of a bitch didn't get away, did he?"

"Jus' hope e ain't bit it."

***

He hadn't "bit it" and, in a matter of time, in the due process of the law, he's convicted of first degree murder. He'd covered his tracks so well with the woman that his story about her was not accepted. It was determined that he got that story from the news and developed it as an alibi.

"It ain't a alibi, Judge. I done admit I killed them fellers. But there was that there lady. An I done it to help her."

His story was not accepted. He had a court appointed lawyer and the fact is the lawyer didn't believe his story either, but out of a perverted sense of integrity he pretended that he did believe it, thereby preventing the appointment of a more empathetic attorney.

The "murdered" men proved to be employees of the salvage yard, and in fact family members of the ownership, which, in the eyes of the court, was enough to legitimize their late night presence in the yard.

Seeing love
a poem

I climb all day some stairs in my head
I have to go fight the devils off
I don't like to face the truth
I turn my back instead

You look out over all creations
You hold no truck with preachers
You honor the old promises

You recognize no nations

this is where I dwell in madness and sorrow
this fear operating from my shoulder
this cursed world without is now within me
this damn mythical tomorrow

Your words of recognition calm me
Your rules of iron, your heart of wax
Your sad brown eternal bottomless eyes
 Your vina, bell, and mrdanga call me

here in these haunted brackish waters
here upon these raw boned blooded knees
here where my appeals have been denied for so many ages
here I turn on the wheel of insane religious potters

seeing love, the world turns away in shame
seeing love we sin the harder
seeing love the armies come to kill it
seeing love the world remains the same

SIXTEEN: A series of events concerning Ansel and his family

When the heart weeps for what it has lost, the spirit laughs at what it has gained.

—*Sufi aphorism*

Ansel and his family

Ansel got a call from his brother at two a.m. that his father had been taken to the hospital with severe pains in his abdomen. He is actually a stepfather but he's been father to Ansel and his siblings since they were quite young and their relationships with him are good ones. Ansel and he have a very good father and son relationship.

"Do they know what it is?"

"Something to do with his small intestine. It's not real clear to me at this point. They're running tests, you know?"

"I want to come if it's serious."

"I can't say, Ansel. I wish I could tell you more."

"How's Mom?"

"You know how she is, she's strong one minute and panicked the next. Do you want me to get back to you in the morning? I mean, I just can't say it's serious. I—well, everything's serious."

Ansel's brother Brent is very religious. He's a "born again" Christian and has been through a lot with his family regarding his outlook on life. There's some history behind his statement."

I know it, Brent. I agree."

"You do?"

"I've had ... experiences lately."

Brent waits for him to go on. When he doesn't, he asks, "Are you wanting to tell me about them."

"Well, it would be good, but not on the phone—when I see you."

"Okay"

"I'd come right now, and I will if I get any indication of him being in imminent danger. I'm involved in a very demanding project. And I'll drop it like that, but, well, why don't you let me know in the morning, early as you want, or any time before that if you learn more, Okay?"

"Okay, Ansel."

"Okay, Brent. Give my love to Mom and Dad and Jody and to yourself, okay?"

"Okay, I'll get back by morning at least."

"Okay, talk to you then."

***

When Ansel gets to work that morning there is a new prisoner on the floor. He isn't told about the new prisoner by the staff, but the news travels fast. Ansel is well aware that news travels fast on the floor but there seems so seldom to be news of any consequence. New prisoners do, of course, arrive on the floor from time to time, but the mental ward policy is to encourage stability, therefore it is generally inhibitive to change. Not that things are ever dull. But even panic and chaos can get familiar to an observer in time. Not to the panicked individual, of course.

What is surprising to Ansel is that he can detect something different in the nature of the panic and chaos this morning. Ahmed approaches him three times in the first hour asking for help in retrieving his medical kit, muttering things like, "Those new recruits aren't trained. They're sending us babies."

And Anthony, feeding off of Ahmed's energy perhaps, is screaming at him, "Shut up you damn fool! Shut up! Shut up! You'll bring the whole goddamned bunch of 'em down on us, if you don't keep quiet. We got more trouble than you know, you damn quack. You ain't no doctor, you're a crazy freak," and other such criticisms.

Stephen's anxiety manifests differently as he lays on the floor below the windows and sobs and sobs, occasionally with violent shaking fits.

Seeing Lao Tse come into the room, Ansel asks him if there's anything that's happened out of the ordinary.

"Well," says Lao Tse, "I'm quite certain that today the stars aligned …" and he goes into some long astrological formation explanation that Ansel doesn't bother to give a serious listen to.

"Oh. Thanks"

"Salright Bro. Glad to help." He starts to walk away but then he turns back and says to Ansel, "By the way, any idea what these freaks are yelling about today?"

"I guess it's just the weather," Ansel says.

"Yeah, I reckon so," says Lao Tse.

***

Ansel goes to a table, sits alone, looking at his notes from last night, regarding his plans for today, still curious about this morning's excessive group anxiety. What he doesn't realize is that a very similar response by the inmates was generated when he and his associates first came to the floor. After his second cup of the tepid, weak brown liquid that passes for coffee on the floor, he gets up to use the restroom. "Great coffee today," he tells the nurse through the barred window as he passes her station.

"Really? That's good buddy."

"Yeah, best ever."

"Now I know you been drinkin' something," she says.

He has to pass Eugene on the way to the lavatory, and Eugene doesn't let the opportunity slip to call him something indecent. Ansel can't make it out. Anyway, he's gotten used to it.

On the way out, he literally bumps into Bascomb, who's on his way in. "Oh, sorry Bascomb, I wasn't looking where I was going."

"Don' worry about it, my man." Then he asks, "Say, have you met the new dude?"

"There's a new dude?"

"Junkyard dog," Eugene mutters.

"What's that you say there, Eugene?" Bascomb says.

Eugene says, snapping, "I said he's a damned junkyard dog."

"Well hell, Eugene, aren't you one to talk. At least he don' need a goddamn muzzle on him like you do." But then a thought occurs to him.

"Come to think of it, though, that's a good name for him. I guess that's what we'll call the poor slob. Whaddyou say, Ansel?"

"I haven't met him."

"Well, you just gimme a sec to drain ma crane. I'll be right out and I'll go introduce him to you proper."

"I'll be here."

***

"Good morning, Charles," Ansel says, greeting the young man. He's learned his real name from Bascomb on the way to the back corridor cell where Charles is temporarily confined to his cell even during daytime hours. Ansel is thinking how young the man looks, like a teenager.

"Charles, this here is Ansel," Bascomb says to the man. "He ain' one of us. He ain' crazy like us. Hell, he ain' even a prisoner. He is here on his own volition."

Charles doesn't respond as he sits sulking on his bed looking at the floor.

"Well, it takes all kinds," continues Bascomb. "Listen here, Bro, we all got names here and it ain' no offense but we all got together and voted," he lies, "and your official name is Junkyard Dog. Hope you don' mind it now, son, it's just all in fun. Anyhow we heard how you took care of couple of scum out there and so you already got yahself a good reputation."

No response.

"We would have baked you a cake or something but the greetin' committee was a little short handed this morning, what with other commitments and day jobs and all that, so we'll just let you get settled in here. Let us know if you need anything. You know, hooch, blow, women, anything at all."

Finally he quits and they walk back toward the hall.

"Who needs a 'greetin' committee when we got you, Bascomb?"

"Thanks Ansel, I'm just working on my social skills."

"Got a parole comin up?"

"Yeah, right on, man."

In the hall the nurse calls Ansel to her window. "Your brother called. Says it's rather urgent."

***

It's a three hour flight, broken up by a one and a half hour layover. That makes it a least an hour too late. But what does too late mean? Would it have been more appropriate he'd been there for the event of his father's death? How would his being there have added to the circumstances? Added his presence, yes, but what could he have contributed? After all, his father was going, no one knew where. Is there anything at all that any one of his family members could do, or could have done to elevate that moment? Or to demean or detract from it? Insofar as the leaving soul was concerned, it seems the answer is "Certainly not." It's all about those who are to be left behind.

These questions are Ansel's as he lays on the unopened bed in his mother's spare room this night. It's very late and the others have all gone to bed,, even his mother, though it's doubtful she'll sleep at all. And what does it matter, this sleep? Isn't it highly over-rated? People sleep and sleep. Meanwhile there are poor souls in the world who are so disturbed, they never get a moment's rest. A moment's peace.

Ansel wonders about his father. Where is he? They will bury his body soon and they will call it the man's final resting place. Why does he doubt that? It's all to comfort those who are left behind. But Ansel knows he is one of those, left behind, and he is not comforted by words. By preachers spilling forth words they've been taught or that they've written, like poetry. Pretty words from the mouths of the ignorant. The unlearned. The inexperienced. Why do they pretend to know about death? The people pay them for their lies. For their comforting lies.

The mind never stops. Does it stop at death? Not likely. If so, if people really knew that, then the case for suicide could be made, perverted as it seems.

'Final resting place.' Somehow the very phrase angers him and it hasn't even been uttered yet in the case of his dad.

Message of George VII
~ to recommend you ~

"'These truths we hold to be self evident.' What comes next, brothers? You know what comes next. Even if you weren't born and raised here in this country, like Amed, or like Toby, or God knows where some of us came from. Lao Tse who's part of an older nation, among nations that were swallowed up by this nation. Everybody knows what comes next.

'That all men are created equal'.

"It's true. I'm of the opinion that it's true. And you who are with me here — wouldn't they call us the damned? Don't we see ourselves as mistakes? If there is a God, are we not his mistakes?

"But I know. One thing I think you, of all people, might understand that others miss, is that 'all men are created equal.'"

He's looking around the hall of silent men. And he's aware that they can hear him though he speaks softly and many are not looking back, but only stealing a quick and subtle glance here and there.

He goes on.

"Because you have been given something special. These broken minds and tortured hearts are our gifts. And the darkest hour is just before the dawn, my dears. And I love you. And I appreciate you. From the depths of my heart I tell you, it is my great pleasure to know you and to be here with you—and to recommend you."

Ansel and his family
–continued-

"Do you think Dad was proud of us," Brent asks. He looks at one, then the other.

The two brothers and their sister sit in the near–empty local coffee shop in their hometown, where only Brent has made his home.

Jody says she thinks so. "He wasn't an arrogant man or the type to be overly judgmental."

"He didn't say it—to me anyway," Brent says, in a tone that confides, or complains.

"He used to tell me he was proud of me constantly," Jody says, grinning.

"Really?" says Brent, naïve as usual.

Ansel looks at her without expression.

"Sorry, I'm joking," she tells Brent, grudgingly.

"What do thou think, Ansel?" she says.

Ansel still has to think about it for a moment. Then he says, "He probably was. But I don't think pride was the biggest part of how he thought of us, you know?"

They wait for him to go on.

"I always felt like he just wished good things for us."

"Exactly," Jody agrees.

Brent looks down at the table, then out the window before he looks back at them."I think he was embarrassed by me."

"You do?" Ansel says.

"Yeah, for my Christianity."

"He was a Christian himself."

"For my evangelism, then."

"Oh," says Ansel, concerned for him.

"I don't thinks so, Brent," Jody says. "He said things to me about how strong you are and stuff like that."

Brent looks at her, kind of shocked."How strong?"

"Yes, he did, more than once."

"I always felt weak and so—I don't know—insubstantial around him."

"He was a strong man," she answers. "Even though I was a girl, you know, I had to be strong, I think, to make him," and she shrugs her shoulders, not sure it's the right word as she says, "happy. One time he told me, and I thought it was true, even though I, personally, was a little embarrassed by your evangelism. He said, 'Brent stands up to his fear.' And I knew it was true."

Ansel returns

On the flight back, Ansel's plane has to land unexpectedly at a small airport because one of the passengers, a young lady, suffers a heart attack and simultaneous stroke. The landing itself is abrupt and unnerving due to the shortness and narrowness of the runway, ill equipped for a large commercial airliner, but it is the fastest way to get on the ground and get the woman to a hospital.

She is hurried off the plane and gotten into the waiting ambulance, but it's at least forty five minutes before it is determined that the other passengers may exit the plane. If they so desire, a bus service will transport them to accommodations until arrangements can be made for them to reach their various destinations. It has been decided that the little runway is too precarious to risk with the passengers aboard.

It is a nice day, overcast but not threatening, so almost all the passengers do exit. Ansel makes a call to Jeff who agrees to make the two hour drive out of the city and pick him up. After the call, he mills around with the others who are variously finding places to sprawl out and get comfortable on the ground, or stand in small groups discussing business, primarily, or exploring the airport and admiring some of the private jets and other small aircraft.

Ansel chooses the exploring option, an activity in which he is soon joined by a gregarious companion.

"Very slick aren't they?"

"They certainly are," Ansel replies.

"Have you ever flown in one of these?"

The man is probably in his mid fifties, a bit overweight, and dressed like a well-to-do African, with a colorful Kufi and Kaftan, although he is Caucasian with a typical Midwestern accent.

"When I was a young boy my father took me along on a trip to Mexico City."

"Ah, and did you enjoy the ride."

"Well at the time I had never flown before so I enjoyed it immensely."

"That's alright. That's alright. But more importantly, I suppose, is the question of your impression of Mexico City."

"There were so many impressions," Ansel says, reflecting.

"I have grown weary of cities," the man states then, as if to an old friend.

"Where do you live," Ansel asks him.

"I live alternately between heaven and hell."

Assuming the man is only being cryptic, Ansel asks if he means, sometimes in the city and sometimes not.

"If that were so I would probably consider my residence as being full time in hell, excuse me for saying so."

Ansel is unsure what to say or do in response at this juncture. But the man continues so he doesn't have to make any decision.

"And what do you do for work, my young friend, if I may be so rude as to ask?"

"I am a student."

"And what do you study, in particular?"

"Psychology, I study psychology." But at this point Ansel is getting a bit peeved with the gentleman and so he says, "And you, sir, what is it that you do? For work?"

"I collect souls. It's true. That's what I do," he answers in a sing song voice and a somewhat playful manner.

They've been walking, and have arrived at a new plane of a beautiful blue hue, and the man was running his hand on the underbelly of the craft as he made the previous statement. He was not looking at Ansel as he made it, but now he does look at him with a sideways look, but without turning his head.

"You know, that lady who had the trouble on the plane?"

"But she didn't die." Ansel immediately feels a ridiculousness at his own statement, as if he were acknowledging that this crazy man in his unlikely outfit had come for the soul of that woman.

"No, she didn't, did she?" He shakes his head slowly, looking a little bewildered. His face brightens with sudden cheerfulness. "Well, I expect she will. Meanwhile, all I can do is wait, just like you. But what exactly do you study in psychology?"

He seems determined not to let go of it.

Ansel, sensing some kind of trap, is glad to see the bus arriving and, even though Jeff is coming for him, says, "Well I gotta go, here's the bus."

"Oh yeah, the bus," says the man, and trots alongside Ansel to get in line.

But the bus fills almost instantly and there they are. Back to waiting. "Listen," he tells the strange man, "I need some time alone, I—I just lost my father."

"Yes of course, I know."

"Oh you would, wouldn't you?" Ansel has just a touch of sarcasm in his voice.

"I thought the arrangements were nicely done. I agree with you completely that the preacher was a little out of his league, good intentions or no."

"It's the intentions they make long ago when they take up a profession, misleading people about what they know and don't know." Ansel knows he's been trapped again, even as he finishes his remark.

But the man only agrees. "You're quite right, quite right, my good fellow. You know, the most touching conversation of the whole affair to me was the conversation you had with your sister and brother in the café."

Ansel is visibly nervous. "What conversation was that?"

"You know; about your father's pride and all that."

"Who the hell are you?" Ansel says, his tone soft, more to himself than to his companion.

"Oh, I'm sorry, I never introduced myself; my name is George."

Ansel reddens in a flash and stomps a foot. *"No it's not!"* His voice rises more. "No it is not!" Ansel surprises himself as he is now screaming at the man.

"You're right about that, young fella, I just made that up. My name is—"

Two concerned men in business suits come up and ask Ansel if he's alright.

"Yes, yes, sorry, I'm alright. It's just this crazy fellow here has sort of glommed onto me and is incessantly pestering me. He really won't leave me alone."

"What fellow is that?" one of the men says.

"This lunatic right here next to you." And then it occurs to Ansel that these other men do not see the man in the African costume who is claiming to be some angel of death.

The professed angel of death shrugs his shoulders and tries to go on. "As I was saying, sorry 'bout the George thing, I just—"

Again the men are speaking to Ansel. "Can we get you something? Is there some medication you may have left onboard the plane or anything?"

"Can you call me a taxi, please? I really need to get out of here right now. Right away."

"Where will you go?" says one.

"I'll—I'll go to the hotel where we're going." "We're concerned that maybe you should see a doctor."

"Well, maybe I should. But I mean, what kind of a doctor should I see? I mean this man tells me he comes for people's souls and then he knows about a private conversation I had with my brother and sister and, and, and—and you can't even see him, though he's here as much as you're here." Ansel is very distraught. He's shaking and some of the time he's yelling.

Suddenly he is apprehended from behind and is being manhandled by several people and laid down on a gurney, which then begins to roll, crunching over the wide gravel strip, surrounding the hanger.

But as they reach the ambulance, which he can see the top of from his horizontal rolling restraint, he is immensely relieved to become aware of the familiar face of his colleague, Jeff, leaning over him and demanding that the gurney operators give him an opportunity to talk to his friend and colleague, Ansel.

Ansel and Azra'il

***

"I don't know what to say, Jeff. The events of the day, and the situation so awkward. They just grabbed me, you know?"

"Look!" Jeff is saying to them, and he shows them his limited credentials." We are doing some extremely important research." He thinks better of telling them where or what, deciding it may not be helpful at the moment.

"This man is a brilliant scientist, who just happens to have been through a lot in the last few days, with his father passing away not the least of it."

"We're not taking him to jail, sir. He's going to the emergency room for help."

"Please. Please let me take him. I will be responsible for him."

"We can't do that."

"Why not?"

"It is against policy, sir."

"Please. There's no one in danger. Please let me speak to your supervisor."

Somehow, they accept Jeff's argument and phone their supervisor. The supervisor is satisfied with Jeff's explanation of the situation, as well as with the assessment given by the EMT, which is favorable enough, due to the present calmness of the patient, and by the presence of Ansel's minimal credentials, which are found in his wallet by Jeff.

***

"Just take it easy, friend, you can explain later." After they are finally moving away in the car, Ansel profusely thanking him and praising him for his efforts and his heroics.

"Alright, okay. I could use a little downtime, alright."

They ride silently for a few minutes. Ansel is nodding off when he hears from the back seat, "Now where were we? So many interruptions."

"Oh God, you son of a bitch!" Ansel blurts out.

"Whoah brother, whad' I do," Jeff asks, startled.

"Not you, Jeff. That devil's back."

"Ooh" says Jeff, who decides against saying more at this point.

"My name is Azra'il," says Azra'il. "My name is Ahpuch, my name is Yama, Cheron, Balor, Dharam Rai." Then he adds, "I find your company pleasant."

"Why don't you talk to Jeff?"

"He's driving."

"You're afraid of a little thing like a car accident?"

"Now wait a minute," says Jeff.

"It is not appropriate," Says Azra'il.

"It's appropriate to terrorize me? Make me look crazy? Make me think I'm crazy?"

"You don't know by now the irrelevancy of that term, Ansel?"

"Why won't you go away?"

"Yes, please go and leave my friend alone," Jeff tries.

"Tell him, that's not helpful," Azra'il says.

"He says that's not helpful, Jeff."

"Oh. Okay. Thought I'd give it a shot."

***

So the ride back is pretty much like that the whole way. But when they get into town, Ansel tells Jeff he doesn't want to go to their apartment.

"Where do you want to go?"

"I want to see George."

"We can't get in now, Ansel. You know the rules."

"Please Jeff, let's go to the prison."

"Well it's useless, but what the hell. It's been an interesting day."

"You have no idea," Ansel says, sighing.

"I guess I don't, Ans."

The cloud cover has been getting gradually darker and by the time they reach the prison it's raining. At the main entrance, Jeff shows his card and they drive into the grounds.

"Don't go to the parking lot, Jeff. Drive around to the front."

"The front," Jeff says, and does it.

"Pull into the loop."

"Okay, the loop."

They stop in the loop. After a minute Jeff shuts the car off. The rain is increasing until it's coming down in sheets. Jeff has to yell to Ansel, "Why the loop, Ansel?"

"I don't know."

"Look, I was just havin' a little fun, Ansel," Azra'il is telling him. "Thought it might be good for your research, you know? Show you what it's like."

"It's admirable."

"Well, you know you guys hang out with the crazies like it's some game or something. Ya'll are in a little bit deep."

"Maybe you're in a little bit deep, Azra'il," Ansel suggests.

"Aw, he ain't comin'." Azra'il has become visibly nervous.

"We'll wait awhile." Ansel assures him.

"Shit," the little man complains. A minute later he says, "Shit, he ain't comin', lets go. Let's get the hell outa here."

"Gotta have a little patience," Ansel says.

Jeff is being remarkably patient as he waits in the loop with his seemingly crazy friend in the extreme downpour. But when he sees two huge guards come out the front, with a prisoner held between them, he speaks.

"Ansel, there's guards coming and they've got somebody."

As he turns to tell Ansel, he realizes an armored Federal vehicle has pulled up on the other side of the loop.

"It was unavoidable, Ansel," George is telling him from the back seat. "Your father had some strange circumstances to work out with his fate. Azra'il was just taking advantage of what he perceived as an opportunity."

Ansel is crying now.

"Your father is alright, I promise."

"What about me? Am I going to be crazy now?"

"No, *he* is gone. He can't come around you any more."

"George. I depend on you."

"That's alright. I have to go now."

The armored vehicle drives past them in the loop and out onto the main drive across the grounds and disappears in the driving rain.

SEVENTEEN: Of His mysterious ways

Welcome to a special place
In a heart of stone that's cold and gray
You with your angel face
Keep the despair at bay
Send it away, and
Show me the meaning of the word
                    —*Chrissie Hynde, Show Me*

Jeff visits Anthony's Mother

They'd agreed upon nine thirty Tuesday morning. When Jeff gets there at 9:35 she chastises him.

"I thought you'd stood me up."

He doesn't know what to say so he says nothing. He's come to the side door that enters into the kitchen. She offers him coffee or tea. He says, "Tea," and she starts in talking while the water is boiling.

"In those days I spent most of my nights up 'til the wee hours worryin' 'bout that boy. He was good hearted, you know. Not like some of them that don't give a damn. Some of his friends were like that, you know. But Henry — my man, Henry's gone on to his maker, just two winters back now — Henry always said, 'It's the company you keep.'

"But when he went off to live near his brother in Texas I sure nuff figured it was a good thing. I thought, 'Well, git him up away from these bad seed here an let him git a fresh start.' But what happened I ain't sure. Tommy ain't sure, an I don't blame him."

"Tommy?" Jeff asks, not sure what she means about not blaming him.

"His brother. Two years older than Anthony.

It was Anthony hisself that got into it. From his innocence partly, I'd say. From his damn gullibility. He come back messed up is all I know. Tommy missin' work and ridin' the train back here with a blitherin' idiot.

"'Oh Lord, my baby!' I cried. And Tommy cried with me. And Anthony didn't cry, cause he had no mind to even get in touch with his heart. Doctors say he took some bad drug. Whether he took it or somebody slipped it to him? Who's gonna say? Sure not Anthony."

"He doesn't seem that way now," Jeff puts in. "I mean, not in touch with his heart."

"Well he come out of it, so we thought."

She gets up to get the train whistle that is the tea kettle. "My poppa was a train man, thirty-seven years for the B&O. I like it cause it reminds me a him."

She comes back with the pot and the cups, carrying the cups by the handles in her right hand that also holds the teapot handle. "Sugar?"

"Yes I will."

She goes on again as she goes to the cupboard for the sugar.

"He started talking agin', like he was gettin' better. But he had them awful dreams and the doctors put him on that Haldol to help him get through that. An yet, after that's when he started up bein' mean. We're a close family, my family. On my side and on Henry's side too. An it was on Thanksgivin' an we was at my sister, Molly's. The men was just relaxin', you know, an us women were jus' about ready with dinner when we hear him yellin' at somebody real loud and cursin' like the devil and I dropped what I was doin' and when I got into the sittin' room, he had one a Molly's buffet lamps an he was holdin' it like a ball bat an cursin at what seemed like maybe the whole room full of men, sayin' like, 'You son's a bitches' an worse, what I don't want to repeat. And Molly's husband Frank come up behind him and tried to get a hold of him and Anthony swung his arms back and forth," here she demonstrates, " and he give Frankie a bloody nose and then he swung that lamp up against the wall an smashed it, glass and pieces flyin' everwhere, an he ran out of the front door of Molly's house."

She is crying now upon the memory and Jeff waits. As she tries to pull herself together, he says, "Did he come back, Melinda?"

"He never come back to that house that day an we went lookin' for him, Henry and I, but we only found him at home, twenty miles away. How he come to git there, we don' know.

"The thing is he got so darn moody, you know? Well you know he ain't tall, an even he stoops a little now, but at that time he was strong an he'd put on weight too, from when they switched him to the anti-depressant drug, you know, and he was a right terror when he got riled up. But the irony of it was that he was still that same innocent, gullible kid on the inside of him."

"A hard combination to deal with, I'm sure."

"You got that right, Jeff. For him and for us that loved him, as well.

You know, I don't know where my manners are. You want some more tea there, hon?"

"I could use another, yes I could, thank you."

She pours it for him. "I'm not used to folks bein' so shy. There's a little more yet, now you jes help yaself if you want it."

"Thank you, I'm not that shy. I just got absorbed in your story."

"Well, I'll go on then."

"Please do."

"The next thing we know is Anthony's hooked up with that woman, if you could even call her a woman. Lord, some of the things I've come to know about her. Well I cain't repeat 'em, much as I know you won't get the proper idea bout her without them bein' said. But I will just say, 'she ain't one for fidelity. An here's my stupid son, all along tryin' to see the best in her, tryin' to make her inta some beloved darling. They got themselves in trouble, sure enough. I guess they don't use that term so much these day, what we used to call 'in trouble'".

"I know the expression alright."

"You probly ain't young as you look."

Jeff shrugs his shoulders.

"The poor thing would ask his friends, 'Do ya think she's true?' ya know, like an idiot. And they'd tell 'im straight what they knew, they didn't have to guess. And this is after she's pregnant, no less. But then he'd flare up at 'em. Tell 'em they was jes jealous and like that.

Oh, she's a piece of work, that devil. She lives over cross town now, and still up to her ol' tricks, I've no doubt."

"And the child?"

"The child, by the mercy of God, was good. I know, I raised her myself. Sweet darling Oluwaseyi, we call her Ola for short. It means, 'God made this.' She's jest finishin' up at the University. She's the only blessedness of this whole affair. She's of mixed race and so, so beautiful. The words jes come up short."

"Does Anthony have a relationship with her, because I wasn't aware of her?"

"His relationship with her is to stay out of her way and to not be an embarrassment to her. I don' agree with it. Ola don' agree neither. But this much I do know, it ain't him coppin' out 'cause he always wants to hear 'bout her from me and I can tell, he ain't putting on about it."

"Well, that's good."

"Yes it is." And she's tearing up again. She looks out the window and Jeff waits. She smoothes her napkin out on the Formica table top with her fingers. He notices the delicate beauty of her hands, remarkable for a woman her age.

"Of course it was only a matter of time before a dumb oaf like that would end hisself up in prison. I'm surprised it took long as it did. They come here to the house and he wasn't home. They come back three days later an he was. He wasn't smart enough to even stay away from here. But then, to be truthful, I've often guessed, that he wanted to be took. Now I know that them prisons are bad, bad places. But I think he knew he just couldn't control nothing out here. His life was like one a them mine fields and no matter which way you turn, you're probably headin for disaster. And maybe there's worse than the disaster you're already in. I know they bounced him around for a couple a years but he's been up there in that tower for a long spell now."

"Does he talk to you about George?"

"Anthony is close lipped by nature but I know something changed him about three years back. He only talks about his friends slightly, but I've been happy to learn that he even has friends, although I don't know why I should be worried that he wouldn't. I'm a Christian, dear Jeff, so I have my suspicions. But he has expressed an opinion, you know, in his own frazzled-like, kinda crazy way, that this George is a man of God. Seems like a strange place for one, but then they say the Lord hisself dwelt in the company of street people and common people and the like. Anthony seems so … attached to him."

There are some moments of silence, both Melinda and Jeff inwardly reflecting, before she says, "His episodes are fewer now, are they not? When he can't make no sense with his talking at all?"

Jeff just says, "I wouldn't think you've ever had an opportunity to meet George?"

"No, I haven't," she says and then asks, "They're still roommates, my boy and George? You know I just don't like to say the word, cell-mates."

"Yes, they are—I very much appreciate your help, Melinda."

"I hope you'll tell it straight." "It's all recorded."

"And you fellas are gonna do what with all the information you are gatherin' up about these men?"

"Well, there will certainly be a report." He hesitates. "The thing is, it's quite a phenomenon about this man George and his relationships with many of his fellow inmates. We are truly finding that the more we learn the more intriguing it all gets."

"Well, there's been a lot of cults that could be well described as intriguing."

"That's true."

"You're not personally involved?"

"I have to admit, it's kind of a test of endurance to remain entirely aloof."

"That's the trouble with religion."

"I suppose it is."

Anthony's prayer
a poem

moving through these dreams so deep
I've awoken as one who is still asleep

what place is this into which I've stumbled?
it's not right, it's all confused and jumbled
a trick of the mind is all I'm sure
these are not lost souls, but souls that never were

I must compose myself, to myself I firmly stated
I must find the world that God created
but I was caught in panic, fear, and trembling
before the mighty host, like fearsome ghosts assembling

all violence and war a'threatnin'
I shut my eyes to stop 'em gettin' in
but to no avail, and I became so nervous
the silent wraiths, gruesome things and wordless

if I should die before I wake
that childhood prayer from deep inside me spake
behind a shield of innocence I would brave my shaky stand
crying out, "oh, please come now and take my hand"

and I called and pleaded, shameless, helpless
and just like a child I was sure you felt this
great fear of mine and my all aloneness
and my never wanting to be on my own-ness
or to have to know this kind of up-grown-ness

an open mike

The prison project is proving to be an experience beyond their expectations. There is an awareness now between the three students that they are being given something invaluable. It occurs to them, and the occurring seems to happen to them somehow simultaneously, *something should be given back*, and they brainstorm, and they sleep on it, and in the morning, Ozwald suggests it.

"There's a lot of stifled creativity up there, you know, like we were saying? What about an open mike?"

And the other two like it. "It has a whole lot of potential," one says, and the other, "Man, there's musicians, poets, storytellers—that's it. But will they allow it, I wonder."

So they make it happen. They bring it up with the powers that be and the powers that be confer and decide that it could be quite interesting and possibly therapeutic. Go figure.

They agree on Wednesdays. "Break up the week," says Ansel.

"But every day's the same," says Jeff.

"True that," says Ozwald. So Wednesday it is.

The first Wednesday gets off to a slow start. No actual microphone is available, they've improvised by inserting a mop handle through the back crosspieces of a folding chair. There is a small audience gathered, but no performers. Ozwald goes up to the mop/mike and gives a bit of an encouragement speech, explaining that there's nothing to be afraid of. A couple of minutes go by and the assembly starts to break up. But then Horatio and Fyodor come shyly forward. They introduce themselves as the Two Tops and do a little singing duet of "Sugar Pie, Honey Bunch", mostly joking around, having a bit of crude fun with the makeshift mike, but prove to have great voices. They follow it up with a serious rendition of "Walk Away Rene", which is very well received and they are showered with a smattering of applause.

That inspires Johnny to get up. Johnny is a tall young man, handsome, multi-racial, relatively new on the floor. Johnny is the perfect example of the enigmatic inmate. To speak with him he shows no sign of mental illness whatever. Neither does he display any typical traits of criminal mentality. The first impression one gets is, "What a nice young man." He's prepared a demonstration of Origami and impresses them with a splendid elephant, who, he explains, is afraid of his next creation, a mouse. The response is minimal. Then he folds a simple airplane, which is a bigger hit, as it flies quite successfully. He promises to show how to make them to those who are interested after the show.

No more acts seem to be forthcoming, so Ozwald again comes up to the mop. "I guess that's it for this time folks, but we'll schedule the open mike for next Wednesday again, so work on your acts and then come on out and show us what you got."

He then joins Jeff and Ansel at their table. "What do you think, gentlemen?"

They have to admit, they're a little disappointed.

"Me too. But maybe it'll take a little time to get it rolling."

"Yeah, it's new to them," Jeff says, encouragingly.

"Yeah, probably next time they'll be more prepared," Ansel offers. "Hopefully, anyway."

"Yeah. Well we'll try it again then, next week and see, huh?"

"Yeah"

"Yeah"

"We should maybe do a Beatles song, the three of us, next time," Ozwald says.

"Why do you say that, Oz," Ansel asks.

"Well, we got the yeah, yeah, yeah thing goin' on, is all," Ozwald answers in his best Liverpool accent.

"Oh yeah; see what you mean."
"Yeah"

EIGHTEEN: Ozwald gains some hard earned knowledge

Oh, to vex me, contraryes meet in one:
Inconstancy unnaturally hath begott
A constant habit; that when I would not
I change in vowes, and in devotione.
As humorous is my contritione
As my prophane Love, and as soone forgott:
As ridlingly distemper'd, cold and hott,
As praying, as mute; as infinite, as none.
I durst not view heaven yesterday; and to day
In prayers, and flattering speaches I court God:
To morrow I quake with true feare of his rod.
So my devout fitts come and go away
Like a fantistique Ague: save that here
Those are my best dayes, when I shake with feare.
                                           —*John Donne*

Ozwald has a headache

Ozwald has a headache. It's focused at the back of his head, emanating from the base of his skull where the top of the swollen trapezius muscles attach, and going forward, across pulsing temples to the eyes in a kind of bandana of pain. His eyes feel as if they're being pulled inward toward the occipital lobes by some over-taut cords, through the imagination of his dehydrated brain. He is surrounded by and enveloped in a dark cloud, which somehow serves as a protection from some of the annoyances of the world, but proves ineffective against the slightest intrusion of light and sound. In short, he has a hangover. The daily experience of being confronted by minds so at odds with the artificial order, or even with the natural order, of the world, is taking its toll on him. And Jeff and Ansel, also, are not unaffected.

Last night they had exorcised their stress with a shared bottle of alcohol. A very big bottle of alcohol. 120 proof. Ozwald, unfortunately, had shared even more freely than the others.

***

"I swear, Brothers," Ozwald is saying to them, "We are some lucky damn science guys."

"Yes we are," the other two agree.

"I mean, we're probably, at least possibly, dealing with some of the most screwed up dudes on the planet."

"You got a point there, Oz," Jeff says. "In fact, it's perfectly questionable whether some of those boys are even from the planet."

"This planet, you mean?" Ozwald says, seeking to confirm his understanding of Jeff's statement.

Jeff tips his head, eyebrows raised, looks at Ozwald, takes a big pull from the bottle that they are passing around, *drinks serious*, and passes it to Ansel. "After hanging with some of them, you start to question all sorts of things, huh?"

"Like, 'Is the world really round instead of flat?'" Ansel says. "I mean, do we really know?"

"There's a fair amount of evidence, Ans," Jeff answers.

"Evidence, shmevidence, Jeff," Ansel answers him back.

Ozwald holds the jug, wiping the spout off with his sleeve. "Some of our boys seem so righteous though, don't they?" he says with the other two nodding in sync. "I mean, I feel like I've been on some heavy drug binge for about two months most of the time but, well, you can't get an education like this in the classroom." He is still wiping the bottle off as he swings his feet up onto the kitchen table and leans his chair back.

Jeff, who is already sitting on the table suggests to Ansel that Ozwald is doing a fine job of cleaning that bottle.

"That's why I get the big bucks," Ozwald states. "No brag, just fact."

"The thing is though," Ansel interjects, missing the bottle talk altogether, "the thing is, it's a fine line."

Ozwald asks him, "What's a fine line, brother?"

"Between our lives out here and theirs in there."

"True that," Ozwald agrees. "True that."

Ansel blurts out, "Some of these guys, my God! Living in constant fear, such hell on earth—Anthony—Oh my God—Stephen!"

"I guess nobody comes in with a clean slate. We've all got history, according to Fyodor," Jeff puts in.

"Fyodor?"

"Yeah, he says some folks have such vivid impressions from past horrors, whether from this world or some other, I don' know. I guess that stuff just followed them on in here."

"Fyodor said that?"

"In so many words," Jeff says, shrugging. "Stuff George taught him I guess."

There was a little lull in the conversation at that point. Ozwald is the first to speak, after. "Let's make a vow, gentlemen."

"Okay," the other two agree.

"What're we vowing about," Ansel asks.

"We're vowing to never become self-important, stuffed up, puffed up psychiatrists, sitting around pontificating about the mentally ill and how to treat them."

"Consider it vowed," Jeff says.

"Ditto," says Ansel.

At this point Ozwald's chair and Ozwald go crashing backwards to the floor with a loud bang.

"'Sa good thing he wasn't cleaning the bottle bout then, huh Ansel?"

"Yeah, it's good."

Ozwald who just lay where he fell, momentarily sits up. "I guess I'm gonna turn in."

"Okay" the other two say.

***

He hadn't turned in. Not to his bed anyway. Rather he'd lain back down and gone immediately asleep. His roommates had decided they'd had enough punishment, as well, after that. Ansel had gone into Ozwald's room for the poor fellow's comforter, which he'd dragged out and covered him with, before he and Jeff wandered off to their own rooms.

Jeff had offered his sympathy before shutting his door. "Sorry you's guys got to work in the morning."

Sometime in the middle of the night Ozwald had found the couch, which is where Ansel found him now after his own alarm had so rudely put an end to the short night.

They drank what was left of last night's coffee, cold from the pot, along with a glass of milk, each, and some stale doughnuts. Ansel found himself a clean shirt and asked Ozwald if he'd like one also. Ozwald said, "Thanks, I would," and told Ansel there was a green one hanging on the back side of the door to his room. After Ansel found it they went out the door and Ozwald put the shirt on as Ansel got in and warmed up the car.

***

I guess I'm lucky I don't have some boss to harass me, Ozwald is thinking, as he sits at his job as keeper of the table closest to the coffee pot. Before he can really savor the thought, there comes to his ears a shrieking and a wailing that makes him question his luck. The sirens of *les miserables*. The horror of every day life in this, his workplace. The waves of sound break sidelong upon the bones of his face and rage through like a flood of pain, into the cavern of his head, crashing against interior walls that swell and throb, but allow no exit.

***

"What is it? What is it? Hath the enemy come?"
No answer comes back, the walls are dumb
From the ruins I look, like a plowed up mole
With eyes sun blind and a blinder soul
But a stronger sense, one without fail
Serves me still in my travail
Is the smell I smell and can even taste
Of things gone bad, of foul and waste
O rude desire, lust ill taken
Of things that should not live awakened

To these ears which hear a little
Screeches, scraping, hell's fiendish fiddle
To these thoughts, bounding and fluttering in madness
Fed by fears of insubstantial but authentic badness

What is this world that manifests obscene
Offensive home of all things unclean
Hairy beast, and mindless brute
Eating flesh and bone and root
Broad daylight sins, and in the depths of waters
The faithless needs of sons and daughters
All examples have the devils told
Since the long lost days of old

***

Ozwald shakes his head, the dark cloud ruffling around like a patch of fog with the motion. "Where the hell was I?" he says out loud to himself, and the sound of his own voice is distant and odd.

"I've got to get it together," he says, again out loud to re-examine the quality of his voice, but a particularly heavy deluge of physical torment swamps his skull and he realizes the screaming and wailing has not stopped, he had only been oblivious to it somehow. He feels helpless to investigate the reason or the source of the trouble. He feels helpless to move. He clamps his hands to the sides of his face and succumbs to the pain and confusion. He is transported. He finds himself in the cell with Stephen. Stephen is standing against the solid back wall, with his back to the wall, his legs spread wide, and his arms reached out against the wall on either side, and he is raised up onto the balls of his bare feet. He is wearing only his prison issue white cotton briefs. He is screaming at the top of his voice and banging the back of his head against the wall.

Ozwald gets up off of the floor where he has been sitting and tries to charge for the door but his legs are numb, as if asleep. He falls, his legs crumpling oddly underneath him and then to the right as he falls to the left. In panic he tries to drag himself to the door. When he does reach the door it is locked. He tries to call for help but it is useless. His call is pathetically lost in the perpetual shriek of the little man against the wall. Ozwald takes two of the cell door bars in his hands and shakes the door but it is unshakeable. He turns to his tormentor, his implausible roommate, and cries out to him to stop, to "Please, Stephen. Stop." But of course Stephen can't hear him. Ozwald pleads and pleads and pleads to no avail. He lays his head on the cold hard floor, exhausted. At last he succumbs to the fear and he is transported.

***

There is a bright light in his eyes. It is so bright that it burns through his pain and the pain becomes an abstract. But as soon as the light is withdrawn the pain returns in its embodiment of violence upon his consciousness.

Now he is aware of someone screaming again. Ozwald must drag himself forward for his legs still have no feeling in them, and he pulls himself in the direction of the screams. Coming through a dark, hot mist he sees the silhouette of a man from behind a kind of curtain. The man is jerking in convulsions and screaming in horror, somehow restrained in a spread eagle fashion.

Ozwald, wary, pulls himself near the curtain, though he is terrified at the prospect of what—who he might find, and then he pulls himself further and around to the front of the curtain.

There are three strange man-like beasts there with the restrained man. They each have a bird-like head with a long pointed beak, like that of a crane. Their eyes are also small and bird-like. Not tall, maybe five feet, they are dirty with bloodied hands and long leather aprons wet with blood. They are dressed like workers in a foundry or a smelter. Large broad workingman's hands they have, and human feet with long terrible claws for nails. And they have long tails, nearly hairless, like rat's tails. These beast-men are absorbed in their occupation of inflicting torture upon the man with great forged metal tools, and they either do not notice Ozwald, or they pay no attention to him.

The man is so bloodied and beaten that Ozwald does not at first recognize that it is Stephen. One of the beasts has Stephen's tongue gripped in the jaws of a crudely fashioned tong while another has a hammer with which he is driving sharp square nails, like horseshoe nails up into the cavities of his nostrils. Blood is coming profusely from his eyes and nose and the tongue is huge, purple and swollen. The third bird-man seems to be waiting his turn as he stirs something in a large caste-iron bowl.

Ozwald now becomes so agitated and horrified that he loses all sense of consequence and he is crawling toward them and screaming at them to stop, to "Please, please, leave him alone!" with nearly the intensity of Stephen's screaming until he finds himself in their very presence. The one stirring the bowl gets up, kicks at him and curses at him with a gravel voice, in a strange language. The kick lands in Ozwald's rib cage but it does not deter him as he makes his way to Stephen. He is attempting to pull himself up with the curtain, but it tears. He attacks the beast with the hammer by trying to tackle him, wrapping his arms around the thing's muscular legs. The other two are kicking him and seem to be cursing him. But he succeeds in knocking the one creature down and somehow gets hold of the thing's hammer and wrenches it away from him.

Then he hears one of the beasts speaking in his horrible voice, but in English, "Where from, where from? Make him stop it. He cannot be here. We have our work ..." and Ozwald is about to hit the fallen one a blow with the hammer but he cannot, his arm won't go, and then, like his legs he has no feeling in his arms, and then he has no feelings at all.

***

When he regains consciousness he is in the infirmary. The pungent smell of disinfectant assaults his olfactory senses and instantly rekindles the flames of his headache pain. "Oh God, oh God, oh God," he cries in his agony.

"What the hell have you got into, son?" someone says.

"Ooooh. I don't know. How did I get here," Ozwald asks.

"Well, you were screaming bloody murder out in the hall, so we brought you in here, and then you passed out rather suddenly," says the man who is probably the day nurse.

"You gave me a sedative?"

"No way, we can't give meds to non-inmates without a doctor's approval," says the voice.

It now occurs to Ozwald that he can't see, but then it occurs to him that he has his eyes clamped shut in reaction to the pain. He moans. "My head hurts so bad."

"I'll call the doctor and see if we can give you anything."

"I've never had anything like this."

"You mean the head pain?" the voice says.

"Yeah."

"Have you ever had seizures or blackouts, anything like that?"

Ozwald says "No." Then he says, "Why was Stephen screaming?"

"Stephen?" asks the voice.

"Yes. I got drunk last night and I had this huge hangover and someone started shrieking and screaming and it was going through my head like a freight train, then I realized it was Stephen, but ..." he doesn't know what to say at this point.

"No one else was screaming, my friend, only you."

"What do you mean?"

"It's been a remarkably calm morning. You have provided the only real entertainment so far."

"Me?"

"Yes, sir. That's what I'm telling you."

questions for Stephen

Ozwald lets it go for a while. Almost a week. They had turned him loose from the infirmary, on the condition that he was to see his regular doctor. He didn't tell them that he didn't have a regular doctor. However, he had no intention of jeopardizing his work on the project, so he subjected himself to the process of finding a doctor.

"The thing is, there's doctors everywhere," he complains to his roommates. "How in the world am I supposed to pick one?"

"I know," Ansel answers him. "It's a big decision and it's sort of a crap shoot, to a great extent."

"So who do you go to?"

"I've gone to this clinic where there's a group of doctors. When I had the flu last year, I started there," Ansel tells him.

"And you like it or what?"

"I don't think I would either recommend it or diss it, to tell the truth. They give you one doctor, but for an emergency you can see one of the others, if yours is not available. What can I say, their intentions seem to be good, but, you know, drugs are the answer to everything."

"I sure as hell don't want any drugs. I don't know what I want, what I need." He thinks about it, then says, "Maybe I need a shrink."

Jeff, who has been silent up to now, says, "Man, you would even consider going to a shrink after what we've seen?"

Ozwald has to think about that. He really has to think about that. "You know I was only saying it, in a sort of offhand way, but that's a hell of a question, Jeff. It's like they tamper with things they don't know anything about, don't they?"

"Yeah, baby," Jeff says, sort of pleased with himself.

"No, I don't think I'll be going down that road," Ozwald says.

Now it's Ansel's turn to speak up. "Wow, you guys are throwing out the entire field of mental health professionals, by what you've seen in a federal prison? That's a big leap."

Jeff shrugs. Ozwald goes to the kitchen for cup of coffee. "Bring me a soda while you're in there, would ya Oz?" Jeff calls to him from his chair.

"What kind?"

"What kind we got?"

"We got Pepsi. You bought it, remember?"

Ozwald remembers. "I'll take a Pepsi."

When he gets back Ozwald tells Ansel he's probably right, and that he was probably leaping to conclusions.

"I'm pretty much staying with the big leap," Jeff maintains.

Ozwald returns to the computer, and his doctor search. "There's some here that claim to mix it up, with alternative medicine. Maybe I'll check one of those out."

***

His visit to the *mix it up* doctor leaves him with mixed feelings. But he agrees to some tests, most of which are prescribed to determine whether he has suffered any trauma to the head. He told the doctor about his fall on the chair, which he doesn't even remember, but it was suggested as a possibility by Jeff and Ansel.

"A possibility?" he had responded, with considerable suspicion to their suggestion. "A possibility to explain what?"

They look a little sheepish, no doubt. But then Jeff tells him, "We're just worried about you, Oz. What do you expect? I mean, you ended up in the infirmary screaming your head off, after all."

"You sure it's not that you guys think I'm, I mean, that it's ..." but he realizes he hasn't told them anything about his experience with Stephen and the two beast/men, so his friends may just be concerned about his health.

"We don't think anything, Ozwald. We're just concerned about your health," Ansel says.

"Okay. I guess I got a little paranoid there for a minute. I thought you were worried about my mental health."

"Well, we've always had our concerns about that, my man," Jeff says, "but no more than usual, I swear." He puts his hands up in an expression of denial.

***

The tests come out negative and Ozwald isn't suffering any recurring visions, hallucinations, or whatever he suffered the day of his hangover. The doctor would have pursued the matter further, had Ozwald persisted, but since he really only went to satisfy the staff at the prison, he lets the medical investigation go. But as he goes along, the experience stays strong in his consciousness, and no effort to push it back, negate it, or explain it into a place of lesser importance is successful. He has returned to work. The staff is satisfied with his doctor report. They've seen it all. One more person screaming bloody murder is not really that big of a deal to them, apparently. But Ozwald knows that, with this persistent preoccupation, he is not up to the work. Finally he decides to have a talk with Stephen. It is a talk that he has feared and avoided.

***

Stephen is a man of extremes. Intelligent and thoughtful, he is quite approachable at times. At other times—at other times his symptoms, for which he is commonly classified as delusional and paranoiac, are manifested in a swamp of tangible sensation, wherein one can easily feel unnerved, even lost, as if he has wandered too far into a place unknown, just by coming in the poor fellow's presence.

When Ozwald finds him standing in his cell, which is where he can most often be found, Stephen happens to be in one of his more approachable states of mind.

"Dear Stephen," Ozwald begins, which is a good beginning. He says it from outside the cell, where he waits for an invitation to come in.

"How can I be of service," Stephen asks, sincerely, but without turning from his position, in which he stands facing the adjoining cell, to Ozwald's left. "Please come in," he adds. So Ozwald does go in.

"I ..." but the 'Dear Stephen' was as far as Ozwald had been able to plan the conversation. "I don't know, but I ... A thing happened to me about a week ago."

Stephen is patient.

"I had a hangover. I was kind of in a fog," Ozwald continues.

"What day was it?"

"It was Monday. We, my friends and I, had been sort of unwinding the night before, with a bottle."

"It's quite stressful here," Stephen says, acknowledging with a nod, his voice now with a slight tremor in it, his right hand twitching almost imperceptibly at his hip.

"Yes. It's phenomenally interesting—but stressful." Then Ozwald says, "Do you mind if I sit?"

"No, no, not at all. Sit."

"Thank you."

Ozwald sits on the bed. He looks at Stephen's back. He looks around the cell. "I was here at work, out in the main hall. The hangover was bothering me a lot. I heard someone begin to scream. It hurt my head and I covered my ears." He puts his hands over his ears as if to show Stephen but Stephen isn't looking.

"The nurse said it was me that was screaming. I had blacked out apparently. I woke up in the infirmary and he told me it was me. That no one else had screamed at all. It was a quiet morning. That's what he said. 'A quiet morning'."

"Hard to believe, I suppose," Stephen says.

"Yes, I found it, I find it hard to believe."

Ozwald goes on in a moment. "I wanted to ask you something personal." His hands are shaking now. He's into territory that must be crossed. He's not sure he has the stomach for it. "I know you've had some experiences with things."

"I've had some, yes."

"With some dark kinds of things."

"I can only assume that it is my special karma."

"I really don't know how to express it. I saw you being tortured."

"Yamadoots."

"What's that?" Ozwald says, not sure what Stephen had said.

Stephen turns around to face him. "It is their job. An eye for an eye. A tooth for a tooth, as the saying goes." Stephen is looking at Ozwald, but Ozwald turns away."I was not screaming," Stephen tells him. "I heard you screaming."

Ozwald's voice was soft. "I tried to help you."

"Yet you're here, as am I."

"Yes?"

"It was George who found you there. Didn't you see him?"

"No"

"Well, you're here—as am I."

a poet in the closet

Ansel and Jeff decide they need to go ahead with the open mike for the sake of trying to get some momentum, even though Oz is unable to participate. They've also learned that some people have been preparing some material and they don't wish to disappoint them.

Jeff assumes the role of emcee for the event, in Ozwald's absence. So it gets off on a familiar and entertaining note with the Two Tops being bold and starting the show again. They are much appreciated as some members of the slightly enlarged audience were eagerly anticipating their repeat performance.

Johnny goes up to Ansel and asks in a whisper if it's alright if he reads something. "Sure," says Ansel. "Something you wrote?"

"Yeah."

So Ansel asks Jeff to introduce Johnny.

There's a little bit of encouraging applause for Johnny, which does seem to help bolster him up somewhat, as he goes up to the mop.

"Thanks." He nervously adjusts the mop handle, "I—I've been a little bit of a closet writer for a long time. So anyway, this is called 'back road pilgrims'. It's not really a poem, I guess but, well, it don't matter what, I guess." Johnny starts reading, repeating the name again, his voice shaky and nervous at first but settling down considerably after he gets through the first few lines.

"back road pilgrims"

"Driving the old boat along the narrow two lane—tall ditch grass, parched to straw lining the way on either side, obscuring the pitted and broken strands that clench still dangerous barbs, as they cling to the disfigured skeleton ironwood posts.

"The night's clear light defines and highlights spire and butte, riders mute in travel, in reflection, and in admiration of creation.

"Sparks hit the black top, in little silent orange explosions, bouncing, swirling, as butts are ejected, un-extinguished, caught in the flash of mirrors.

"Carefree travelers are these? No, only actors, filled with human cares, concerns, apprehensions—actors, reticent, furtive, true to craft.

"The earth is a big ball, beautiful and foreign, inhabited by ghosts in all manner of astonishing costumes, all strange, one to the other, orphan intelligence, stranded, uninformed.

"The road is going, the road is not knowing, the boat is chrome and golden luster adrift on the heat of the desert, headlights searching, insects singing to the engine's drone, hands on the wheel, the hard resin feel, feet on the floor, arms in the windows, hair in the wind, dreams of memories in the past, hope with reservation in the destination, pale stars in the sky unfathomable.

"This band of pilgrims, a speck of dust set in motion, a drop of water in an ocean, a passing thought in creation, a remote breath of imagination, no doubt significant, infinitely eminent.

141

"An old mare is crossing the road. The acute senses of these beasts are their friends. Senses that caused so much trouble, playing mischief in her human form, from which she spun helplessly back into the eternal wheel.

"Here where men would call her free, call her a wild thing of nature, born to run with the wind, in pageantry and power and grace.

"Her senses now fail her. Blind of eye, and in her own silent world, she has come down from the highlands, following a phantom's trail.

"Some miles back, other, keener senses have detected her movement and dark shapes have fallen in, loping behind. She is neither wild nor free. She is imprisoned in a frail form, a skeleton frame, a certain fate in a determined existence.

"The headlights are strong. The boat is sound. The road is gray. The fire is orange and bright and yellow, from the offered light, he holds the wheel true as he turns and leans to receive it. The cigarette glows and the warm mellow smoke is pulled deep into the lungs. Returning his eyes to the road, a sudden image, an explosive sound, the shattered glass and mangled steel as the roof is torn loose and folded back, the coasting on, engine idling, until running into the shallow ditch and stopped against a field approach, her great head thrashing about, long neck writhing, the soft and terrible groan of her species in agony, legs twisted or amputated, gut torn open and spilled upon the twisted, broken bodies in the front seat, the back seat passengers completely hidden beneath her.

"All things come together in the order of time.

"Those dark runners, hesitate, tentative at first, daunted by the strange smells and the soft sound of the engine, but tempted by their hunger and their lust, they approach, and standing on powerful back legs, one reaches in, while others whine in anticipation, and she tastes the taste of the blood of these abandoned things and then leaps in.

"And following her lead, the others are emboldened and they come up, snarling and bickering for position in the rather cramped quarters."

**

Johnny looks up, not knowing what to expect. "That's it," he tells them. Ansel and Jeff offer polite applause. But then from the little audience comes more genuine applause, and enthusiastic comments, like cheers from peers. "Yeah Johnny!" "Dude, that was awesome." Johnny smiles, shy. "Thanks you guys, that's nice of you." He goes and sits in the same place in which he had been sitting, where he receives more congratulatory remarks.

Jeff and Ansel look at each other and give *thumbs up*.

**

After the event breaks up, Ansel asks Jeff if he has the scoop on Johnny.

"You mean like, 'What's he in for?'"

"Yeah"

"'Cause he seems like a pretty cool dude, doesn't he? I know, I think so too."

"So? Do you know anything?"

"No. But I sure aim to find out."

"Good. Let me know, if I don't find out first."

"No doubt."

NINETEEN: Some lessons in love

physician heal thyself
Ozwald

We had just gotten to work that morning, the cell doors were not yet opened, when some guard that I'd never seen before came up to me and told me that I was wanted in the medical room. Jeff had gone to use the restroom and Ansel, who had planned another attempt at an interview with the inmate, Charles, more commonly known as Junkyard Dog, had already headed back to Charles' cell.

The medical room is a separate room from the nurse's station. It is used for the more serious emergencies and has a windowless, lockable door. When I went into the room, which was not locked, they had him on the floor, bound in a straight jacket, with two guards, Ed and Clarence, holding him down. Clarence had his knee in George's back and Ed was finishing up with the fasteners of the straight jacket. The nurse had a syringe and was waiting to administer the contents as soon as the guards would give the word. George was still struggling frantically, but to no avail. Besides the straight jacket, he was also gagged. I learned later that the purpose of that mandatory procedure, with George, was to prevent him from alarming the other inmates who seemed to depend upon his stability.

After the shot was given, George calmed down, they picked him up and laid him on the cold and crisp white sheets of the hard hospital bed.

"May I try to speak with him," I asked the nurse after the guards left the room, seemingly ignoring my presence.

"I guess it's alright," said the nurse.

"George, I'm sorry to approach you in this way," I began, my voice quavering, George not looking at me. "I'm taking advantage, I know. But why are they treating you this way?"

When he turned to look at me, I was afraid. Some part of me has developed a respect, an anticipation, an apprehension of the *looks* of George, even with the buffer of distance, which I do not have here. I am also very conscious of the fact that George has never spoken to me directly before. When he does look I realize the implications of my concern. His gaze went into me, through me, shattered me, destroyed me, paralyzed me.

Yet his words expressed his own confusion and frustration. He seemed not to be speaking to me at all, but only thinking out loud. Somehow it was my fate to be there, embarrassed as I was by my own presence in his time of despair and humiliation.

"The people seem to come out of nowhere. I don't seek them out, all these strangers. I don't find it all that comforting to have lifelong strangers. They don't like me—not really. Sure, I can impress them in certain ways. Sometimes please them, somehow. But they sure as hell don't like me. Not all of me. They don't think like me. They don't feel like I do. Who are they anyway, these people that have come out of the void?"

There was nothing in my world that could possibly respond. His words burned into some part that was left of me, though, at that moment, there was no me, but only the experience of his eyes and his voice.

Then I heard myself asking him a question. I had not thought about the question; it came from me, I'm sure, but from some part of me operating independently. "George, did you come there when I saw Stephen?"

Then George spoke to me directly. "Have you not seen so much that you know so little, Ozwald? Who will help poor Stephen if I don't do it, even now? And these others? All condemned. Who will love them? Do you think that love is talk?"

He turned away and after a while, I don't know how long, I realized that I should leave the room and I did.

***

It may seem strange that I was allowed to come into the room. It seemed strange to me. That also was explained later. We, Jeff and Ansel and I, were told, upon requesting a meeting with the prison authority, which was granted, that they, the administration, wanted us to be aware of the reality of this George. That, like so many other charismatic Gurus and so-called prophets, he was really a madman and a charlatan, a wolf in sheep's clothing.

"Why do you encourage him then?" we ask.

"What do you mean," we are asked. (The names and positions of the prison authorities involved in this discussion we are not at liberty to disclose.)

"You allow them freedoms. Freedoms that seem to be quite unorthodox, and that are not granted other prisoners. They are allowed to assemble and associate freely, choosing to come to the hall during daylight hours or to stay in their cells. They can even leave the floor, some of them, on a limited basis."

"These are practical things. As we have already mentioned, there is a certain sense of stability that George helps to maintain on the floor. He has a calming effect on the other inmates, which of course is an asset to our staff. We simply take advantage of that."

Naturally, Jeff asks what we're all thinking. "So you don't mind if he is misleading the others?"

"What concern is that of ours? This is a prison, not a church, or a temple."

"Then I'm still confused as to why you would want us to be aware of George, the charlatan, as you have called him," Jeff continues.

"Your impertinence seems rather uncalled for, young man, given the broad range of freedoms you and your colleagues enjoy here in the process of your research."

This time it's my turn. I think we were all a little more vocal here than we would have been, but for the strong image of George being manhandled and gagged in the infirmary.

"We don't intend impertinence, Sir. But the findings of our research we hope to base on facts, and truth, to the extent that is possible. It seems that since the prison administration decided in our favor originally, and by that I mean that we were allowed to come onto the floor and enjoy these freedoms, which I agree are quite, " I change it to, "quite extraordinarily liberal—well, it just seems that there is a reason, as there is a reason for everything."

That's what I said, although looking at it now I see a certain ambiguity to my statement, as, seemingly by the reply that I received to the statement, did the unnamed authorities who heard it.

"The reason." Here he opens a file, which has been lying on the desk before him. He leafs through the first few pages and then explains to us. "The reason, as you were told upon the acceptance of your original request to implement your project was, I quote, 'in line with the continuing efforts of the United States Penal System to support the advancement of science, as it applies to the treatment of prisoners and the implementation of prison policies.' Does that answer your question, Ozwald?" the man said, with what I detected as just the slightest hint of condescension in his voice and manner.

After that I thought better of trying to make the point that I had unsuccessfully attempted to make a moment ago. I think Jeff would have attempted it, but Ansel and I were concerned about that, since Jeff would probably be successful in making the point clear, due to his gift for lack of subtlety. So when he began to speak we elbowed him in the ribs from either side, not being subtle about it.

"Yes Sir, I think it does answer the question," I said.

committed to the bone

The morning that Ozwald is called to the medical room to witness George's disturbing episode, Ansel succeeds in drawing Charles into a brief conversation.

As he approaches Charles' cell, Ansel does not speak, or otherwise announce his coming, his intuition telling him that Charles is very sensitive to his surroundings and also very aware of his surroundings. He quietly walks up to the cell and sits outside of the door. Patiently, he sits there and waits. After twenty minutes, Charles says, "What do ya want?"

"Not much. Just hoping you'll talk with me a little bit?"

"What ya want that for?"

"Well, I'm a student. I want to learn," Ansel tells him.

"I ain't no teacher."

"I know."

"I ain't useta talking ta people, much," Charles says.

"People aren't often that easy to talk to," Ansel says.

There's a long silence at this point. Then Charles invites Ansel to come into the cell. "Come on in if ya want to."

So Ansel goes in, sits on the floor inside the cell.

Charles says, "They got me in here for murder, but I didn't have no choice, killin' them two. I never hurt nobody before, like that."

"Justice isn't always served. I've learned that here," Ansel says, sincerely. After a little bit, he goes on to say, "Charles, I was wondering if you've heard anything about the inmate George?"

"Cain't be here without hearing about him."

"What do you make of what you hear?"

"My loyalty's ta Jesus."

"Oh, I see."

"I don't expect anybody can see how somebody else's loyalty is."

"No, you're right, Charles. I'm sorry if I implied otherwise."

"No offense taken. But I only got one heart. Jesus got it."

"I'm glad you told me," Ansel says.

"I prefer it, just me an' Him."

"Okay. But thanks for talking with me."

"Okay."

nothin bad about nobody

"I ain't ga-gonna say n-nothin bad about nobody, Jeff, specially n-not my friends," Anthony informs Jeff.

"What makes you think I want you to say something bad about him?"

"Well, well, well, well, iiiiiif it ain't bad, how come you d-d-d-don' a-ask 'im yourself?"

"Come to think of it, Anthony, I can see now how it could look that way to you. But you got it wrong. We just thought that if we asked him, you know, straight up, that it might, well, embarrass him. I mean, he seems like such a nice guy, and you bein his friend—"

"Johnny is a n-n-nice guy. I'm not so sh-sh-sure about you, though Jeff."

Jeff finds himself sharply struck by Anthony's assessment of him. Uncharacteristically, he's at a loss for words. Finally, he says, "I'm sorry, Anthony." He puts his hands in his pockets, shrugs his shoulders. "Well, never mind," and he turns away. But in a moment Anthony comes after him. "Jeff."

"Yeah," Jeff says, turning back around.

"Okay Jeff, Ja-Ja-Johnny blacks out."

"Blacks out?"

"Y-y-y-yes. An he r-r-ran over two liittle kids, blacked out."

"But that condition. It should have been manslaughter."

"N-no license, Jeff. M-maaarrrijua-jauna too." And Anthony looks at Jeff for a long moment and he sees that Jeff is affected by what he has told him. Then he continues. "He's v-very s-sad, Jeff."

TWENTY: A series of low burning fires

I need a lover and a friend
All friendships you transcend
And impotent I remain.
— Maulana Rumi

Through me many long dumb voices,
Voices of the interminable generations of slaves,
Voices of prostitutes and deformed persons,
Voices of the diseased and despairing, and of thieves
and dwarfs,
…through me forbidden voices…
—Walt Whitman

A man talks
Jeff

This is off the record. This is *not* in the report. I was sitting in the hall, trying to work on my notes. It was unusually quiet, almost peaceful. Peaceful, that is, for a place without peace. The afternoon sun was coming in through the little windows and I was getting kind of drifty; just started meditating on the dust floaters in the sunbeams. Gradually, I became aware of a conversation. Horatio and Johnny sitting three tables away. I could only hear a few words here and there. I know it seems kind of pathetic, but they had their backs to me so I picked up my notebook and moved closer, to where I'm only one table away in a flagrant eavesdrop. I guess the guards saw me. But we're talking about men whose job descriptions include depriving others of their privacy. They didn't say or do anything. I confess, I didn't care what they thought, as long as they didn't call me on it. I suppose I also took it for granted that no one else would notice or care in that world of strange men where odd behavior is the norm.

Again, this in not in the report. I had to take notes. I won't guarantee that every word is right. It's close, though.

***

"A man talks," Horatio is saying. "He turns to his fellow man and he talks. Tells what is on his mind. No, that's not true. He rarely, almost never, tells what's on his mind. Not what's burnin' down low and steady in his mind. Seems like a man is preoccupied with trivial stuff, politics, the weather, you know what I mean? An' on we go about it. 'This man ain't doin us right up there in that buildin'. How'm I supposed to make ends meet?' While the other man he's a thinkin', Damn fool don' know what he's talkin' bout. He's so lazy is why he cain't make no ends meet?

So then they go on about the weather. 'Damn, it's hot.' You know. Then a man goes home to his woman an' he talks at her. 'That damn fool, he don' know what he's a talkin' bout.'

So the fire is burnin'. An' the man, he throws dirt on the fire and it don' go out. You know what I mean, dirt, Johnny?"

"Well, I guess you mean like the things we do to try and forget. To escape," Johnny answers.

"Yeah that's it. Only it seem like the fire burns on dirt. Burns a little hotter even. Still, it's a small, low fire. But it don' never go out. I expect that's what is meant by a man bein' burned out. I seen it in my grandpa and in my own dad. Ever man is afraid. Don' know where-from we come or where-to we gonna go. We put on the man thing. 'Well then, hell, I'll do what I want,' says the man."

"It's a matter of trust, I think, Horatio," Johnny suggests as Horatio gives him an opening.

"Maybe so. I think I get ya there, but tell me more," Horatio says.

"I don't know, exactly. But it seems like we protect that fire. Maybe we know it's burning us up, burning us out. But still, who can we trust with it? I know, it sounds crazy the way I'm putting it."

"No it don't," Horatio says, assuring him. "Like we don't trust nobody with the truth. I know it's true, Johnny. It just don' seem to make sense."

The two men sit for a while in silence. We're all facing the windows. Maybe we're all watching the dust floaters. But then Horatio makes Johnny a proposition.

"I tell ya what," he says with what I take as a kind of shy, if not embarrassed chuckle. "I'll tell you what's on my fire if you tell me what's on yours."

Johnny readily agrees to this arrangement. I'm glad, because I'm very curious. But now I'm starting to feel a little guilty. Maybe not guilty enough though, 'cause I don't get up or do anything to make them conscious of my presence.

Naturally, at this point both men begin to look around to see who might be listening. I shoot a glance down at my notebook. When they see how close I am behind them, I'm not more than ten feet away, they look at me until, feeling their unrelenting eyes, I look up and see those looks that I can only describe as incriminating.

"What?" I say, feigning innocence, but soon having to give up my feeble attempt to appear absorbed in my work.

"Afternoon, Jeff," Horatio says, with sarcasm in his greeting. Johnny doesn't say anything.

"Gentlemen," I respond.

Horatio turns to Johnny. "Johnny, what'ya say we invite Jeff to join us?"

"I don't think so," says Johnny.

"I figgered that," says Horatio. "I don' think so too."

"Well I'll just saunter off to another table," I say.

"We'd appreciate it," Horatio says, but at least now he's smiling. I don't think Horatio's really capable of holding a grudge.

I've thought about that conversation from time to time. I sure would have liked to have heard about those fires. I've begun to try to assess my own low burning fire. Somehow, I think if a person could really pinpoint the source, define the nature of that fire, the person would know something worthwhile. Well, I haven't got very far on that.

Walt Whitman
-a low burning fire-

"Listen, Doc, I gotta talk to ya; I gotta ask ya somethin." Walt Whitman is soliciting Jeff who is sitting at a table working on his notes.

Jeff gets up and walks over. "I'm not a doctor, Walt," he explains, "but I'll listen if you want."

"Well, you're workin' on it, aren't you?"

"I am intending to eventually obtain the status of a doctor, but I'm not intending to be a therapist. I'm more interested in theory, really," Jeff further explains.

"Ya, that's really groovy, Doc. Kin I talk to ya or what?"

"Uh, of course."

"Good, 'cause I see you talking to about everbody in this joint but me. So what am I, just some kina wall decoration or something?"

"We've talked …" But Jeff starts to realize he's making this thing more difficult than it needs to be. It occurs to him that the man just wants to talk. After all, this is really a prison anyway, not a clinic. People can talk. "Look, I'm sorry; sure go ahead and talk. I mean, let's talk. Just try not to call me Doc, okay?"

"Deal, then what do I call you?"

"Jeff."

Walt nods, affirmative.

So Jeff pulls up a chair. "Do you mind if I take notes, Walt?"

"I'd be a damn site disappointed if you didn't." I don't know if you're aware of it, but the other night, I took a run for it."

"You tried to escape?"

"Yes I did, Jeff. In my own way, that is."

"Oh. I see. You tried to escape *altogether*."

"Yeah, they slipped up. They cut me loose to put me to bed, but they got distracted, by that nut Stephen, wailin' about something I think it was, and I hit the corner right as you go into the corridor. Bunged myself up pretty good, but they got hold of the cable at the last moment, nuff to slow me down just a little and foil my escape."

Jeff is conscious of a certain physical sensation like a painful sympathetic cringe that rushes through his body, as Walt relates that brutal charge of self destruction into the corner of the wall.

"Anyway, what I wanted to talk to you about Jeff. When I was in the infirmary getting my *head examined*—pardon the expression—I got in kind of a dreamy mood, I don't know; nostalgic like. I was remembering something that happened long, long ago in a little town. It's really weirdin' me out. It was nothing. Why in the hell would I think about it?"

"You're saying it was a *fond* memory?" Jeff says, in order to clarify.

"I wouldn't say fond so much as just a memory of an event. An insignificant event."

"There's nothing unusual or wrong about remembering incidents from the past. I mean, everybody does it."

"I don't."

"You don't?"

"Never."

"Okay," Jeff acknowledges.

"So?" Walt Whitman says, inquisitive.

"So—I don't know. Why don't you tell me about the memory?" Jeff suggests, to move the conversation along, feeling that this isn't going all that well.

So Walt Whitman tells him about his memory.

"The thing I remembered happened in the area where I'm from. Not in my home town, but in a little town, near there, where I lived for a time as a young man. That town had been swallowed up by suburbia, yet it had successfully maintained many of its small town ways. Kids ran free. Folks didn't worry much about crime. Quiet streets with little traffic, that sort of stuff. And there was one thing; they didn't deliver the mail. Ya had to go to the post office for it. You get the picture, right Jeff?"

Jeff nods that he does.

"This situation was not without benefit, Jeff. Besides being a kind of encouragement toward getting some exercise by being required to get out of the house and walk there, that is, unless you were damn lazy enough to get in the car and drive over, there was the social aspect. People actually saw their neighbors occasionally, found out what they looked like.

"So one day, as my memory serves me, I coincidentally met a man at the post office. We knew each other to some degree. I had to walk by the other man's house on the way to get the mail.

"In this instance, I was untying my little dog from the Local Traffic Only sign, at the entrance to the alley behind the post office, where I was in the habit of putting her, having retrieved my mail, when the other man, having gone quickly in and out of the building, sees me.

"'He's ready to go,' the fella says to me.

"'Yes; he's a she though,' I answer him.

"'She's a pure Beagle, is she,' he asks as we start walking.

"As soon as we're across the street, I bend down and undo the clasp so she can go on her own as the three of us walk the trail through the woods.

"'No,' I tell him, 'She just looks that way, but she's a mixed up old girl.'

"Well, we start in to climb down the little hill and then over the clearing that takes us down behind the row of houses, and naturally we stop on the path as it goes past that man's yard and there we continue on with our conversation. But after awhile, I begin to turn and back up as I'm turning, like I'm gonna go on home, but it's just a false start. And the other man turns toward his house but, the same thing you know, and he turns back and we go right on talking.

"'We had Golden Retrievers,' he tells me. 'Just lost our old boy this last winter.'

"'I'm sorry,' I tell him.

"An' he goes on to say, 'He was doing pretty good that night. He couldn't hardly walk for the last while but I always went out with him when he had to go, you know, helped him back in if he couldn't make it up the stairs. But he ate good that night, I gave him some ice cream and he seemed alright, and I left him in the porch where he was comftorble, an' I went back in and we watched the news, but when I came back out in about an hour, he was gone.'

"'It's not easy to lose somebody, I know,' I say, cause I do understand, of course.

"'Well, no,' he says, kinda shakes his head a little.

"'We talked the one other time, I don't know if you remember,' I say to him.

"'Yeah, you was lookin' at an old truck I had for sale.'

"About then a man on a bicycle goes by saying, 'He's ready to go,' referring to my dog, who has made her own beginnings down the road,

155

only to turn back when her man don't come along. Somehow people seem to notice when you're dog is ready ta go somewhere.

"'I wanted it, but I didn't have a good place to keep it, so …' I say about the truck.

"'I've always got one or two, as you can see,' and he points to the line of old vehicles he's got lined up there across the ditch where folks can see 'em from that path that folks take through the woods. 'I've made them all roadworthy,' he says, kinda proud like a fella would be about his hobby. He's got 'em under a fiberglass car cover an' all, over there, to keep the rain off 'em.

"From there the conversation goes on about one thing and another, and the talk turns to our origins.

"'I'm not from here. I was born over in Sankit County,' he says, 'I was thirty years in the Army.'

"'Really.' I find that interestin' and I tell him, 'There's a base near where I come from in Washington. I used to drive through it on my way to work. It was kind of strange, because I'd drive a perfectly good road one day and the next day the same road would have huge holes and pieces blown out of it. They played war games out there at night I guess.' I never was in the service, so I tell him that.

"And he tells me, 'I was there once a few years back in the seventies. I've got a cousin over on the east end that lived out there. He's been all over, though. He was in the Air Force, did his training out in North Dakota.'

"'Been through there,' I say, 'Got caught in a hailstorm. Couldn't find a tree to get under, even.'

"By this time my dog has made several more false starts and that other man does start himself down into the ditch and he begins walking through the line of cars and trucks that he has made roadworthy. An' I turn down the road on my way an' we're still talking, only now with our raised voices, but without turning, and each of us, well aware that the other man can no longer make out what is being said."

Walt Whitman stops at that point, and he's looking away and Jeff doesn't know for sure if the story is done or if he should just wait, or say something. But then he hears a sort of stifled sniffle, and he realizes that Walt Whitman is crying, softly.

Jeff sits still, somewhat uncomfortable, to be sure, but not knowing quite what to do and also, the psychologist in him somewhat intrigued by this sudden show of emotion, given the inmates affectation of bravado heretofore.

After a little while, Walt Whitman, says through the tears that have now manifested, "What's that about, Jeff? I mean, that ain't nothing."

"You mean the memory is nothing?" Jeff says, unsure.

"Yeah."

"I don't know, Walt. I know you said it wasn't, but it seems like a fond memory to me."

"What the hell's the world coming to?"

"It's a good question. I don't know what It's coming to."

critics

Horatio and Fyodor have revved up the crowd with their latest, kind of a Gladys Knight and the Pips routine, in which they recruited Ozwald for the role of Gladys. Ozwald readily accepted the role, emphatically declaring confidence in his masculinity. Johnny has revealed another of his rather dark creations, garnering another appreciative response, and as he makes his way back to his seat, there is another participant making his shuffling, now sidestepping, way to the mop. He makes a full circle around it, appearing to inspect it from all sides. The little audience, noticing the newcomer, has become silent, probably in disbelief.

When he has concluded that the mop is satisfactory to his unspoken criteria, Anthony steps up to it to speak. "These are s-some examples of my wo-wo-wo-wo-work," he says, holding up a small notebook. He opens the notebook for his own viewing, holding it at waist level, turns a few pages and looks at one for a period of time. The crowd waits, likely more out of a sense of trepidation than out of patience.

Anthony holds up the notebook, showing the open page to the audience. There's some sort of circular greenish design or illustration on the page. Ansel and Ozwald look at each other, unsure. The rest of the audience is still, still. Anthony again peruses the notebook until he finds another work that he wishes to exhibit. He holds it up for their enjoyment and this one appears to be of a reddish brown hue and a somewhat indefinite form.

"Anthony?" Horatio says, out of the silence.

"Yes, Horatio?"

"They're kind of hard for us to see from here."

"Oh." He thinks about it, then says, "M-m-m-aybe I could pa-pa-pa-pa-pa-pass it around."

So he hands the book to Ozwald who is sitting the nearest, and then returns to the mop. Ozwald and Ansel look at the still open page.

"Do you want us to look at only certain ones, Anthony," Ansel asks.

"N-no, y-y-you can look at them all i-i-if you like."

"I didn't know that you were an artist," Ozwald says.

"Yes, I am. I w-wo-work ah-lone."

So Ozwald and Anthony browse through the notebook, which contains a series of works, paintings in a variety of shades and shapes, very abstract. Then they pass it on. The different members of the audience page through, mostly in pairs, sometimes with curious over-the-shoulder lookers as well. Generally, everyone is examining the little designs with respect, shown by their various nods, smiles and other expressions of attention.

When Johnny's turn comes to look, and his turn is last, as he is sitting alone in the back, he comments, "Anthony, your work is quite abstract; do you think you could explain it to us, somehow, maybe your inspiration or, something about your style—possibly."

There are two or three audible, "Uh-oh"'s. and someone puts in, nervously, "I like it, Anthony."

But Johnny goes on to say, "It's just that it's kind of hard to understand."

Anthony stands, looking at Johnny.

The members of the audience, including Ansel and Ozwald, are looking back and forth at Johnny and Anthony.

Anthony's face has assumed a high level of intensity, a ruddy darkness in its aspect, prior to boiling over. Then it boils over.

"Y-y-ya-you d-d-da-dumb ssssson-a-b-bitch, J-J-J Ja-Ja-Ja ..." He just can't get Johnny's name out. "Ha-how c-c-ca-come y-ya-ya? Oooooooh, f-f-fa ..." He shuffles away from the mop and runs a few steps toward the corridor and then he turns back. "Some f-f-friend, J- Johnny."

Johnny is looking at him, in tears now, "I'm sorry, Anthony," he says, his tone pleading. But Johnny knows there's nothing he can do. Anthony will have to have time. Time to forgive. Time to let it go.

TWENTY-ONE: Of Lovers and cynics

Rainy day people always seem to know when you're feelin blue
High steppin strutters who land in the gutters sometimes need one too.
—Gordon Lightfoot, Rainy Day People

Clifton
-good people-

"There are some good people in this world. I've only met a few. But she's shown me again an again what it means to be a human being.

"We met in the ghetto. That's a good place to meet a woman. You don't get the blues so easy when your expectations start out lower. Ain't so far to fall, if you see what I mean. She had her dreams, though. Ain' no doubt. She was a writer of poetry. She was a vision of poetry, an she was a writer of poetry. In her poetry she spoke to the heart. It was flowery, but the flowers in her poems were natural and oh so beautiful. Not put on, my friend. Not put on.

"You're probly thinkin', What's this fool talkin' bout poetry, who can barely spit out the English language enough to ask for directions to the john? An' that's a good question, but all's I can say is I don't think it matters. If it's a matter of vocabulary, well hell, that's why the good lord created the dictionary ain' it? I guess you get my drift.

"So we met in the ghetto at this little dive bucket greasy spoon. That's where I was workin'. She was with her girlfriend the first time she came in. The waitress came back talkin' stuff about her because, turned out she was a vegetarian. We didn' get so many a them in those days you know. So I got to make her biscuits and I made 'em from scratch without eggs like she'd asked and I was pleased to do it. I whipped up a special gravy from just soy sauce and black pepper an a pinch of flour an' I tasted it an' it was pretty good. I told that waitress to wise up and treat her right. Well, I kept up watchin' and she seemed to like what the waitress was tellin' her, how I'd made this biscuits an' gravy up special for her. And after she had a few bites she looked over my way, an' I tried to pretend I didn' notice but I caught her smile and the next time she looked I smiled back, you know.

"She came in a few days later on, an' by then I'd had some time to get my nerve up an' I told the waitress, I was goin' out to meet her. So I took off my apron and I checked the mirror; couldn't find nothing wrong that a different face wouldn't fix, and out there I went. She was with her friend again an' when I went up to the booth, they both said 'Hi' to me real nice, and I said 'Hi' back an' I asked if I could take their order. Then she said she wanted to thank me for what I'd done the last time and how most times people just looked at her funny when she asked for food with no eggs an' that. Well, by then, just by bein' in her proximity for those few minutes and listening to her voice, I was getting in kind of a trance an' I barely made it out a there and back to the kitchen without becoming a complete blubberin' idiot." He shrugged and grinned. "The long n' short of it is, she accepted me for what I was—what I still am. We got married the next spring."

Ansel is thoroughly enjoying the story. Clifton's romanticism is refreshing to him, coming as it does from someone within these surroundings of such concentrated, often self-inflicted, daily misery and confusion. Clifton goes on to tell, in considerable detail, the happy tale of his married life.

"We'd be living the good life, even today, Ansel, if I hadn't been cursed with that damn tumor in my head, which caused me to start acting out and doing things I would never have done, in my right mind. I started getting in fights, I lost my sense of humor altogether. In the madness of that tumor I hurt a man real bad. I hit 'im in the face with a wooden post. He never saw it coming. I took his money, which he dint hardly have none to begin with, and I bought a spoonful of heroin. That girl she forgave me even that, and she helped me get into a reg'lar nuthouse instead a the pen; cause the guy, he was never the same after that, and I was into it pretty good, but my lawyer got me the deal.

"She was there the day I got out too, and she took me home, still full of love and hope for me and a new start for us. But the next fella I hurt ended me up in here and the last I heard she was doin' pretty bad. Got depressed and lost her job an' all that. I tried to get word to her to just go on with her life an' fine somebody new, but that didn' cut it with her, I guess, 'cause just like me, always lovin' her, she wouldn' let go a me neither. Hell of a fix, this love bisnez."

He looks Ansel in the eye. "How bout you, Ansel? You got somebody to love or what?"

"No, I've not had that fortune smile on me yet, Clifton."

"Fortune, yes. It's a setup for heartbreak, though. God, yes. It sure is."

***

"Terri called, asked us to stop by her work and have a beer with her," Jeff says in the elevator. "Up for it?"

"Salright, brother," Ansel answers with a smile.

Jeff turns up his collar in anticipation of the cold December wind and opens the door. He looks at Ansel as they are walking down the stairs from the main floor to the parking lot. "You seem kinda specially cheerful."

"Had a good day at work today. Somebody told me a love story."

"Who was that?"

"Clifton."

"Cool. Why don't you tell us about it after we pick up Terri? She loves a good love story."

"Really," Ansel says. Then, in the car he says, grinning, "So you're her good love story now, huh?"

"It's true. What can I do?"

pop the bubble

It's the day before Christmas. Although there's a little decorated tree in one corner of the hall room that was donated by one of the local missions, the floor is otherwise unfestive. However the city below is lit up like a veritable blaze of commercial holiday glory.

"Warms the heart, doesn' it?" Bascomb asks Jeff as they stand by the windows looking down upon the scene.

Jeff looks at him, skeptical. "You're serious?"

"You don' find it beauteeful?"

"I'm a confirmed Scrooge when it come to this sort of thing. Cutthroats selling tinsel."

"I like that, dude," Bascomb says as he laughs. "'Cutthroats selling tinsel'." He turns around. "But what about our rather more modest effort here?" he says, gesturing with his arm toward the tree. "I trust it is more to your liking?"

"It's kind of the other end of the spectrum, huh?" Jeff says, smiling at Bascomb's antics. Then he asks, "So what happens here tomorrow? Will there be a feast and presents?"

"No doubt, there will be some type of festivities. I'm sure they will cheer us up some way or another. 'God bless us everyone,' and all that. The ladies from the mission will pay us a visit, I'm sure. Of course they will have the guns pointed at us, all the while. Tough love. It's the best kind, really."

They stand, admiring the tree. Clifton comes into the room, carrying a small red and green package. He approaches the tree and kneels down in front of it. Small and thin in stature, Clifton looks like a boy before the small tree. Bascomb and Jeff look at each other, wondering. Clifton reaches out and lays the little package, so delicately, onto one of the bows. Then he clasps his hands together and appears to pray for a short time, before rising and walking away, head bowed down, to the other end of the room and into the corridor.

"What you make of that?" Bascomb says, still looking toward the corridor where Clifton disappeared.

"I don't think I'd dare to venture a guess," Jeff says, "curious though I certainly am."

"That makes two of us."

"Ansel was very impressed by something Clifton told him about his relationship with his wife. Wonder if that could have anything to do with it."

"Ansel got sucked in by that too, huh?"Jeff is surprised, wondering. "What do you mean?"

"That dude's never been married. He's a crack head; has been for years."

"How does that translate to, 'never been married'? Besides, Clifton apparently admitted he has a problem. He told Ansel he has or had some kind of brain tumor or something and that he was a heroin user."

Bascomb leans back up against the wall, sighs a big sigh. "Listen, Jeff. You guys, you and Oz and Ansel, you guys are cool. I like you. Most everybody does, I would say. But you ain' in the same boat with us. You come in the morning and you go back to your apartment at night. You see us, you talk to us, you get to know us. But you don' really get to know us. If somebody could really get to know us, well then, maybe there would be some hope for us."

He shakes his head and puts a palm up. "All I'm saying is, don' forget that we're a bunch of sick motherfuckers. It is not likely we are going to be life-long friends. And it is not likely we're going to tell you the truth."

Jeff dwells on that for a bit, then says, "Don't you know I'm the cynical one of the three of us? Shouldn't you have given that speech to Ansel?"

Bascomb can't help appreciating a comment like that.

"Dude, maybe you are friggeen crazy, after all."

"Don't go getting all gushy on me now, Bascomb."

Bascomb shakes his head.

"Bascomb."

"Yeah?"

"I wannna know. Why do you say Clifton's never been married?"

"I do know it, for sure. He has never been married and he has not got no brain tumor. He's a crack head, man. Take it or leave it. I can' tell you why I know for certain personal reasons. It is a dream he has concocted. He believes it himself. But that does not make it so."

***

That night Jeff tells Ansel what Bascomb told him. Ansel is upset. "You're telling me what Bascomb told you about what Clifton told me?" he says, in his frustration.

"Bascomb wouldn't tell me how he knew, but he insisted that he did know, with certainty," Jeff says in an apologetic manner.

"You know what I think?"

"What?"

"I think you and Bascomb should put your heads together, you know and maybe you could start a, a prison gossip column. You could like pin it up on the message boards of all the floors and give everybody a chance to get the latest."

"I'm sorry, Ansel. I thought you'd want to hear the truth."

"Let me know when the first issue comes out. I can't wait," Ansel says over his shoulder just before he slams the door to his room.

What is the price?

"What is the price of insanity? The benefits are obvious. You can act however you want, and you don't have to work."

"Yeah, I see you've got a good grasp of it, man," Jeff assures him.

Jeff and another graduate student, acquaintances from an undergraduate psych class, are discussing their current projects over lunch, after running into each other outside of a little Mediterranean restaurant near the University campus. It is a discussion Jeff realizes he would have been better off avoiding, but, as is his way, once he's into it he doesn't back out of it. His strongly opinionated lunch companion is into experimental psychology.

"Go ahead, be facetious, but I'm telling you; I worked in a mental hospital for a while and that was my experience. People copping out. Afraid of life."

"I'm not being facetious," Jeff informs him. "I'm being sarcastic. I haven't seen any fakers on my watch. Listen, I don't know if you really care, but on the other hand, you asked, 'What is the price?'."

"Okay, dude, what *is* the price?"

"Okay." Jeff pauses, rubbing his hands together in a namaste type of position before his slightly inclined face. Now he looks up at the other. "You gotta allow me a little latitude here."

He doesn't really expect much latitude from this person, but the fellow says, "You got it."

Jeff begins again. "Maybe you don't realize it, but I thought I was obvious. I'm a skeptic, a cynic, I have a reputation for that, just like you. I'm always looking for the motivation."

He looks out the window. Big flakes of snow are falling, drifting lazily onto and amongst the pedestrians. "Just look out there, man. All those people, coming and going about their business."

The other skeptic/cynic looks, as asked.

Jeff goes on. "They're all very different, but they have one thing in common."

His antagonist is silent.

"They don't know why, but they're all afraid. Most of 'em do a damn good job of covering it up, but they're actors. Just like you and I. Actors. Actually you and I are particularly good actors, Zac. Because we're tough guys." Jeff looks at Zac. True to form, no reaction. "See, I've just accused you of insincerity, and no discernable reaction whatsoever. That's good acting, dude."

"I didn't realize you were accusing me, Jeff. I only thought you were bonding with me," Zac says with a wry smile.

"I am bonding with you, Zac. But it takes two to bond."

"Chrissake, gimmee some latitude, I'm new to this," he says, which finally makes Jeff laugh a little bit.

"Alright, alright. My point, though. My point is that fear is so powerful that it has the whole damn human race acting—acting as if we're not afraid. Afraid of our own fear. Afraid to be seen with our fear."

Both men look out the window. They watch the flakes drifting lazily down upon and between the pedestrians.

Zac is the first to speak. "I suppose it's possible that this fear becomes too much for some people. I suppose it's possible that people cannot be held responsible for their fear, for their inability to control it, to act it away."

"We do have a responsibility to resist fear, to stand up to it within ourselves. I agree with you on that, Zac."

Zac doesn't say anything so Jeff goes on.

"But it's like the flu. There's the flu that you fight. You take something. You go to work, carry on. But then again, there's the flu that knocks you down. It can even land you in the hospital. Life threatening.

"I've met some people there, Zac. Some strong. Some weak. But I've seen some strong men, good actors, cut down to nothing by things— things I can't understand. They've done things, some very bad stuff, some of them, no doubt. So they're stuffed up in that hole up there where they live like worms in a can. But they're men, not worms. And after being exposed to it, to their situation, for some time now, nothing's clear for me anymore. Except that I'm trying to face my fear. Be brave enough to admit it."

"Aw look, Jeff, I was just bein' a hardass," Zac admits. "Devil's advocate, you know. Trying to get a rise out of you."

"Salright, Zac."

"Takes all kinds, right? I mean, where would the world be without rednecks?"

"It'd be a damn sight more sensitive, I expect. More honest, too," Jeff says, grinning.

"Yeah, well we all face our fears in our own ways, ya know. Whaddya say, maybe I could go to work with you one day, get my own firsthand impressions."

"It'd be fine with me, but I don't think it's gonna work. We have a contract with them, you know. It kind of forbids that kind of thing."

"Yeah I figured. Well, I got to get to a class, but I just want to tell you that I do appreciate your honesty, my friend," Zac says.

"And I appreciate your saying so."

Zac leaves and Jeff stays at the table by himself, looking out the window. The waiter comes by, "How we doing here? Can I get you anything? Dessert?"

"No, thanks, maybe some more of that great coffee."

So this is what it feels like to be vulnerable Jeff is thinking, to feel you've said all the wrong things, or said all the things wrong. And what does it matter? He's just some crazy intellectual redneck anyway.

His coffee comes and he sits and looks. He realizes he doesn't really know what's next. Those damn nuts are getting to me, he thinks, shaking his head. It's a good thing this project is almost over. I'm beginning to think that being an uptight basket case is normal.

He takes out his phone and calls Terri, but no answer. He looks at the time on his phone and realizes she's at work. He's embarrassed with himself because it didn't even occur to him that she was at work. He thinks about Ansel getting so upset with him last night. He wants to apologize to him but Ansel's at the prison now.

Yeah, it's a good thing, he thinks. Almost over.

things that go bump

There's a car sitting along the side of the street, Old Ferris Road, #381. The woman sitting in the car is nervously checking the rearview mirror, as well as doing a kind of visual sweep of the area out the side windows and the windshield. It is a relatively warm winter day, sunny, but blustery, and little flurries of snow and dust are kicking up here and there in the large vacant lot across the street, occasional gusts of wind buffeting the car. The traffic is very light here, and she feels a strange sense of remoteness, even though she is deep within the city. The sudden gusts seem to her as phantoms, alive, with the dread of unfamiliarity and a kind of dense bad energy, as if inhabited by swarms of angry and depraved spirits. Out the passenger side windows, beyond the tall chain link fence that collects the varieties of plastic, paper, and aluminum trash along its base, she has a view of the first few floors of the dark gray monstrosity where he now lives. She leans across the front seat and peers up at the full dimension of his home. "My God, what a monument," she says softly. She sits back up behind the wheel. "What a monument to our *civilization*."

"Goddamit!" she bursts out. The only one, she is thinking, then saying out loud, but only above a whisper, "The only one you ever brought to me that I could love. In all my life, nobody ever captured my heart before. And now you let him get up in that horrible place."

The nervousness has abated now, being superseded by her grief.

"How are people supposed to love you, God? You make it so hard and then you expect us to love you. People get crazy, you know. It happens. They don't get crazy on purpose." She knows she's being unreasonable, but she also knows she means it. "What about all the babies? All these men's babies. They're going to grow up with all the same problems their poor daddies had to live with and then those poor babies, will they end up moving in there to live too? *That is not a place to live, God. Not a place to live!*"

A sudden loud crash outside her door startles her, causing her to spin around in alarm, the blood violently rushing to her extremities, and for an instant she is frozen in terror. But she sees nothing outside the window. Then she twists around, frantically looking out all of the other windows. Nothing.

I should look outside, she says, her lips moving, but no sound comes out. Someone hit my car.

But she can't bring herself to it. She is terrified that any moment some horrible person, crouched outside of her car, below the windows, will pop his head up and be looking at her. She can't move. If she could move, she would start the car and step on the gas and drive away.

Nothing happens. It's blowing harder now. The car is rocking in the wind. "Or maybe someone's rocking it," she says, crying to herself now. She continues to look out all of the windows, but doesn't dare to get close to them, for fear that the person will look up at that moment and scare her to death.

After awhile she thinks, But I'm scared to death already. What's the difference? Still, she waits. She tries to get up the nerve, or whatever it takes, to do something terrifying when one is already terrified.

Finally she decides she will not look. She will start the car. The car doors are locked. She has had them locked all along. She will start the car and as soon as it starts she will step on the gas and tear out of there. Even if the man breaks the window at that moment, she may be able to get away if she speeds off.

From her position close to the middle of the seat she reaches over to the key. She puts her left hand on the wheel, hesitates for a moment, and then turns the ignition. The car starts. She is shaking so badly. She steps on the gas with her left foot, floors it. The car lurches forward and as she scoots behind the wheel to handle the car, there is a scraping, dragging sound. He's hanging on and dragging beside the car, she thinks. The wheels are spinning, squealing and throwing gravel from the side of the road. The car pulls up onto the street, and a car that has come up from behind has to swerve over, honking all the while. She lets off the gas to avoid fishtailing into it. When it gets by she realizes she doesn't hear the dragging sound and she thinks to look in her rearview mirror. A metal garbage can is rolling off of the street behind her.

She drives, perhaps a quarter of a mile, thinking about it. Maybe, she thinks. Her pain of fear is slightly relieved. She drives looking out her side mirrors now, trying to see the sides of the car. She moves the electronic button to adjust first, the driver's side, adjusting it up and down, in and out—then the same with the passenger side. She sees nothing. She slows down, trying to calm her nerves. "It was only a garbage can. Maybe the wind blew that garbage can up against the car."

She pulls the car over as soon as she comes to a suitable shoulder. She doesn't want to sit in it, afraid, anymore. She jumps out. Nothing, on her side. She dashes up to the front of the car, slips in a patch of snow, scraping her hands on the rough pavement, catching herself, and then runs ahead of the vehicle, looking over her shoulder. She runs about forty feet and stops, turning around to face the car. Nothing. She moves quickly to her left. Nothing on the other side. Giving the vehicle a wide berth, she runs as fast as she can, through the patchy snow cover, across the lawn of some business, and when she goes by the end of the car, seeing nothing, she turns to her right and checks the driver's side again. She stops, heaving and panting, out of breath, and looks at the car from fifteen feet away. She approaches the car, stands by the door. Looks at the side. There's some minor scratches.

"They might be from that can, or they might have been there already. I was watching the rearview pretty close. I never saw anybody."

Suddenly, she makes a mad dash, a tight circle around the car, keeping her hands on it as she goes, to keep from falling. She feels silly, but relieved at not finding anyone leaping in front of her or jumping out at her.

A long deep breath. She looks into the back seat. "Had to look." She gets into the car, starts it, pulls up and turns right, into the parking lot of Canada Mills, "whatever that is?", turns the car back to the driveway and turns left, back toward the prison. When she gets to the spot where she had been parked she slows, sees the can up against the chain link fence, then drives on. "Oh God, I just don't know," she is saying, both to herself and to God.

TWENTY-TWO: George takes his followers into his confidence

You are my Father, You are my Mother, You are my kinsman, You are my brother.
You are my Protector at every place, then why should I have any fear?
— *Guru Arjan Dev*

Christmas in the big house

It's a monumental job for the ladies of the missions to bring Christmas to the prison. First, it takes a monumental portion of tolerance and good will, just for the authorities of a variety of missions, sanctioned and supported by religious groups that are as often as not at odds with one another, to come together at all, let alone in a united effort. Then come the endless organizational requirements. Lists upon lists concerning details such as donations and budget, volunteers needed, volunteers available, assigning duties to the volunteers, menus, deliveries and shopping, food storage, and so forth and so on. It is perhaps the ultimate catering endeavor.

Coordinating the effort with the prison staff is an exercise requiring the extremes of patience and attention to detail, due to the ever-present safety and security concerns, all of which are typically in a state of transition. There are, in fact, certain persons who essentially donate their time, throughout the year, to the single event of the prison Christmas Dinner.

Why do they do it? No doubt, for a great variety of reasons. It's doubtful that an exuberant display of gratitude and affection from the prisoners is one of them.

***

While the ladies are setting up the tables with the pots and baskets full of food, there is the typical hubbub in the hall, as at any function where a large group of people are waiting, expectantly, to be fed. But then the room goes strangely silent, the only noises those of the sliding and rattling of metal chairs as most of the inmates takes seats, and the soft buzz of the serving ladies, but they also cease their nervous chatter and their talk of the arrangements at hand in an abrupt manner.

George walks over to and sits down casually on one of the long folding tables near the windows, leans back onto the support of his arms, hands braced flat on the table top behind him. He sits quietly, looking around the room, reminiscent of some great lion, having just entered his den. inspiring the others into anticipation and regard. And the ladies have now relinquished even their utensils and they stand, in surprisingly patient acknowledgement of this unscheduled part of the program. In the rather phantasmal silence he begins to speak.

message of George – VIII
~ this dark tower ~

"Here we sit in this dark tower. A bleak symbol of the power and glory of the mighty race of men. A holding tank for some of the failures of that great race. Actually, they would not consider it a holding tank, but rather more of a waste disposal." Again, his large dark eyes regard the room in silence.

"So—Is there anything I can say to encourage you on this day, Christmas day? I want to offer some encouragement, some hope. Because it seems the best way to honor that great giver of hope, whose birthday I celebrate today. But what can I put forth, that will stand against a wall of bitterness and cynicism? The power of love is strong. Nothing in this world or any other world is stronger, or faster, or more intoxicating—I thought you might like that one," he smiles," *or more enduring. But it's not for everyone. It's only for those who want it."* And now he brings his legs up onto the table and sits cross-legged. Some of the ladies look around to get the guards' reaction to this breach of manners, but they see nothing noticeable.

George goes on. *"There's no excuse for what the businessmen of the world have done, in their greed and their blindness to the significance of this day. The businessmen certainly don't want love. But then, who really does? Out of all the billions of people in this world, I wonder who does want love.*

"Generally, I think, we always push love back for some more attainable desire. In all fairness, I don't think we know what love is. We've been so long without exercising it that we don't have any memory of it. Not just us, in this particular predicament, but all of the souls in all creation. Because love is like the sun. It shines all the time. Even at night. And we could not exist for one moment without the perpetual sustenance of the Creator's love. Scientists can go to hell for all they know.

"The reality is, we want love only when He makes us want love. It's not in our hands.

"Maybe we think, 'I want love, I pray for love, even, but all I'm given is more of the same—my selfishness, my sex cravings, my cruelty, even my mental illnesses. All I can say, all I can encourage you to do, is to keep asking for love. In the face of it all, ask for love. Don't relent. We've been coming and going here for an eternity. Maybe He thinks we're not serious.

"We're no worse off than that bunch out there, with their sparkling lights and their bells and their Santy Claus. We're paying off some debt here, anyway. Who can say our lives are a waste of space? Some of us want love — at least some of the time. That's no small thing.

"Thanks to the ladies for thinking of us and serving us. Don't pity us. Pity the world at large, understanding that all are prisoners. Also, please understand that some of us have ceased to eat animals, recognizing them as our brothers and sisters"

in his unique confidence

After the party, when the dishes have been cleaned up and the ladies have gone home, there is a little time before the nighttime lock-up in the cells. There is a gathering near the far wall, between and seemingly meant to include Walt Whitman and Toby. George is sitting on a folding chair, facing the wall and the men are lounging around, some on the old sofa and the tattered upholstered chairs, most of them on the floor. The mood is jovial, but intimate. Someone asks him a question about his past. This is followed by the shaking of heads and the rumbling of grumbling, because everyone knows George doesn't talk about his past. Most of them consider it a type of offense to ask. "You don't ask a man about what he don't want to talk about," they say and feel. It is like an unwritten law. Something akin to what is known as "honor among thieves". So they are generally affected with a sense of wonder when he begins to talk to them in response to the man's question.

"Looking back on my life, it is no surprise to me that I became a victim of the mental illness. Right from my childhood I saw the bad things and even had many bad things happen to me personally. My mind was pushed beyond the limits that it could contain and I acted out, without any control over myself. Like many of you I saw the examples of violence and brutality and meanness routinely and I had very little experience with love or kindness. My mother did love me, I think, but she herself was a victim of circumstances, which perhaps led to very unhealthy choices on her part.

"I was drawn to the intoxicants, which can give some temporary relief from the pain. Unfortunately they prove, in the long run, to be another source of misery. I became an addict and, in time, a homeless person. If I was born with any virtue, I will say that there was no virtue left in me by the time I reached adulthood.

"I met my wife in a rehabilitation center where she worked and at which I was a patient. She was a very positive influence on me. With her help I reformed and got free of my addictions for a time. We had children and life looked hopeful and good. But the impressions of the

171

past are extremely powerful and when I lost my job I turned to alcohol, thinking I would allow myself to get drunk just that once and then go back to being responsible the next day."

At this point, Anthony begins to wail, which is probably in sympathy with George's story, but is also quite distracting. But George smiles at tells him calmly,. "It's alright, Anthony. It's alright now," and poor Anthony calms down so George can go on.

"Well, as you know, it doesn't work that way, that you can indulge in a strong habit one day and give it up the next. It's only a trick of the mind that we follow such a foolish line of thinking.

"So my life became very troubled and through a chain of events, most of which I have no knowledge, due my extreme use of alcohol and other drugs, I was convicted of crimes and sent to prison. I was paroled after one year but I fell right back into my habits and found myself again immersed in a life of utter despair.

"Such a pathetic life seemed to be my destiny, but then my destiny changed. A man found me in the park one cold night, where I lay in a stupor, having been beaten by thugs. Without his help, I surely would have died of hypothermia. He took me to his home, doctored me and fed me. In the comfort of his home, my true destiny was awakened, because he was a man who was more than a man.

"In his company, I learned that there is a knowledge which goes where the intellect, even the intellect of the finest minds of the world, cannot go, can never go. That knowledge is older than the world itself. It is primordial and ultimate and sacred. And it is not impersonal. Rather it is the most personal, the most intimate, because it is the source of and the manifestation of love."

He is silent for a moment and then he adds, "Only because of my meeting with such a personality, I can say that I will never have to return to the bad ways or the intoxicants again."

Here Jean-Paul interjects. "George, some of us have seen you in places that are, I don't know how to say it, otherworldly, I guess. You have come there and helped us."

"If I have it is all because of my benefactor," George replies. "I am not just being self-effacing when I say this. I have done nothing to be put in the position that I am in. There is no merit in me that qualifies me for it.

"I must tell you that those great ones from the past, the enlightened ones, they worked so very hard in their devotion, most of them for many years before they were even given a glimpse of the esoteric inner knowledge, and when their teachers, their masters, became pleased with them, they elevated them to their own stature. Those masters chose their successors for their most exceptional qualities and then made them take over their work of taking the souls home.

"But what have I done? I have been a failure and a quitter in life. If I ever had any good qualities or talents, I wasted them."

"We l-l-love you, George. N-n-no one else was eh-ever for us," Anthony says, pleading with him and yet trying his best not to cry.

"I know you do, Anthony. I'm just telling you these things, in this way, today, so that you will have some understanding of the great sacrifice that was made and is being made for us here, so that we might be delivered from our trappings, our strange destinies, and go home at last."

There is a pause. George seems to be finished speaking and the group absorbed in the peace and the mystery of the moment. But Stephen has something to say.

"George. You say that you have done nothing, but I have *seen* you make the sacrifices." He looks around at the others. Then he tells them, "George is paying, alright. He is paying the debt for us that we could never pay."

The night horn blasts into their consciousness and the group gets up quickly and disperses, the men hurrying to their cells. The guards approach to release Toby and Walt Whitman from one confinement so that they can take them to another.

TWENTY-THREE: A most personal tale of separation and heartbreak

Oh man, don't be saying mine, mine; there is no guarantee of breaths.
Your life is as fragile as sugar candy thrown into water.

— *Kabir*

Mr. Santhanam

Upon his arrival at Mr. Santhanam's home, Jeff is greeted cordially, invited in and offered tea. However, he soon learns that the old man has only disdain for his grandson, which he expresses with much bitterness and sarcasm.

"If you want to know about Raja, I will tell you that he is bad news. He has been trouble, from his boyhood on. He never cared a lick for his own culture or the beliefs and traditions of his family. If it had been up to me I would have disowned him. I would have barred him from our door." The old man puts his forearm across his face and he pushes forward as if he is shutting and barring the door.

"You don't feel that he has redeemed himself or ever could redeem himself in some way?"

"Well, if you call making a home of the Federal Penitentiary a method of redemption," he points his index finger up into the air and wags it back and forth," then he is redeemed. And good riddance to him, the lout."

"Have you had any dealings with him, Mr. Santhanam? I mean since he's been in prison."

"I have not."

"Did you go to his trial?""No"

"And you've never visited him?"

"What did I tell you, young man? Are you interrogating me? What would I go there for? Should I bake him a cake and slip him a file into it? No! He did the crimes. Let him pass the times. If you think he's so great then take him into your own home and see how things devilup."

He is fairly shouting and Jeff apologizes. "I'm sorry, Sir, I didn't mean to insinuate. It's just that I have knowledge that he may possibly soon be released and I was, well, I wanted you to know, that if—if he was bad, well he seems—"

Mr. Santhanam says, "I'm doing my best to listen to you, but by all means, just say it."

"He seems … not bad."

"Not bad—that's quite a recommendation."

"He'll have no place to go."

"And you're working for him?"

"As I told you, I'm just a student doing research."

Mr. Santhanam stands with his hands on his hips. He is looking right at Jeff and shaking his head back and forth. Then he says, as if he's bestowing a generosity or a benediction, "You go ahead and take him. He's yours. You can research from the comforts of your own home." The old man shows the *student* the door.

of Saints in the stairwell
Ansel

"You know people say, 'Man, you're a Saint!' or 'That woman's a Saint.' or 'He's a Saint.' They throw that stuff around and you know they don't mean it. It's like a compliment that they take back in their hearts at the same time as they give it.

"Have you ever had anyone say it to you? I don't know, they've said it to me and I think, 'I'm not a Saint and I really don't appreciate your so-called compliment.' I might not say that, though. I might just say, 'Aw heck, you know I ain' no saint.' I guess I sometimes take some unimportant stuff too seriously."

I'm in the stairwell with Horatio and he's performing one of his jobs of mopping the stairs. I don't remember how we got onto the subject. Horatio likes to talk. He's opinionated, but also reflective and seems to have a big heart. I can see his point about Saints.

So I say to him, "What would he or she be like—a saint? Is there such a thing, really, or is it just a label?"

He stops, leans on his mop handle to think about the question. "Well, there's them that've seen—like visions, for one thing. That'd be about everbody in this whole building, save some of the hired help I s'pose. So that don' seem to be it. Unless we're all Saints."

I shrug.

He goes on. "There's them that're supposed to of been so good all their lives and helped all kinda people an' like that. That type seems closer to it to me, though I can't say what would make one for sure. Maybe God has to make one from scratch?" He cocks his head, eyebrows up, big eyes looking at me. Then he takes up his work again.

"Horatio, do you think George is a Saint?" I don't even know what makes me ask. I was raised Christian. Later, I was more or less adopted by Ozwald's Hare Krishnas. Certainly George doesn't fit any description or preconception of a Saint that I ever had before. That I ever learned.

But when I say that to Horatio, "Do you think George is a Saint?", he stops mopping again and to my surprise he does a few little backwards dance steps, very nimble, like a moonwalk, but different.

"Now I feel just stupid," he says. "Now I feel just plain stupid."

"What do you mean?"

He is squirming around and I realize he is genuinely embarrassed. I give him time.

"Here we are talking about 'What's a Saint?' 'What's a Saint?' and soon as you asked, I couldn't believe it. There ain't no definin' it. It's just George. And there ain't no definin' George. But that's what it is. Made from scratch. God's recipe perfected, I'd say. We're some lucky devils." He's chuckling. "Mysterious ways. My, my, mysterious ways."

Of Saints in the Stairwell

***

Later I wrote, "This is a phenomena that has me baffled as a student of psychology, as a student of science. These are men committed to a life without any of the basic freedoms we take for granted in society. They are ridiculed and punished, often needlessly and uselessly by the nature of the system and by individuals sanctioned by the system. They subsist on poor food, and have generally inappropriate and insensitive health care. Entertainment is barely existent. There is a considerable amount of potential danger from the ravings of homicidal lunatics as well as sexual predators within their immediate society. On top of all that, each individual has his own internal nightmares to face, which are largely responsible for landing him here in the first place. Yet there is a stronger community of hope and a more believable faith in spiritual deliverance here than any I've ever personally witnessed outside."

Ansel (much later)

In the year following the project at the prison, we completed our report. We had a strong sense of mutual respect, if not outright pride, in that we had collaborated successfully from beginning to end. We didn't always agree on the interpretation of any specific, but each of us gave our own individual interpretations anyway which we felt gave the report that much more credibility for the variety of opinion. And of course we each, personally, dealt in depth with the subjects of our individual interviews.

The strong probability that our project was ultimately sanctioned as part of an experimental project by the prison administration, we concluded to be largely irrelevant. If anything, it added an element of intrigue to supplement the already fascinating collection of anecdotes. Regardless of the perceptions of the system's powers that be, we understood there was something happening that was larger than and totally unaffected by any of their manipulations.

We were frankly riding a big wave of enthusiasm and optimism. We had a story to tell and we could hardly wait to tell it. But even a big wave runs out of steam at some point, though it passes wildly beyond the shore and races, reveling in its freedom, out across the inland. When the wave finally exhausted itself, and we stood with our wet feet on the solid ground, we all knew we couldn't publish. Not the way we had it. No one would be able to accept the details of our report as being valid. We would be taken as hoax-meisters, writers of phantasmal fiction at best—gullible fools more likely. Ozwald and I were convinced that we had witnessed, arguably, one of the most significant manifestations of human potential, relative to, although completely transcending any relevance to, parapsychology, behavioral psychology, transpersonal psychology, community psychology, etc., etc. And we were almost certainly going to be taken as charlatans. Jeff is more of a skeptic by nature, but I do believe that, although he is certainly not as openly expressive about it, in his heart, he is quite sympathetic with Ozwald's and my rather fondly enlivened opinions.

So we went back to work. We bent down, we got on our knees, and we picked up those precious pearls, before they could be eaten with the slop of life. Before they would be dragged into the wallows or broken upon the rough and splintered boards with the scratching and straining of beasts. We spent four more months on the report and although the clinical sterility of it was heartbreaking in some ways, it was ultimately a source of relief. I thought of how my mother advised me once, when, as a teenager, I was bragging to my family about my beautiful date to a certain high school function, "Don't tell the other boys about your girlfriend. Save your appreciation for her." I understood that she meant it was a matter of respect.

***

When George's hearing came up, no one was prepared for it. For the result of it. He was paroled. After three years of affirming his guilt and confirming his status as a danger to society, they turned George loose.

The first to go was Milton. They found him with his throat cut in the lavatory. They had only begun to investigate when Ahmed was found in the stairwell hanging by the neck from a 3/16 inch steel cable, which was slung over the edge of the fortieth flight banister where it was attached to the top of the handrail. A simple, slightly loose, cable clamp along with a knot tied in the cable end served as the mechanism for constriction at the man's throat. To say they *found* the men in either case is misleading, because knowledge of subversive activity was almost instant due to the camera security system. However the cameras had in both cases been covered with spray paint by the perpetrators of the crimes, if you hold that suicide is, in fact, a crime; and it was the eventual finding of the investigative team that the gruesome deaths were attributable to suicide. The men, in any case had acted fast. There would have been almost near instant notification of activity in the two locations, but the bodies had already breathed their last when the guards arrived. Ahmed's neck was found to be broken, no doubt from the violence of jumping over the railing. It's interesting that the two who did themselves in both came from cultures long associated with the Guru phenomena. But it would seem to be scientifically impossible to tell if their suicidal choices were influenced by their connection to those cultures or if they were only victims of themselves, or both.

Ozwald and I repeatedly requested permission to come back and do a follow up. Our requests were not granted. A few years later, there was a major change at the administrative level, and we were allowed to return, but for the time being, we were locked out. We couldn't even go up as normal visitors. What little info we got from the prison was from public Prison Records, and entries there were scanty at best. We know the maximum security was further maximized. There were no more suicides to our knowledge. We can only assume that George's gang lost their freedoms. We have almost no knowledge of the condition of the followers.

We were able to learn some fragmented details from Horatio's sister, whom we located, living in Philadelphia. She, like Horatio, is a warm and gentle soul. It's funny how I've taken to using that word, soul, now. I guess I'm losing my science more as I go. You know how people say, 'losing their religion'? I guess I'm losing my science.

It turns out Illy, which is short for her beautiful name, IllishaImelda, has maintained her relationship with her brother for all the years of his incarceration (thirty two at the time of our meeting with her). She invited us to her home after we contacted her. Harold had talked to her about us, and she trusted his impressions of people. She offered us tea which we gladly accepted.

Illy believed that Harold's crimes were truly only crimes of misunderstanding, as well as of ill fortune. As she tells it, "He was committed to the sanitarium when he was only a boy. When he was ten years old he began to have seizures. Our parents took him to various doctors but to no avail and his condition got worse. The seizures were the cause or the result of his brain damage, it was never determined which came first. But as Harold grew bigger and stronger, Momma and Poppa couldn't control him, and they felt they had no choice but to commit him. I don't hold it against them now, although I was angry at them for it at the time. Oh, but you young fellows didn't come here for me to go on about Harold, did you?"

Although we were anxious to learn what we could of the events following George's parole, we also realized there was much to be gained from Illy's confiding to us about Harold's history. We told her as much, and so she continued.

"Well, I'll try to keep it short," she said. "In the 1960s they opened up the doors to most of the mental institutions around the country. I guess you prob'ly know that. All of them that wasn't considered dangerous and that were able to function, although I have no idea how they defined that word, function, were let out. It was a crime in itself in many respects, even though the spirit of it, to not confine people and shut them away only because they were different, was good. My Harold, like so many others, didn't know how to live in the world. Even though I took him in, I couldn't keep him at home all the time, nor did I want to. But out on the street he'd get in trouble for things. He'd talk to folks, friendly like he is, you know. Some of them don't like that. He'd talk to kids. Some of their parents didn't like that. Did he ever tell you what he was convicted for?"

We said that we had some knowledge of it but that we would appreciate hearing it from her.

"One day a young white lady was molested in an alleyway. Poor Harold heard her crying out and he went in to help her. You know how big he is and fierce looking, so when he came running onto the scene, the two guilty fellows took off running. He didn't chase them down, he stopped to help the girl, ya know? And as luck would have it, this was one of the times when the police happened on the to scene real quick.

Naturally, they suspected Harold. And since the girl was drunk and wasn't able to tell one man from the next at that point, the crime stuck on Harold. They sent him to the Federal Prison and, due to his past record in the sanitarium, he was assigned to the mental ward."

We told her that it was completely believable from our experience with Horatio. Horatio had been one of my case studies, but all of us, including Ozwald, had gotten to know him because of his friendly and outgoing nature.

She went on. "After Harold met George, a few years ago, he was like a different person. I don't know how to say it, because the last thing I want to imply is any kind of homosexual relationship, because that was absolutely not it. But it was like he'd fallen in love. He was almost aglow with it. And he was so innocent. I mean he's innocent anyway. But his enthusiasm about George was kind of contagious, really, and I came to the conclusion that if George really was a holy man, albeit an extremely unorthodox holy man, maybe he found that innocence in those poor folks with all their mental problems. Does that make any sense at all to you gentlemen?"

We found ourselves nodding, involuntarily, but naturally, that it did.

Illy sat for awhile and we sat too. The afternoon sun shone through a crystal in the southwest window of her sitting room and in that multicolored dance of light we were momentarily content with entertaining the prospect of *higher things*.

Then she began to tell us of a conversation she had had with Harold after George's parole. He had been crying and it was obvious that nothing she could say, especially through the 'terribly severe' medium of the thick glass barrier, would console him. So she had sat and just let him cry.

She told us that after a few minutes, he told her a couple of things that might be of help or interest to us.

"He told me about Milton and Ahmed. Of course you already know about that. But then he said how the whole place just went still, except for the occasional outcry of some fearful soul or other. Those who were completely in their own world most all the time, I guess. But Harold told me that even the hardest of men, the coldest, they were all weeping, silently weeping. Even that Toby, that he'd told me about. A man who eats dead people, crying at the loss of George. I was very moved by that." Illy was holding back her own tears with that admission.

She went on, after composing herself a little bit. "He said that he'd talked with a couple of the other fellows in their gang, you know, Bascomb and Jean-Paul. He said they'd all agreed that George was still with them. They had all had some type of experience that that was true. It wasn't a matter of believing it, he said. They experienced it, he said. But he also said it didn't ease their suffering, really, because they just missed being with him in person so much."

She also told us that the guards had made things harder all around and that none of them were now allowed off the floor, under any circumstances, without the escort of one of the guards.

Belated
a song

i celebrate your birth ... belated
as i remember what it's worth ... that you created
an anthem for our souls ... and so we waited
to see where you would go ...we waited

i hang on every word ... you utter
like the wings of an anxious bird ... that flutter
and i know that i must leave ... this clutter
but you're gone and i just grieve ... and stutter

i saw a shimmering light, my brother
way out past the farthest hill
i wonder if we could sing another
song to help my mind be still

did i want to be like you? ... yes a dreamer
did i stay up all night too ... like a believer?
did i sing and bare my soul ... within a fever?
and worry my loved ones so ... by my demeanor?

what no one else would say ... you dared to
in the rudest light of day ... you said a prayer too
like a ghost in a ghostly land ... i'm compared to
with my burning heart and hands ... and my vacant stare too

i saw a shimmering light, my brother
way out past the farthest hill
i wonder if we could sing another
song to help my mind be still

i heard your guitars ... amid the others
as they wept among the stars ... like lonely lovers
for a world torn apart ... sisters and brothers
scattered ever near and far ... and born of mothers

On Holiday
a poem

i'm sorry that I was not able to love you until you were gone
down the dark roads of these ages, I am a mendicant of these hells
on the sharp stones of my sins you cut your feet
coming for me, my brother, my kinsman
past the crimes of my lust, oh your innocent eyes
as we lay, victims in the dust, in the mud
as we get up and curse and cheat and run forth
as we forget … as we remember

that I lived to be a poet of love more than a lover
by the pretense of love we contrive
in a world full of hate and desire where I cast my lot
when my love comes round then my lover's gone
though I wail in disgust, I lose heart too soon
then though I look out through the dim and misty woods for you
then that I peer round and about me
then that I whisper meekly in my forlorn realizations
only then that I sense the utter distance and the magnitude of my
                                              solitude

when I cannot sleep and am afraid to eat
when you've suffered too much though you are an ocean of suffering
when you've reminded and reminded until your sweet voice is
        broken and done
when you've coughed and coughed the illness of us
when you've seen that I would not let go, my cold fingers clung to the
        pitiful plough
even as the life ebbs out of me, even as you weep
I lay sprawled on the floor, on the rough brown boards
the cold light of winter getting in and pressing against
I would fall if I could but I am already fallen
"Open your eyes, damn fool!" they advise and condemn
I know I've opened them too far, much too far, for too long
I know that all calls to life are useless calls to death
Set me up, I am asking you
Put me in a wakeful position
Set my mind on holiday, and let me read the book of you
Let my heart sing the song, the great longing of you

I would like to sit on the rough brown boards forever and dream of
    you
I would like to bring you back
I would bind you with the bindings of my love, if you would only
    allow it
If I have lost my mind, is there not now room enough?
I would try to make a comfortable place for you to stay
to decorate it in the simple way that you like
Is it not up to you? You can come back. But I cannot go.
You come again. Touch my eyes, my tears. They'll be fine without me.

PART TWO: GEORGE ON THE OUTSIDE

TWENTY-FOUR: Varieties of panic and sympathy

This material world is no place for a gentleman.
— *Bhaktisiddhanta Saraswati Thakur*

driving home

George winds tentatively down the hill, not sure if it's on this road or whether he has to make a turn at the bottom. At the bottom there is a sign for route 38, which rings a bell so he turns sharply right but, as soon as he gets onto that road, he doubts it. Too narrow; too much like a sidetrack and it starts to take him back up the hill. He decides to turn around. But just as he begins to make the left into someone's driveway, he sees the shop out of the corner of his eye. He has to wait quite a while in the driveway for an opening to back the big car out onto the lane and then drives the half block to the shop.

As he starts to enter the lot there's a car coming out toward the same entrance/exit so he waits for it to come around to the left but the driver hesitates directly in front of him until finally he has to pull left and let the other driver exit to his right. "Have it your way," he mumbles to himself in a frustrated complaint, "I guess any side will do." As he parks the car he is judging himself harshly for the criticism.

***

The parking lot is dark and damp when he comes out, carrying the vacuum cleaner. He puts it on the floor in the back seat and gets in. He backs out carefully, turning in the seat and peering through the dirty back window.

Out on the street, as he comes around the corner, he remembers that he needs gas, badly. The price isn't that bad at the station next to the shop, so he pulls in. The car fills on the passenger side so he pulls to the left of a row of pumps. Another driver pulls in off the street and into his row in front of him as he's getting up to the pump. He waits. The other car waits for a couple of moments, then pulls out around and he pulls forward to the end of the row while the other driver comes into line behind him and backs up to the pump that he had gone past. When the middle-aged lady gets out at the same time as him, they smile and go about their business.

He opens the flap, takes the gas cap off and lays it on top of the car. But he doesn't feel good about using his bank card at the pump because it doesn't seem to be working right and it wants him enter his pin, so he walks in to pre-pay but is told, "That's the only way the system works."

"I guess I don't want to do it then," he says, and he walks out. He realizes he's trying to make a statement because of something he read in the paper, questions the value of that, but gets in anyway and drives out of the station lot. On the first curve at the start of the hill, he hears a sliding and tumbling noise from the car. After a moment, he knows.

"The cap, I never put the cap back on. I never closed the flap, even." He turns hard into a private residence driveway on the far side of the road, but before he can back out there is a stream of cars coming down the hill. The back end of the car is out into the road just a little but they can get by and he waits … and waits. Finally there's enough of a space to pull out, but before he's out all the way, another stream of cars behind him. He's gone maybe half way up the hill and he's going pretty slow coming back down, hoping for a spot to pull off near the bottom. He sees a driveway, another residence, no lights on at the house and no cars in the driveway. So he turns in but it's a rough entrance and he has to go slow. Now they're honking from behind. He's glad to notice a kind of parking spot off the side of the drive and gets pulled in there, starts to get out. From the last car of the stream, there is a guy yelling and the guy even stops his car momentarily to yell at him at the top of his voice, "What the hell are you doing? You stupid asshole!" before driving off.

He walks to the other side of the street, figuring he's below the place and starts walking up the hill. It's not well lit on the street. But he assumes it would have gone off that side of the car. He has to walk close to the street, mostly on top of the snow bank, to see over the top of it. He also is looking across the street, just in case. Seems like he should be able to see it although it's black, as is the street, and the snow is dirty and half black itself.

When he notices that he's walked up the hill almost as far as the place where he turned around, he turns, walks back down. He's thinking that the gas cap flap is still open. He's not even looked at it, but he knows it was his gas cap he heard. He walks below where the car is parked. Nothing. He crosses to the side the car is parked on, wondering how far it could have bounced or rolled. He thinks he sees it ahead, still on top of the car, but that proves to be just a shadow from the chrome hinge of the tailgate. He wonders whether to give up. *No, not enough of an effort.* He goes past the car and finds the cap, some fifty feet uphill of the car. "Thank You."

At the car, he screws the cap on, shuts the flap, gets in and drives up the hill. A momentary peace. But soon the cars are behind him again. As the road opens up to two lanes each direction he stays in the left lane to make his turn. At the light there are cars behind and to the side of him. Suddenly there is a deep roaring noise that penetrates his car and sets it to vibrating as if it were emanating from within his own car. He is very startled and suffers a cold terror as the roar continues, pulsing through the car and through his body like the heartbeat of some horrible beast. He looks around in panic to try to ascertain the source of the violent sound, but, to no avail. The light turns green but he is stunned and doesn't notice. He hears horns blaring behind him through the roar and he steps on the gas, goes forward and makes the turn, his body now shaking involuntarily. He decides that the other drivers seem to be going along normally, so he draws courage from their behavior, but he keeps checking out his side windows and the rearview mirror, to observe them. They all move along as if in a psychotic procession to the music of the damned. After four blocks he notices the cars behind him as they turn off onto a side street and, as they do, the noise subsides and is gone as he drives on. Could that really have come from one of those cars? the thought occurs to him, but it's difficult for him to accept it—much less explain it.

***

Coming into the dark entry, he has the machine protectively in his arms, so he sits on the wooden bench in the dark and struggles with getting off his shoes without hands. When she hears him fumbling about, she comes out and sits with him in the dark.

"Are you okay," she asks.

"It's not a simple question."

"I know."

"Well, it may be a simple question, but there's not a simple answer." He's smiling at that but she can't see it in the dark.

"Are you smiling," she asks, guessing by the tone of his voice.

"Are you?"

"I am now."

"I am now, too."

"Why are you smiling," she asks.

"Because you're here."

"Oh. Did you get your shoes off?"

"It warrant easy out here in the dark.""It warrant, warrant it?" She takes his hand and holds it between her hands.

"I've just made tea."

"Let's go drink it then."

Inside he sees she also has food ready for him. He asks about the kids."They're out with their friends."

"I'm sorry I'm late."

"You're not late," she tells him.

"I just made it early."

"I'm not good with time."

"Any time is alright. You were gone, altogether, so long and I ..."

"Well, I expect I'll get better with the roads as I go over 'em more," he says so she won't have to cry.

"They're not well marked around here," she says, crying anyway.

He takes her in his arms, gingerly, unused to any physical affection. "You didn't have to wait for me, but I'm glad you did."

She walks over to the table."I didn't function so well without you, George," she tells him, back turned to him.

He doesn't know how to react or what to say to that, but after a little thought he says, hopefully, "You know, I learned quite a bit."

"I can tell," she says turning around.

"Really?" He smiles in hope.

"You're very kind and ... understanding."

"Thank you," he says.

"You too."

"Did they get it fixed?"

"Well, it may take years. I mean, I don't know if I'll really get *fixed*, altogether."

"I meant the vacuum cleaner."

"Oh." He puts his head down.

"No, it's alright honey." She comes over to him. "It's funny. You know it's funny to make a mistake like that."

He lifts his head up. "It's not wrong?"

"No." He smiles a little wider. "And it's funny."

She laughs a little at that.

the fire escape

It's four a.m. and the fire alarm is sounding. The resulting chaos on the floor has the guards nearly as confused and disoriented as the inmates.

On duty on the floor are Clarence, Ed, and Clancy. Clarence and Ed are charged with getting the relatively mobile prisoners into the main hall room. This they are accomplishing with methods not unlike those used in the moving of livestock in a slaughter house. Electric prods produce results faster than verbal ones. There is no time for someone like Fyodor to relate stories of other great escapes, or for Confucius to argue the relative merits for or against the lifesaving process in the first place. All of the appropriate cell doors are opened at once and starting from the center of the rear corridor the two guards start driving them out of the cells and herding them in opposite directions through the right and left corridors.

Unfortunately even a cattle prod has its shortcomings where fear is the ruling emotion and where common logic is entirely absent. Jaiden, for instance, seems convinced that the guards are merely there to beat and torture him for another sexual misconduct on his part, about which they are mistaken. "I didna!" he screams, "I didna do it. Ask 'em. Did I do it? Tell 'im, 'I didna!'" He's either oblivious to the fire alarm or, at least, does not understand the meaning of it, in which case it likely increases his confusion. The prod only hurts and terrifies him as he cowers smaller and smaller into the corner of his cell at the foot of his bed.

Stephen also is completely bewildered and, darting past the guards and shrieking as he gets shocked, he is going in small circles and eventually begins running laps through the corridors and into the hall and back around through the corridors.

"Where the hell's the fire?" someone is yelling.

Meanwhile Clancy, with the help of the night nurse, is responsible for the restrained and infirm inmates. Walt Whitman is restrained already in a strait jacket in his cell, so Clancy simply lifts him onto a gurney and has the nurse push him into the main hall. He happens to be one of the first to arrive at that destination. The same process with the *dead man* and Clancy has him loaded and in the corridor amid the mass confusion by the time the nurse gets back. However she doesn't see him, because of his being surrounded by the others being driven through.

Clancy has gone onto Eugene's cell in the opposite corridor. He is tying an old fashioned gag in Eugene's mouth to prevent him from biting and handcuffing him with his arms behind his back. Since he's personally escorting the prisoner down the corridor by the time she reaches Walt Whitman's cell, she is still confused and has no clue where Clancy might be in all the tumultuous activity. She is in a near panic frame of mind herself because she has great fear of some of the inmates on this floor and now finds herself in this chaotic situation with no protectors in site, and the inmates milling around freely.

They are in fact milling around *quite* freely, at least within the right corridor, because Clarence has lost control of them in his effort to catch Stephen who has circled twice past him, after having eluded Ed who originally "freed" him from his cell in the left corridor. Ed previously felt compelled to abandon Jaiden in his cell and now, having lost two of his charges, has begun to lose both his confidence and his will to accomplish his task, but is still going forward on the power of his training and finally gets his group to the hall.

When Clancy goes back into the corridor he finds the *dead man* approximately where he left him, but not seeing the nurse he feels that her safety is in jeopardy, so he continues down the corridor where he finds her in Horatio's cell, where she has locked herself for her own protection.

"Can you help now?" he says to her after, more or less, learning what happened.

"I don't know. I feel very—unsure."

He unlocks the door and tells her to just stay with him. It is about this time that they begin to smell the smoke. Clancy and the nurse hurry the *dead man* to the hall and then return for Toby.

Out in the hall they are loading the prisoners into the elevator as fast as they can because the stairway seems to be the source of the fire.

***

There are three floors above them. One is for the psychopathic murderers, terrorists, and other extremely dangerous criminals. Above that is death row, and the top floor is "official prison use", which includes facilitating emergencies such as the current one. The building is designed with multiple elevator shafts, to the extent that there are elevators exclusive to certain groups of floors and the top four floors comprise such a group. The emergency procedures are such that floor #41 goes up first, then #42, and finally death row and the floor above that. The roof, even though a portion of it is designed for and fenced off as a type of small outdoor exercise yard for the mental unit patients, can accommodate large military transport helicopters which will temporarily relocate the prisoners. Floors numbered #30 through #40 also go up, but via a separate elevator system.

There are multiple escape routes for all floors below #30 and all those people will escape to ground level where they will be detained, temporarily in the large, secure, general population, outdoor exercise yard.

***

The crowding of inmates into the elevators proves to be too much for some of them and they break and run. Just as Clancy has Toby nearly secured, the nurse informs him that two prisoners just ran by the cell in the wrong direction.

The typically silent Toby says, "Where's George?"

"You know he's gone," Clancy says.

"George is na gone, Clancy," Toby argues.

"I don't know what you're talking about," says Clancy, frustrated. "He's never gone."

"Well, you better git 'im to calm these suckers down, Toby."

"I don' know where he is."

"I can't tell ya what a big help you're bein here, Toby."

"Dake me back do them, Clancy. Please?" Toby pleads as they are exiting his cell. Clancy hesitates in the corridor. The nurse can't believe it. Her voice rises in renewed panic. "You're not going to listen to this monster are you?"

"Clancy, George will help," Toby says in his terrible voice.

So Clancy turns toward the back corridor. They find Anthony and Johnny trying in vain to hide in a back cell with the door locked. Clancy unlocks the door but he doesn't go in. He looks at Toby. The nurse looks like she's seen a ghost, or worse.

"Anthony, ha you seen George," Toby asks.

There's no answer. Toby asks again. "Anthony, ha you seen George?"

"Geor-George ain't h-he-er no more, Pumpkin Head,"

"George is here, Anthony," Toby gurgles, "George is never na here."

Nobody says anything. The nurse turns around and runs for the hall.

"Toby's right, Anthony," Clancy says.

"Yeah, he's right, Anthony," says Johnny.

"Ya'll sons a bitches are gangin' up on me ain't ya?" says Anthony.

"George don't want us dead an burned up back here, Anthony," Johnny tells him.

"Ok, b-b-b-but-but, I can't ride with the elevator so full. I'll ride with ju-just ya'll."

"Okay," Clancy agrees.

When they get to the hall they can see smoke through the stairway door window and they can feel the heat coming off of the big steel door. Clancy tells Ed the agreement. Ed says, "Just get in!" as the elevator arrives. They get in and at least four other inmates enter in with them before Clancy can get the door shut, but Anthony and Johnny let it go and they go up.

***

The building was ultimately saved. The fire was severe, but the building had been meticulously designed to confine fires and other emergencies to the section of their origin. There was extensive damage on the 24th floor, and varying damage going up, but it was repaired in six months time and the majority of the prisoners were returned.

Jaiden was a casualty. When the firefighters reached the floor, moments after being notified of its having been evacuated, the smoke was released from the stairwell. By the time he was discovered in his cell, he had died of smoke inhalation. The *dead man* did not survive the stress of the evacuation. He was pronounced dead on arrival, by the medical team at City Jail, where a number of the rescued inmates were temporarily relocated.

TWENTY-FIVE: A blessed reunion

Let us all go to Sirsa. I am in pangs of separation of the beautiful Beloved—let's go, let's go.

—*Kirpal Singh*

outside

After so many years of life lived almost exclusively behind bars, Horatio is paroled. On the day that they release him, his faithful Illy is there to pick him up and take him to her home. It is better for him on the outside now. He's calmer. Also more wary and thus more reserved. After George was released, he had grown somewhat introverted. It is a quality that proves valuable on the outside. Put it all together, he had learned to handle himself in a much more independent manner than when he was set free from the sanitarium those many years ago. He had always loved Illy and appreciated her loyalty and the respect that she unfailingly gave him.

Before too long, he settles into a quiet life with her. She calls him Harold and he is happy with that. Her financial situation is such that he no longer needs to work a job, and that fact in itself keeps him from many of the typical crisis situations that can so easily occur when one's security is dependent upon the pleasure of an employer. Instead he pitches in around the house, with cleaning, other basic chores, and maintenance. He walks to the small neighborhood grocery, when necessary, and when nothing is needed he strolls in the neighborhood park. For the first few months he can't help but feel that he sticks out, that he is different. But his age and experience help him in that regard, because he has learned that everybody's different, so in time that knowledge also becomes a part of him, rather than just a mental concept. Even when some boys cross paths with him in the park and he hears them referring to him as "Big Bubblehead", he is not affected *so* badly. They're only boys. That's how boys act, he realizes.

Horatio will not die in prison, is a message of love he sends to himself. So he spends his days, and the days flow through the seasons. He finds comfort in the changing seasons and comfort in his relationship with Illy, who has adapted her lifestyle so lovingly to accommodate him. She became vegetarian several years ago, inspired to do so during her visits to the prison when Harold would speak with conviction on the merits of nonviolence.

In the spring and the summer Horatio is outdoors more than in. In the fall, he takes brisk walks and finds pure intoxication by the rush of the wind and the anticipation of the winter. And when the winter then comes, he revels in it, takes the cold breath into his lungs, and he breathes deeply of it. "Life!" he says, his arms raised up high and fingers outstretched. "It is life and it is natural." He also has friends. The man in the produce section at the grocery is his friend. Also the fellow who walks around the park picking up trash that thoughtless people throw away. There is even a lady who is his friend. In nice weather she sits on the park bench by the pond and writes poetry. She spoke to him for the first time on the day when those boys were rude to him. Talking to her had kind of made up for the small rudeness of the boys.

"How could he not?" Illy says to her friends when they get together for lunch or for cards. "How could he not have friends? He's always been friendly and charming." They are convinced for the most part, although they don't really know him and cannot help having certain concerns about a man who spent his whole life locked away.

***

He sees George on a winter's day afternoon on the bench outside of the filling station. Horatio is coming home from the store. It is a blustery kind of day, not bitter cold, but with a bite in the wind. At first he assumes he's suffering a phantom vision, a sad creation of his own longing. It would not come as a surprise, such a phantom vision, considering that Horatio has dwelt with such a sense of loss for so long now. There is a pain that has never healed or even lessened with the passing of time.

But as he stands, enrapt by the vision of the man on the bench with the light parka hood up over the head which is bent down, and who appears not to notice him, Horatio becomes convinced. *Oh my, it really is him.* He leaves the sidewalk, feeling awkward, and approaches the figure. Dried oak leaves that lie in the dusting of snow crackle under his feet as he steps over the low concrete barrier and into the lot..

"George," Hotatio says softly when he is standing beside the man.

George looks up and Harold sees that George's face is bruised, purple and swollen, and it is a great spasm of pain for Harold to see that. His eyes well up with a flood of emotion and he cannot speak.

But George says, "Horatio, my dear. How I've missed you."

And Horatio falls onto his knees on the cold concrete and he lays his head in George's lap. His great sadness comes forth in his sobbing, and he is crying. "Oh George, Oh George, I'm lost, I'm lost in the world."

George is caressing the back of Horatio's head and he is telling him, "You are not lost, because I found you here. So how can you be lost?"

After awhile, when Horatio calms down, he asks, "Who done this horrible thing to you?"

George replies to him in a way that he has never spoken before to any of his followers.

"Horatio, I must tell you that there are many long horrors interwoven with the histories of those who love me. When He who sent me gives the order, I am pleased to follow the order. The dear souls among which you are counted are of the oldest and the most weary. But more than that, they are the sufferers of past deeds unspeakable. Are they are not the unloved? The unforgiven? The unremembered?

"Now, in the fullness of time immemorial and unimaginable, are they going home. In His will, it is for me to forgive the unforgivable, to remember the unrememberable, to love the unlovable. Still, the debts must be paid. And who can pay them? I'm telling you now, my dear, so that you will know and have comfort in knowing, that I have been given a store of inexhaustible forgiveness. Inexhaustible wealth. Because He who keeps the accounts demands payment in full. And like a loving father will pay the debts of his children if they are neglectful, so I pay the debts of those of mine who cannot pay themselves."

Horatio has been sitting on the bench with George and looking steadily into his eyes as George has been revealing these things to him, and it is as if there is nothing else in the world. It is as though they are alone in the sanctity of a private room in some serene temple of God. Now he realizes that George's bruises have cleared, as the face of George has, again, become radiant and bewitching in its beauty.

"Your bruises, they're gone," he hears himself saying in the midst of his intoxication.

"We learn that all sacrifices are but the blessings of Him who loves us. In fact, all creation is the manifestation of sacrifice. Love is the glorification of sacrifice. So don't be fooled by appearances. I have to go where I am told to go."

But Horatio is suddenly possessed by the fear of George leaving him.

"Stay with us George," he says, his tone and expression pleading. "Illy has room."

"I can't do it."

"Then what will I do? I can't live."

"Don't say that. It is a falsehood. Remain devoted. Remember me. Give of yourself. The world is hard, but it is temporary. Patience is devotion. Endurance is devotion."

Horatio hasn't seen or heard the car that has driven up behind and parked outside of the walk where he first stepped into the lot. But George rises and informs him that he has to leave as his ride has arrived. Horatio stands when George does but he remains still, hands in his coat pockets, as George walks to the car, which is driven by a pretty woman, opens the door and gets in. George turns to smile at him through the glass of the window and the car starts up and then pulls out into the street. With his eyes only, he follows the car until it is out of his sight.

***

When he comes in through the kitchen door, Illy is sitting at the counter with a cup of tea. "Hello Dear, how was your outing today?"

"It was very nice, Illy; thank you."

"Would you like some tea?"

"Yes, I b'lieve I would."

As he sits she gets up and goes to the cupboard for a bag of tea, then over to the stove for the water. He watches her. "Illy?"

"Yes, Harold?"

"You're a better than any sister I could imagine, hard as I tried."

"Oh, Harold." As she turns back with his teacup he sees that her face has turned a little red.

"I saw George, Illy."

She looks at him, astonished. "Where did you see him?"

"At the fillin' station."

"You spoke to him?"

"Yes"

"Was he … fine?"

"Well, when I'm with George I learn things."

"Do you want to tell me what you learned? I mean you can. You don't have to," she says, confusing herself somewhat.

"I think I learned that George is always fine."

She smiles at him, but there is really nothing to say, so they drink their tea and they are content and quite comfortable in their silence.

Never Again
a song

You know I never did give love
i never knew the way
You know i never did give love
i only took what You gave
You know i never did give love
i only came to hear what You had to say

198

and You said that never and never again
never and never again
never and never and never again
do we want to come to this place again
See them sitting in the field
out in the heat of the sun
See them sitting in the field
waiting for you to come
See them sitting in the field
and ' I'm thinking to get up and run
but never and never again
never and never again
never and never and never again
do we want to come to this place again
These are the days of fun
here in old America
These are the days of fun
here and the world over
Well if these are the days of fun
I'm thinking to go out and have me some
but never and never again
never and never again
never and never and never again
do we want to come to this place again
You know i never did give love
i never knew the way
You know i never did give love
i only took what You gave
You know i never did give love
i only came to hear what You had to say
and You said that never and never again
never and never again
never and never and never again
do we want to come to this place again

Spirituality cannot be taught, it must be caught like an infection which is passed on to others who are receptive.

—*Kirpal Singh*

the questioner meets George

"Everything you say discourages me," The questioner complains.

"Am I now to be held responsible for your impressions?" the fellow replies offhandedly.

"So you take no responsibility for what you say?"

There is no answer. The men sit in the dark. The little fire illumines their grim faces and casts fantastic wavering shadows high up onto the blackened brick walls on either side of the narrow passageway. Out on the street front there is much care given to appearances. Fine cloth awnings extended beneath ornate and gilded names create a warm sense of welcome to curious passersby, who pause to look into the windows as one might look beneath the bushy eyebrows of a kindly old gentleman, stealing a glimpse into the windows of his soul. There is no care given to the back. Out of sight, it is out of mind. Place of utility. Of loading in and garbage out. Of darkness, and the unknown.

But places of darkness are not barren and lifeless. They are home to creatures of darkness. In perfect symbiosis, one world is part of the other, though they cannot know each other.

"What I say is what I mean," says the man into the darkness. He pokes at the fire, adds another broken piece of board.

"I know. I know it." The questioner is apologetic, shaking his head. "I just get too damn desperate."

"A man who is not desperate is a fool."

"Do you think so?"

"Thinking is a dead man's sport." Then he asks, "How is it that you've come to find me in this place."

"I was told that you—*had something.*"

Again they sit silently in the chill and the gloom of the night and the dark. High above, between the towering walls, a murky violet haze moves in slow tumbling motions, like an inverted and poisoned canal. There are two other men who have been sitting by the fire wrapped in their grimy blankets against the cold and now they have lain down, each on a length of cardboard for a bed.

The man with the questions now finds a certain quality in his own desperation. It is the quality of waiting. Now he watches the man across the fire. The man looks to be hard and there is an aura of ferocity about him. There are vague rumors—a recovered addict?—he had been some kind of a prison guru. But there is something else, as well. For a man of the street, for a homeless person, there is something—it's not clear. The dark stubble of beard, framed by the ragged hood of an old sweatshirt. The gaunt features, the rough hands. These are the obvious marks of his human condition. Yet there is also a rumor of another life, of a wife, a family.

He watches as the man sits cross-legged before the fire with eyes shut. He notices that the man's breathing is, well, it's hard to tell if he's breathing. But he's sitting fully upright. He looks regal. He seems … like a man turned to stone. Like a sculpture of a homeless man in a threadbare blanket. And so, within the tangle of questions, it occurs to him to wonder, Can this man truly be homeless? And why? Even in these base surroundings, he appears to be a man in control.

He thinks of his questions. He gets up, walks around to the little pile of broken boards and carefully places one on the fire. Then he returns to his place and sits in his long warm coat. His questions seem to have no meaning. He notices that one of the men who had lain down earlier is shivering and coughing softly. He stands, takes off his coat and lays it over the man. Then he sits. He still has his sweatshirt. He's not cold. He shuts his eyes as he sits. He forgets himself completely when he sees the man across the fire.

***

When he opens his eyes, he is alone. Daylight, such as it is in this strange place, has crept in. A door opens and a young man comes out with a large plastic sack. The fellow is somewhat startled when he notices him sitting there, and stops, unsure. But as he only sits, the young man continues to the dumpster, then hurries back to the door, looking back at him as he goes in. He hears the click of the door latch and the sliding of the bolt.

an early spring morning

On a mild, early spring morning in the city, some years earlier, four hundred and twenty-eight men and women dressed in black came out of the front doors of an old hotel in a single stream, simultaneously forming a marching unit of four abreast as they exited, and proceeded down the center of 84th Street, the barrels of their weapons propped against their shoulders. That end of 84th was quite narrow, run-down, and used only by slow moving local traffic. The walks were in even worse condition so the street was used as the main footpath by the local residents. But as the unlikely armed marching troupe approached, the pedestrians and bystanders made room for them, silently for the most part, though there were the occasional calls of attempted humor, "What time's the battle, soldiers?" or "Ooowee, Johnny come marchin!", things like that, assuming the marchers were part of some parade, or perhaps a movie production. Some adolescents fell in behind, ignoring the sharp commands of those in the rear, "You kids get the hell away from here. We're not joking!" They did fall back when two of the soldiers turned and aimed the barrels of their guns directly upon them.

When they reached the little court yard park, they turned into it, promptly effecting its evacuation with rude, unambiguous gestures at the few confused occupants, and began to walk the perimeter, the most forward groups of four peeling off in succession until all the outer edges were lined with the outward looking grim faces. Almost immediately, and even as they raised their rifles to their shoulders, there was a deafening explosion of gunfire, which came from all quarters of the tall buildings surrounding the park. Those blackly attired souls fell, slumped, were thrown back, in twisted disarray upon one another from the heavy pieces of lead that crashed through their bodies. A few that remained standing for an eternity of a few seconds, fired futilely at targets they could not see before being assaulted, as their comrades had been, by an unfathomable torrent of ammunition hurtling through the air. A few terrible voices crying out in agony were all that could be heard after the firing stopped. Mingling clouds of dark smoke rising slowly against the faces of every building.

***

The bodies are left to lie for the remainder of the day, and so the park takes on an added dimension of the ghastly.

"Why doesn't somebody do something?" a lady who had walked up to one of the policemen assigned to the site said.

"Mayor's orders, Ma'am."

"Well then, somebody should call the Gov'nor."

"The Governor is of the same mind as the Mayor, Ma'am. They don't want people to forget what happened here," the policeman informs her.

"Well, I never heard such a God-awful thing in my life. The dogs will come and start in on 'em, and the birds."

"We're keeping the dogs out, Ma'am. Dogs aren't supposed to be running around loose anyway. Do you have a dog that runs around loose

Ma'am? 'Cause if you do and it comes around here, we're going to either send it to the pound or shoot it; I hope you understand that."

The woman is getting frustrated now. "What the hell are you talking about, young man? We're not talking about dogs here. We're talking about hundreds of folks, real people, slain in the courtyard park—"

He has no patience for her. "Ma'am, I have to tell you that you're beginning to interfere with my performance of my duty. You go on back home now, or back to work, or wherever you were going when you came up to me with your questions."

"This is where I was goin'. There ain't no place to work today. You didn' know that?" She's beginning to raise her voice. "Even if everbody round about is scared, I told my sisters, even if everbody is scared, I don't care. I'm goin' ta find out some answers to what we're all sayin' and wonderin'."

"Well, you're not going to get them from me, Ma'am. These people that died here were criminals of the state. They openly threatened the security of this city, this state, and the United States of America. We simply, and efficiently I might add, put a stop to it. Now if you don't do as you're told and go away peacefully Ma'am, I'm going to arrest you and send you to jail. Is that what you want? Because I am more than willing to accommodate you."

There were other similar conversations throughout the day. A few particularly agitated people did end up being arrested. When night fell and enough threats had been made and enough folks had been arrested and put in jail, the antagonism of the citizens, at least the overt antagonism, abated and the city began to clean up its mess.

***

All day long, the man with questions had been watching. From the steps of an apartment building across the street, he observed them come pouring out of the hotel, their faces showing not fear, but purpose, as they went to their certain deaths. From the shelter of an entry to a long-closed local telephone office, he saw them willingly destroy themselves before the power of the administration. And he stayed the day long, observing, mostly from a bus stop, two buildings down on 84th, where no buses had come nor would come that day, the ensuing vocal bitterness of many members of the local citizenry and the enduring callousness of the authorities.

He had known it was coming. There was no averting this madness. It wasn't exactly suicide. They were going to be coming after them anyway. They would have picked them off in small groups, made it look legitimate. Many of those who died in the small park were his friends.

Some he had been friends with for a long time. He knew the general consensus among the group. "At least let them be shown for what they are," they had been saying. "Lay the cards on the table. Let the people decide who's righteous and who *really* is the threat to freedom, even to democracy."

"But revolution?" He had left the question open ended.

The answer came swiftly, "Don't you see, man? They are the ones who have perpetrated a revolution. They have taken the country from us, without a fight, until now. We are not revolutionaries, we are the defenders."

For how long had it been coming? This usurping of freedom. Of the freedoms on which the country was supposed to stand. Freedom of speech was the first victim. It usually is. In the name of security, wartime is the excuse. The other freedoms are picked away at, slowly. But the reality is that he never saw politics or social systems as the answer. "Yes," he would say in agreement with his friends, "there are answers in politics—just not *the answer.*" People had made sacrifices and been sacrificed for politics and social ideals through all of human history. The history of the oppressors and the oppressed. He deeply admired his friend's convictions. How could he not? Their bravery, their concern for others, their sense of justice. But in the end he chose not to die with them.

Somehow he felt that the real enemy had not yet even been identified. Those misguided creatures who killed his friends? He was convinced they were victims themselves. At the same time, who in the world knew anything about the truth? He had never come to any total political conviction, even after the better part of a lifetime in pursuit of such conviction. But *truth.* He was less than a beginner in that field. He *was* aware that people spent their whole lives in search of truth. Renounced yogis engaged in severe austerities in remote and solitary locations. Cloistered monks, bound to severe vows and tedious service. Myriad ways and means, both worldly and otherworldly, to a very uncertain end. An end that, he thought suspiciously, most never found. Anyway, would one recognize the truth if it was found to be, or placed, directly before him? How does one recognize something one has no concept of?

Still, *journey of a thousand miles* and all that. He'd hoped to find something he could bring back to them, like, "Look, my friends, you don't have to do this." But there was no time. When it was over he'd left the country. He'd spent ten years overseas. China, Tibet, India, Jerusalem, South America. In that time he'd come to be the owner of certain convictions. He'd learned that self-defense was necessary, but that violence was not—and that violence ran much deeper than he had known. He understood that all life was connected, and that all things were made of life. To purposely or even neglectfully harm any life was to harm one's own self. No prayers, no ablutions, no sacrifice, no pilgrimage could wash that away.

When he came back to the states, he was not the same person in many ways. He had learned less resistance, yet more restraint. He still grieved for his friends who had been lost to that extreme of violence. The world was a place of beauty and terror. But he had always known that. He was still looking. He had confirmed that teachers, gurus, shamans were abundant. The world was not lacking in them. Interestingly, he had not grown cynical. In fact, the portion of cynicism that he'd begun his search with was now less. But he'd not found a good fit. It was inspiring to him to see how many souls in the world were actually sincere. The opportunists, though multitudinous, are not the only ones on the planet. The trick is to curtail the opportunist in one's self.

The questioner returns

The following evening he goes back to the alley. He really has no more questions. What can there be in a verbal answer? He is thinking. Some mysterious Zen Koan? An ancient and all-inclusive proverb? They would hardly seem to have potential for true enlightenment. The fellow didn't seem to be much of a talker anyway. Seemed kind of gruff. Suppose he had his reasons.

When it comes down to it, he's not at all sure why he's going back. At the fire, they greet him with nods and a gesture to sit. Nobody says anything. They sit cross-legged by the fire in their rags for blankets and do whatever it is they do. He watches the fire as they close their eyes. No one has asked him to tend the fire, but he wonders who else will do it. It is a very small fire. It would surely die out within a short time. So he watches it and he watches the man. The rough unshaven face. The gaunt, street-hardened look. A couple of hours go by. Despite his best intentions toward the fire duty, he falls asleep.

***

In a dream he sees the same man, the man he has come to see, running through the city. The man is dressed similarly to the way he is currently dressed. Like a homeless person. But he is running with great urgency. It is still nighttime but as he runs, the pale glow of approaching dawn becomes apparent over the skyline. On and on he runs, without pause, without faltering. At times as he runs, ghostly apparitions and strange, troubled beings rush out from blind alleys and other dark places when he goes by and they look down the street after him. Sometimes they call out to him to, "Come back, oh please," but he pays them no heed and he runs on.

And then he enters an area that appears vaguely familiar as the day begins. He runs through many neighborhoods, small business districts and industrial areas until the sun is full up and the day is well underway, when it becomes, in the dream, completely familiar territory. The houses, the sturdy old maples, the neighborhood shops. Just two blocks over, parallel to this one is 84th, where they marched so willingly to their deaths.

Suddenly there is a roar of sound, as if a great battle has begun up ahead, and at that moment great shards of metal come tearing through the man as he runs; some strike the walk or the wall behind him after passing through him and ricochet off into the distance, and some bury themselves with a loud thud sound into the electrical power line poles behind him, while others, after their violent exit from his body, continue on unimpeded. The man falters now and falls, his body twisting and crashing to the concrete without any sense of harmony or coordination. And then he lies in his blood.

In his horror, the dreamer with no questions wants to go to him, struggles to get to him, but he cannot. In that place up ahead, that terrible place, the guns are still firing, but then they go silent. To his amazement he sees, in his dream, how the man lifts his head and for a brief instant, he catches his gaze. And in that glimpse, in that silent communication, however fleeting, there is no fear or confusion. Then an old dog comes from across the street and, whining softly, the dog nuzzles the man and then begins to lick the wounds as the man lays his head back onto the rough concrete walk.

***

When he wakes, he is alone again. He looks at his watch and it is at least an hour before sunrise. Someone has put a blanket over him and the fire is going strong. He gets up, sits by the fire in silence and dwells on the dream that he'd had. One thing is certain—once again he has questions.

TWENTY-SEVEN: Responsibility and Fulfillment

The walls were of concrete block with a stuccolike graffiti-proof coating. Light came from one small barred window and a large fluorescent light that burned day and night. Etched into the window by some sharp object was the prophecy, "Yes, Jesus and God will help Ernest Shaw to come home now."
    — *Sol Watchler   - former chief judge of New York State   in his own prison memoir, After the Madness*

follow up
Ozwald

There was a message on my answering system. I was being asked to call a certain individual at the prison. I didn't know what to expect. It had been a long time. I called.

"Ozwald, I'm glad you called," the individual answered.

"What is it about?"

"I've recently replaced the former administrator of psychiatry, and I have been studying the history of the past few years in the mental unit. I had become interested in the George phenomena even before I came to this facility, although the information available was quite limited."

"Yes, those were the days," I said, not quite knowing, myself, if I was being facetious, or openly genuine to this man I had just met on the phone.

"I was also interested in the study you fellows did, here. Rather, I mean that I am interested."

"In what way?" This time I knew I was being guarded.

That individual went on to tell me he was convinced the original project had been somewhat manipulated by the former administration and that he felt that was unfortunate.

I told him that in all honesty, it didn't matter because what happened was bigger than any manipulations that may have occurred. Goddamit, I didn't care anymore what people thought.

Then he asked me if we thought there might still be value in a follow up. I was floored, really. "I don't think Ansel's available. He's just started a pretty involving job in Europe."

"What about Jeff?"

"I don't think he'd want to. He's always said that he wouldn't."

"What about you?"

"When can I start?" I asked him, shamelessly.

***

So in a couple of weeks, when the paperwork had been completed, I found myself back on floor # 41. Things had changed, of course. But many of the same characters were still there, including certain men I had come to think of as dear friends extraordinaire, like Stephen, Toby, Walt Whitman. Where else would they be anyway? But Horatio had been released, thank God. That gentle soul never hurt anybody. Hope he's able to function, though. Bascomb, that marvelous entertainer, was out as well. Fyodor was still in. That surprised me. And Lao Tse, the Apache poet, Thomas Small had been transferred. I understood his health wasn't good and he had been moved to a smaller facility in New Mexico that was closer to his family, so they could more readily visit him. Johnny was still there also, though he was up for parole the next month and the word was that he was expected to get it.

One person I had never really spoken to—he was Jeff's case—was Jean-Paul. He always struck me as a fascinating individual, and so I took this second chance opportunity to have an interview, slash conversation, with him. As a matter of fact, he approached me near the end of the very day that I had decided to ask him *tomorrow*.

Jean-Paul
-responsibility-
Ozwald

He came up to me in his quiet way. "Dear Ozwald."

"Jean-Paul," I said, greeting him with a smile. "Do you prefer I call you Jean-Paul or your given name, Lin Chung?"

"Oh, I like Jean-Paul. George called me that, Ozwald, so I'll stay with that.

I wanted to ask you—please tell me if you've any news of George." His eyes are hopeful and yet doubtful.

"Oh, I'm sorry Jean-Paul, I have nothing. We, Jeff and Ansel and I, have made so many inquiries. But so far without result."

"I thought so. I thought you would have told us right away if you knew anything."

"I would have."

Jean-Paul looks down at the floor. Then he puts his head way back, looking up at the ceiling, shaking his head slowly. He breathes a deep sigh. "Can you do an interview with me, Ozwald?"

"Of course, Jean-Paul, I was going to ask you tomorrow. What did you want to talk about?"

"I wanted to talk about responsibility. George's idea of it."

"Okay, I appreciate it. Tell away."

"Tomorrow?"

"No, please. Today is fine. It's good."

***

"We used to hang out in Milton's and my cell quite often. I don't know any particular reason for that. But George was always so kind to me, and with my physical handicap, maybe he figured I'd be more comfortable. This might sound conceited or something, but I honestly believe that George cared about me so much that there's nothing he wouldn't do for me. But I don't mean that the way it sounds. I mean there's nothing he wouldn't do for anybody. Anybody at all. If events in a man's life conspired against him, boxed him in a corner, you know, something he couldn't handle, like his life was a train wreck waiting to happen. Where other men would stand by, helpless and sorry, George would throw himself down on those tracks and try to derail that train before it could destroy that man.

"You know, Ozwald, most of the time, we just had fun goofing off and wasting time. Killing time. But once in awhile, when it was just us friends together in my room or wherever, he'd get to the point. I mean by that that he'd give us some special kind of message. And you'd think it would, but it didn't, make us proud or anything, like we were so special. I don't think it ever did. It did make us learn something, because he was so sincere at those times."

"Are you thinking of a specific time like that?"

"Yes. The responsibility talk, we call it. He gave it in Milton's and my cell. It was so interesting how he'd turn things around when he'd talk, so that when you'd think he was taking you one place, sure enough, you'd arrive at another.

"Well, he was talking about how it wasn't good for us if we used our illnesses to our advantage. How when we were 'clear' we should be clear, and not acting or posing as if we were under the influence of whatever it is that we get under the influence of. How we should try to do good and try to be vegetarians and try to help those less fortunate than ourselves.

"It was like he was teaching us to be more than just a bunch of unfortunate misfits, feeling sorry for ourselves and how the world had dumped on us and how our families, in some cases, and how even God had dumped on us and all that. And I think we were receptive to that

211

and it made us feel stronger and maybe able to rise above our shortcomings a little bit.

"Then he said he felt there was something more than that, though. And this is one of the reasons why I love him and why I'll never stop telling the story of that man. He said that it is the responsibility of God, or any man of God, to inspire the souls. That he was given that and that it was his full determination that we should be inspired by such a love—those were his words, by *such a love*—and that we should not be beaten down by any God into submission. And the thing is, coming from George, though he doesn't talk about himself, I get the strongest impression that he knows all about being beaten down in the name of God."

"From what I've seen of his records, Jean-Paul, I would say they confirm that."

"It figures." I confide in Jean-Paul at this point. "It's interesting to me that I've heard more about God and people talking about God here in this prison, on this ward, than I've heard anywhere else, outside. Well, other than in the context of being in a church or with some other religious organization."

"Maybe it's because we've got less to lose here. George once said that it's to our advantage, spiritually. And I think maybe we don't have to worry about our pride too much. Most of us have already lost face with John Q. Public on just about every level imaginable."

"Strange, but I can see the advantage," I say.

"On the other hand," he says with a big guffaw and holding out the piece of arm on which there is no other hand, "we're not to take advantage of our conditions."

"You're hilarious, Jean-Paul," I say, playfully mocking him.

"I rarely joke," he says, not smiling.

I get the near certain impression that he's embarrassed.

an altercation

"You know how it goes, Ozwald, is that if somebody admits to being a sex addict, people think, 'Well sure it's a problem but …' well, Hell, that's all legitimate and everything, they even get the admiration ya know, like they're a sexy person or something. It's like a goddamned advertisement. But if that same person was to say that they are a porn addict, for instance, or a some kinda pervert, they immediately make themselves vulnerable. Everybody gets disgusted, right off. Get all superior."

"Well, I have to admit, it does seem like there's a difference," Ozwald says.

"There's often no real difference. I know most folks wouldn't agree, but it's the truth. I'm not talking about child porn and I'm not talking about—"

He gets interrupted in the middle of his little harangue as an altercation breaks out at the next table. It's Confucius and Fyodor.

Fyodor is yelling. "Damn, what the hell'd ya do that for? You broke my nose, ya dumb son of a bitch." Blood is running out between his fingers, dripping onto his clothes and the floor.

Confucius taunts him. "You think you're smart? You think you're somebody?"

"I'll kill you, ya little panty ass freak!" Fyodor kicks Confucius, who is still sitting and sends him and his chair sprawling. Confucius has just managed to raise his arms enough to defend his face from the kick of the powerful Fyodor, so he's not badly hurt. As he struggles to get to his feet he is assisted, by some help he really doesn't want.

"Let's go Confuse Us. Time to take this party to the hole," the guard is telling him.

The other guard has his stick raised, threatening Fyodor, who is still talking through his hands. "The son of a bitch elbowed me in the nose. What the hell am I supposed to do, kiss his ass?"

"On your knees!" the guard is telling him,, menacing with the stick.

Fyodor gets on his knees. The guard goes behind him. "Hands behind your back, Runell."

"I'm bleeding all over here, man."

The stick comes down hard on the back of his shoulder and Fyodor is down. But as the guard bends over him he swings back with his arm and closed fist. The backhand blow lands and the guard is knocked back.

"You wanted my hands, you bastard, come on I'll give you the other one too." He is cursing at the guard as they both get to their feet. But by then there is yet another guard who stuns Fyodor from behind and he stumbles forward, in shock and pain and into the other guard, who knocks him down with his stick. Once he's down the fellow kicks him in the ribs from his side and the guard with the stun gun, does the same from the other side.

"Fuckin' with the wrong dude, Freddie," the guard growls in his ear. "Now we're goin' to see the man upstairs."

Together the guards cuff him as he puts up little resistance, and they get him up and take him to the elevator, Fyodor and the one guard, both dripping blood from their noses. They open the doors and the two bleeding men get in and go up.

Ozwald and Johnny have watched the event in silence and alarm. They now look at each other, recognizing that they are mutually disturbed by the violence of it.

"That's really bad," Johnny says, voice shaking.

"I know. Those guards are some reactionary guys, man."

"'S the pen. That's the way it is."

"I know, sometimes I forget, and I think it would be different on this ward, this floor, you know because of the mental illness, no offense, Johnny."

"It's still the pen, though."

"Yeah. Who's *the man upstairs*?"

"Oh, it's their pun, you know. Like the wrath of God. In other places it's called the hole. But here it's upstairs, the top floor."

It strikes Ozwald as odd that he hadn't heard that reference before. But he realizes he hadn't been aware of anyone from the floor being sent to the man upstairs.

visiting the man upstairs

Lying on the long metal box that is his bed, Fyodor is trying to focus. George has shown him a way to focus his attention that will help keep him from hallucinating. The nature of his illness is that his attacks are preceded with a migraine like aura, so in an effort to brace himself against that old nemesis he is implementing George's advice to the best of his ability. He is having some success in his efforts, yet his mind tends to wander off here and there.

For thirteen days he has seen not another soul, only his one guard, his keeper. It is not a dark place. "Or is it?" He wonders if there is not a kind of darkness that lives in the light. The light is never turned off. After the seventh night, he tried to break the light, thinking, It'd be better to always be in darkness. But he could not. The source of the light is a round fixture, fifteen inches in diameter, recessed into the middle of the ceiling. It is a typical opaque white glass, behind a heavy metal mesh cover. The ceiling is twelve feet high. Fyodor tried throwing his shoe at the light. But the shoe is soft rubber and canvass. "Shoes ain't good for nothing these days," he had grumbled. "What if a man needs a hammer? How the hell is a man goin' to hammer a nail with a shoe like this?"

Laying here now and remembering the incident, he grumbles again. "The goddamn building isn't tall enough, they got to make this friggin' hole twelve feet tall—deep," he decides to correct himself. He realizes he's just daydreaming and works to pull back the focus he was attempting. He feels the efficacy of that effort and knows some temporary peace.

For an hour, perhaps two hours, he remains still and quite focused. He has few thoughts. And in time, as he lays on his back with his eyes closed, there comes a different quality to the light. He does have a passing thought, and the thought is, There is no darkness in the light. He has no consciousness of the time, but a time comes when tears spill over from his eyes and they roll down his cheeks and into his ears and he experiences a kind of happiness like the happiness of a child. Fyodor lies there and though his thoughts are beginning to crowd back into his mind, he doesn't want them to, and he keeps his eyes closed against the world. He begins to cry in deep sadness over his entire life, and also from a very powerful sense of futile lives past without number and the probability of lives forward without end. And within him, though it is beyond his understanding, he feels a great longing for the innocence of which he has just been reminded. "Oh Lord!" he cries in his despair. "How far away. How have we come so far away to this counterfeit world? Where is the road to come back? Someone needs to show the road." He is sobbing. And in this forlorn state of mind, in this locked room, and in this recognition of the hopelessness of his condition, of his orphaned predicament, his eyes flutter briefly open and George is sitting there on the metal box bed with him. Fyodor shuts his eyes, thinking he cannot bear to learn that George is not really there, that his imagination is playing a trick, but George puts his hand on Fyodor's shoulder and Fyodor open his eyes full of the wetness of his tears and looks at George, who is looking at him.

"You came," Fyodor says, almost in a whisper.

"I wanted to see you," George says. "They were generous enough to let me come in."

"They let you come in?"

"I bribed them," George says, smiling.

"Really?"

"Really, sort of."

"George, I just had a kind of—a kind of awakening, I guess."

George smiles and pats him with the fingers of the hand that is still on Fyodor's shoulder.

Fyodor says, "I want to go home now, George."

"Me too," says George.

the return of Fyodor and Confucius

In a demonstration of perfect justice, Confucius and Fyodor return to the floor on the same day. They've been visiting the man upstairs for three weeks. They return with little fanfare, however Fyodor does get a warm reception from his friends before returning to his cell, exhausted. Confucius simply returns to his cell.

After a couple of days, Ozwald presumes to pay a visit to Fyodor. He finds him, obviously still needing a lot of recuperating time, but looking better, having cleaned up as well as having had a few substantial meals. Somehow the man has retained his good humor and his usual pleasant demeanor.

"How's it going, science dude?" Fyodor quips when he sees Ozwald.

"I was going to ask you the same question, philosophy man."

"Hell, I'm alright. It ain't like I've got a lot to lose. Of course, it ain't the nonstop party up there like we got goin' down here, though."

"I don't suppose it is."

"You're lookin' good, Oz. Got a smoke?"

Ozwald has, of course, come prepared. "Don't think I'd come to visit empty handed do you?"

"I don't suppose you would," Fyodor says with a big smile.

"I've got questions, as usual," Ozwald tells him, lighting his cigarette.

"I supposed you would," Fyodor says smiling again.

Ozwald sits down on the floor, against the wall, Fyodor sitting on the bed. "I just can't help wondering what the big fight was about."

"I take some offense at your calling it a fight, my man. The little twerp sucker punched me in the face when we just sitting together, having a discussion."

"Sorry for the offense, then."

Fyodor blows a series of perfect smoke rings. "You hip to Howard Fast?" he says.

"Well, not hip, but aware of him. He was a controversial author of political fiction, am I right?"

"Controversial, bein' the point of our discussion-slash, argument."

"You mean yours and Confucius?"

"Zactly. I'm a big Fast fan. Confuse us is as ignorant as he is arrogant, so he's callin' my man Fast a stinking Commie and other such derisive terms. But I'm cool, I'm takin' it in stride. I figure it's his problem, know what I mean?"

Ozwald nods. He's finding this surprisingly intellectual side of Fyodor to be just as entertaining as his usual, less conspicuously intellectual, harangues.

"So I'm explainin to the fool," Ozwald is all smiles recognizing that Fyodor probably has some right to indulge in these demeaning descriptions of Confucius, considering the hell he has just finished paying for their *discussion*, "you don't know anything about him. You haven't really read his books. You're condemning him on fucking hearsay. True he joined the communist party for a period of time, but he became disillusioned with it when he saw the results of it put into action in Russia.

"So Confuse Us tells me I sound like a sympathizer myself. I say, 'What're you, some kind of latter day Joe McCarthy saint or something?'"

Ozwald can't help but smile at that. Fyodor grins back at him.

"Yeah, that's what I said to 'im. That's about when he started turning kind of a funny color of red, fuchsia maybe. So I go on to tell him that Howard Fast was a beautiful soul, full of love and compassion for people, something he, Confuse Us, seemed to of took especial exception to and with no warning at all, he cracked me with his elbow—you know how we were sitting side by side there at the table—well it was a goddamn easy cheap shot, and he broke my nose, which, by the way, has been broken a number of times already and is *just a little bit* sensitive."

"It looks better now," Ozwald offers meekly.

"Does it? It's had some time to heal I guess."

The two men sit for a minute in silence and then it occurs to Ozwald, and he says more or less to himself, but in the way one does when thinking out loud, "He told me he'd never read a book in his life."

"Well, he damn sure never read Howard Fast, I stand by that."

TWENTY-EIGHT: His Will is Sweet (Little girl on a stoop meets George)

God cloth'd himselfe in vile man's flesh, that so
Hee might be weake enought to suffer woe
                              —John Donne

Empty Bowls
- a song -

One a those strange guys
we met on down by the bins
had a little accident
they found him in his sins
the others they up and went
but I'm sure we'll see their skins

Even with their curtains drawn
the people this demands
are not in hiding
they're quick to show their hands
there's no confiding
with the people this demands

"Saw it in the moonlight once"
the law he said to me
"It takes a martyr
to find eternity
It takes a martyr
to want to be set free"

Ahh …
Ahhh …
Ahh …
Ahhh …

Even the mystery
of an unexpected fate
cannot depress me
I know we have to wait
for our success we

just line up at the gate

After waiting countless years
three old restless souls
were tired of lying
to fill their empty bowls
and now they're dying
but it's just their restless souls

Ahh ...
Ahhh ...
Ahh ...
Ahhh ...

little girl on a stoop meets George

There is a little girl sitting on a stoop in the shade of the morning. She had seen the man fall on the sidewalk where the sun had already reached with the warming of the day. She had hesitated for a moment, but then had run down to try and help the man.

"Are you hurt?" she says to the dreadful and dirty man in her pity, placing her hand over his eyes to shade them from the bright sun, but, although he opens those shaded eyes and gazes at her most kindly, he gives no answer.

He has fallen full across the walkway and, as she kneels down to him, a couple of passers-by step into the street to go around. A lady from a window of the building next door calls out to her.

"You better get away from him. You don't know *who* he is."

"But he's hurt." She's now seen the bleeding that has stained the inside of the man's jacket.

"You just get away. It's not safe. Or I'll tell your momma."

Reluctantly, the little girl rises up and goes back to her stoop where she sits near the bottom and watches.

When my poppa gets back, he'll help the man, she thinks. She wants to run and tell her momma but she knows Momma is asleep and will get angry at her if she wakes her. "But when will Poppa get home?" She has no knowledge of that.

Now, without her there by the man, the people, when they come by, aren't going into the street but are simply stepping over the man and going their way.

"Be careful of him," she calls out to them. "He's hurt, please don't step on him."

Some boys come by and they tease her and make fun of the *'drunken bum'*.

"He's not drunk," she retorts, "he's hurt."

"How do *you* know?" they taunt her.

"He's bleeding."

The boys look closer to confirm this, and of course it is confirmed.

"He's still probly drunk, though," one says, now more sober in his tone.

"It don't matter." Her voice is soft. "He's hurt."

The sun is beginning to feel hot and the boys step into the shade of the wall next to her steps.

"Well," says one boy to the other two, looking down and shuffling his feet in the narrow strip of tattered grass there, "What can we do?"

They don't answer, so the little girl does. "Well, you *could* get him out of the sun. You could get him out of the walkway. Anyway, I'm going in and get him a drink of water and you can give him that.

So now they feel embarrassed by her reproach and then suddenly they feel gallant. They go back up to the man and one of the boys takes charge.

"Perry, you take him by the wrist and Emil, you take him by the other wrist." He's the biggest and strongest, so he says, "And I'll get his legs."

At first they are surprised at how heavy he is, and they lose grips and stumble or fall, mumbling curses. But they gain determination and gather their strength. They slide the poor man toward the shaded patch of grass where they had been standing, and the little girl comes to assist them by holding the man's head up and walking backwards, all crouched over and grunting and straining with the boys. Then the little girl runs in and gets the water. When she returns, and while Perry holds up the man's head, she gets the glass to his mouth and he does, in fact, drink some of the water.

The lady from the window sees all this, shaking her head in frustration, but she is also now moved to pity by their courage and by the selfless actions of the little girl and her reformed companions. So she goes to the phone book and finds the number, calls the mission and tells the person who answers all about it. The person replies that they will send a couple of fellows over to have a look. Then the lady calls out to the children who are still very worried and have not been able to come up with a plan as to what to do next.

The sun is climbing in the sky; the shady spot will not be shady much longer, and the man is still bleeding.

"We should call nine one one," Perry says.

"No," says Emil. "Then the cops will only come."

"But won't they help him," asks the girl.

"No," says Emil, "they'll only haul him off to the slammer."

"Oh," she says.

The others also seem to accept this bit of sage knowledge, which Emil impresses upon them is based on first hand experience.

So when the lady calls out to them and tells that she has notified the folks from the mission and that they are coming to help, they are greatly relieved. Even so, after a bit of thought, certain practical concerns come up.

"I guess they'll try to convert him if he ain't of their faith," comments the biggest boy.

"Yeah, they're Protestants alright," Perry agrees.

"Course, he could be of their faith," Emil puts in.

"S'better than nothin' though, huh?" the biggest asserts.

"Oh yeah," they all nod and agree. "Yeah, they'll help him."

POSTSCRIPT

Perhaps some summing up would be in order, some closing comments on this idea of a spiritual benefactor, especially for the benefit of any dear reader who would find only tragedy in this little story of George. Although part and parcel of most of the world's religions, the concept is one that is yet shrouded in mystery. I'm quite certain that anything I added here would only be a continuation of the same style that you've already become familiar with in reading to this point. So, rather than my going on, there is a parable that Sant Kirpal Singh Ji used many times that seems more apropos. This particular version, I found published in the January,1970 Sat Sandesh Magazine. It is part of a talk by the Master that was given the title, "Out of Bondage".

Jesse S. Hanson

"There are many prisons in the world,
and supposing a man visits one of them
to give an uplifting talk to the inmates.
He notices the lack of good food there,
and so makes arrangement for the food
to be improved at his own expense. Another
man also visits the same prison and
seeing that the prisoners' clothes are torn
and ragged, he kindly supplies large quantities
of new clothing for their use. A

third visitor finds that the prisoners' cells
are dark and unventilated, and so he volunteers
to remodel the buildings to provide
better living quarters. All these
things have vastly improved the life of
the prisoners, but unfortunately they are
still prisoners. Finally another man
comes, and he opens the gates of the
prison saying, "You are all free, I release
you." Who do you think was the greatest
benefactor out of all these men?

When true Masters come, they release
the soul from the wheel of births and deaths."

Character Profiles

Ahmed
>-physically average, Muslim
>-disciple of George
>-was a doctor in a war. is still living the war mentally
>-in prison for practicing medicine without a license

Azra'il
>-Caucasian man in African apparel that Ansel meets at a small airport
>-claims to be an angel of death

Ansel
>-physically average height, thin, white
>-one of the grad student interviewers
>-Christian background, from the Midwest

Anthony
>-George's roommate
>-disciple of George but not one of the gang
>-stutters badly and loses focus of his thoughts
>-becomes easily angered
>-physically, thin, hunched shoulders, white - from a small town rural background

Bascomb
>- real name is Jesús
>-physically average Latino, intense sky blue eyes, clean cut grooming
>-from Albuquerque
>-one of George's gang and disciple

biggest boy
>-one of 3 young boys that help the little girl take care of George as he lays wounded on the sidewalk

Bony
>-mentioned as an old friend of Ahmed's; they were in a support group comprised of war medics

Brent
>-Ansel's brother

Charles
>-see Junkyard Dog

Clancy
>-one of the night guards
>-only guard that George communicates with
>-physically tall, 6'5", thin

Clarence
>-one of the prison guards on the floor

Clifton
>-physically thin and small black inmate
>-reclusive
>-not part of George's gang
>-his story is that he is married, has a brain tumor and is a heroin addict
>-Bascomb insists that Clifton's story is all a fabrication and that he is simply a crack head

Confucius
>-real name is Carol J.
>-not a member of Georges gang, but was given the name Confucius by Horatio, due to his tendency toward philosophizing
>-inmate who is quite sure that he is a species of one
>-most of the other inmates call him Confuse Us
>-serving 6 years for two separate counts of assaulting police officers for no apparent reason

Coreen
>-oldest sister in "family ties" story
>-Eugene's sister

dead man
>-severely emaciated inmate who experiences his life with the knowledge that he's dead
>-formerly a musician and artist
>-doesn't like George

Ed
    -one of the prison guards on the floor
    -fundamental Christian
    -condemns George and the attention he receives as the work of
the Devil

Ella
    -George's mother

Emil
    -one of 3 young boys who help George as he lays wounded on the
sidewalk

Eugene
    -tied to the wall in hallway because he bites
    -smart, violent, prone to fits of cursing, depressed

female nurse
    -has to help Clancy in the effort to evacuate the inmates during
the fire in the prison

floors
    -forty-four floors altogether in prison building
    -main concern of story is floor 41
    -mental unit is comprised of floors 31 through 44
    -floor 37 is unknown
    -floor 44 is for official prison use (one of its functions is solitary
confinement and it is called "the man upstairs" by the inmates)
    -floors 31 and 32 are women's floors

Fyodor
    -real name is Freddie Runell
    -one of George's disciples and gang members
    -named after Fyodor Dostoevsky because he loves to hear and tell
stories
    -physically strong, average height, black man

George
    -physically average, white
    -dark shoulder length hair
    -short dark beard
    -originally from West Virginia
    -abused by his stepfather, who was a fire and brimstone preacher

-originally committed to mental institution because he became a danger to his mother using scissors and tools as weapons

-was given spiritual enlightenment by his benefactor and given the mission of bringing spirituality to the inmates of the mental ward of the Federal Penitentiary.

George's wife
-in the house when George returns from getting the vacuum cleaner from   the repair shop

-picks George up at the filling station where he meets and talks with Horatio

Henry
-Melinda's husband, passed away 2 winters ago

-Anthony's father

Horatio
-real name is Harold

-physically large, black, extraordinarily large forehead

-came up with the idea of spiritual names

-one of George's gang and disciple

-in prison due to being wrongly convicted of rape

-suffers from seizures and brain damage

IllishaImelda
-Horatio's sister

-called Illy for short

-lives in Philladelphia

-has always maintained her relationship with Horatio

Jaiden
-inmate who violently abuses himself sexually

-not one of Georges gang or disciples

Jeff
-one of the student interviewers

-the project was Jeff's idea

Jesse
-worked with Fyodor (Freddie) on the city maintenance crew

Jean-Paul
-for Jean-Paul Sartre

-real name is Lin Chung
-Chinese
-has no right arm and the left arm has no hand
-disciple of George and member of George's gang
-his crime was an act of violence with the handless arm
-long hair, scruffy beard
-cell mate is Milton

Johnny
-inmate
-friend of Anthony's
-writer, poet
-physically tall, thin, multi-racial

Juan
-friend of Bascomb's that was murdered as a teenager
-physically Latino

Junkyard Dog
-inmate (arrives later in story)
-physically young and even younger looking
-real name is Charles

Lao Tse
-native American
-real name is Thomas Small (took the name Lao Tse because people say, although he doesn't completely agree, that Taoism is like Native American philosophy)
-poet
-one of George's disciples and one of his gang

lady in the car
-lady sitting in a car on Old Ferris Road outside of the prison

little girl on the stoop
-helps George as he lays wounded on the sidewalk
-gets 3 boys to help as well

male nurse
-in the medical room when Ozwald is called in and George is being restrained

rude driver

-man who screams obscenities at George when George is looking for his gas cap

Melinda
-Anthony's mother

Milton
-real name is Raja Santhanam
-physically thin, tall Indian, large facial scar from knife wound
-one of George's gang and disciple
-American born, American accent
-cell mate is Jean-Paul

Mr. Santhanam
-Milton's father

Ola
-Anthony's daughter
-short for Oluwaseyi (God made this)

Ozwald
-one of the student interviewers
-raised a Hare Krishna on a farm community in West Virginia
-interviews Toby

Perry
-one of 3 young boys who help George, as he lays wounded on the sidewalk

prison mental unit administrators
-original administrator is one of several persons present during a meeting with the three interviewers regarding the treatment of George
-replacement administrator who invites Ozwald to do a follow up

Sal
- was in a support group with Ahmed on the outside comprised of veterans   who had been medics in various wars; was actually prejudiced against Ahmed though

Stephen
-real name is Stephen
-has visions or hallucinations of a hellish nature
-physically thin, white

-disciple of George, but not part of the gang

Stook
-friend of Ahmed's who comes regularly to visit him
-was in a support group with Ahmed comprised of veterans who had been medics in various wars

Swumpa
-the king of the giant squid
-lives in the depths of The Indian Ocean

Terri
-Jeff's girlfriend
-likes love stories

the beholder
-girl who is a prisoner in the attic of a large old house
-spends almost all of her time looking out the little attic window and has never seen the ground, or other humans
-wearing a too large flannel nightgown
-very small, about two and a half feet tall, with legs and arms like broom handles, and with doll's feet, and with hands like the feet of a small bird. The eyes are big and the face is small, gaunt, and so pale, like the transparent membranous skin of some tropical fish.

The three student interviewers
-Ansel, Jeff, Ozwald

the questioner
-a spiritual seeker on the outside
-finds George in his role as a homeless person
-formerly a student of social and political sciences

Toby
-humanoid inmate, tied to the wall with 1/4 inch steel cables
-ancient being
-scavenger – survived throughout his long life by eating death, but has become a vegetarian due to George's influence
-has had variety of names down through the ages including: *Akkāl-dehānt*, the gluttonous eater of death, *Isibungu* the worm, *Hara Popa'a*, the shame or the wrong doing foreigner, and *Ofo Ogo*, the long lived ghost

-also called Pumpkin Head in the prison due to the shape of his head

the man upstairs
-the name given to floor 44 which is where mental patients are sent for solitary confinement

Verna
-neighbor friend of Ella's in West Virginia

Wade Federal Correctional Institute
-the prison where George and his friends and followers are incarcerated

Walt Whitman
-tied to the back wall of big room, as is Toby
-part time member of George's gang
-attempts suicide whenever he's not restrained.
-incarcerated for habitual rape

Zac
-acquaintance of Jeff from an early college psychology class

Zeke
-a prison guard that Jeff has spoken to regarding the cell bars

Regarding Federal Prison Mental Wards

Due to an increasing amount of information on the subject, many people are now aware, or are becoming aware, that many of the mentally ill residents of the United States, as well as those of many other countries, are not being treated in modern mental health facilities designed solely for that purpose. For the most part, the severely mentally ill are not seen, neither are they heard, so the average citizen has little reason to think of them at all. They are not seen nor heard from because they are generally absent from the common spheres of our experience. In other words, they are institutionalized. And what is the nature of the institutions that deal with the greatest percentage of the mentally ill? For most, the only institution available for them is the Federal Prison System.

It's obviously an imperfect system, however some changes are in the works, both within the prisons themselves, as well as in the courts. For instance, there are now laws in some states against the practice of placing mentally ill prisoners in solitary confinement or "segregation".

But there is a long way to go and the problems as well as the solutions are very complex. It also occurs to me that the prison of the future may be even more likely to assume the role of mental health facility. With an ever increasing world population, reflected by an ever increasing population of "misfits", who pose a variety of dangers to society, it seems likely that either the prisons will have to increase their mental health facilities or the mental health facilities will have to increase their prison-like facilities.

It was never my intention, in writing this novel, to argue a point of view regarding the proper care and treatment of the mentally ill. But for the reader who may question the possibilities regarding such a group of men as are in my story, being incarcerated in a Federal Prison, I have included here certain references in support of such possibilities.

Jesse S. Hanson

The following is taken from an article printed in the Boston Herald, March 26, 2007, titled *"Cruel and sadly usual: Prisons shouldn't be mental wards"* by Jamie Felder:

"Twelve years ago a federal judge ruled unconstitutional California's practice of putting mentally ill prisoners in solitary confinement. It is, he said it is 'the equivalent of putting an "asthmatic in a room with no air."' Since then, inmates have won settlements or court orders in 12 states to keep prisoners with serious mental illness out of "solitary" or what corrections officials prefer to call segregation.

~

Prisons now house three times more people with serious mental illness such as schizophrenia, bipolar disorder and major depression than mental health hospitals. The federal Bureau of Justice Statistics says half of state prisoners nationwide have a mental health problem. They end up in prison because the community mental health systems are in shambles - fragmented, underfunded and unable to serve the poor, the homeless, and those who are substance-addicted as well as mentally ill.

Nationwide, half of the state inmates with mental health problems were convicted of nonviolent offenses, primarily low-level drug and property offenses. Alternatives to incarceration may have been appropriate, but the court's hands are tied by mandatory sentencing laws.

Once behind bars, the mentally ill find themselves ill-equipped to handle the stresses and rules - formal and informal - of prison life. They are more likely to be victimized and more likely to be injured in a fight than other inmates. They are more likely to break the rules. They are more likely to behave in ways that annoy, disgust and even enrage security staff who have scant training in how to recognize, much less cope with, symptoms of mental illness."

The above article in its entirety was found at:
http://www.gmhcn.org/files/Articles/CruelandsadlyusualPrisonsshou ldntbementalwards.html

And from the Wall Street Journal, May 3rd, 2006, Gary Fields writes in his story titled *"No Way Out - Trapped by Rules, The Mentally Ill Languish in Prison"*:

"For years American prisons have been grappling with a surge in the ranks of mentally ill prisoners, caused in part by the shuttering of state-run mental-health facilities a generation ago. The Joseph Harp prison spotlights an often-overlooked aspect of that problem: how it has become self-perpetuating. Once imprisoned, mentally ill inmates are rarely paroled. Some 'max out' their sentence, serving at least 85% of their term, and are released. With nowhere to go, and with a recidivism rate higher than that of the general prison population, they often end up back where they started."

~

The National Alliance on Mental Illness estimates there are 300,000 people suffering from mental illness in state and federal prisons, compared with 70,000 in state psychiatric facilities. "Our jails and prisons are our largest mental-health facilities now," says U.S. Sen. Mike DeWine, a Republican from Ohio who has co-authored bills to create federal programs to improve services for mentally ill inmates.

~

Many states, responding to budget pressures and changing ideas about how to treat mental disorders, closed their residential mental institutions. Oklahoma was one of the last. It shuttered Western State Hospital in Fort Supply in 1997 and turned over the inpatient psychiatric hospital at Eastern State Hospital in Vinita to the Department of Corrections, a process completed in 2001.

The idea was that community agencies would take over treating and monitoring these patients, but in almost all cases they haven't picked up the slack. The number of long-term, non-criminal psychiatric patients housed in Oklahoma's state facilities is about 200, a fraction of the 1,300 they held in the 1980s, according to the state's department of mental health. Griffin Memorial, the remaining state hospital, houses about 162 of those but generally only for two weeks at a time until patients are judged stable enough to be released into the community.

~

Corrections and mental-health officials are trying to ease the situation by developing new programs, such as mental-health courts that would steer some mentally ill defendants away from prison."

The above article in its entirety was found at:
http://www.mindfully.org/Health/2006/Prison-Mentally-Ill3may06.htm

For Further Reading on the Subject

Deinstitutionalization of the mentally ill

http://mplf.org/text1/deinstitutionalization-S8296-001.htm

Some Resources about real-life Godmen:

websites dedicated to Sant Kirpal Singh Ji:

http://www.ruhanisatsangusa.org/

http://www.kirpalsingh-teachings.org/

websites dedicated to Sant Ajaib Singh Ji:

http://www.santji.allegre.ca/lifesj/lifesj.html

http://www.ajaibbani.org/

Some Other Resources:

http://dsal.uchicago.edu/dictionaries/platts/

[akkāl A *akkāl*, s.m. An enormous eater, a glutton.

The end of the body, i.e. death:--*dehāntar* (°*ha+an*°)]

http://isizulu.net/

http://homepages.ihug.co.nz/~swamisat/ROWAN/long_gloss.html

About the Author

Jesse S. Hanson is a North Dakota (rural Midwest USA) native, writer/musician. Jesse and his wife, Lilasuka, currently reside in Pittsburgh, Pennsylvania, USA. He has also lived for a considerable time in the Pacific Northwest (USA) and briefly in the Southwest (USA). — "I suppose restlessness is a part of my nature. I'm never quite at home anywhere in the world. And that is part of why spirituality is the backdrop for of all my writing." Jesse was initiated into the timeless path of Surat Shabd Yoga by Sant Ajaib Singh Ji of Rajasthan in 1976.

Jesse and Lilasuka (pronounced Leelashooka) are part-time performing folk/rock musicians in the greater Pittsburgh and West Virginia Panhandle area. Their band, The Primatives, for which Jesse is the songwriter and guitar player, has two CD's to its credit: "The Lovers of Kali Yuga" and "Primitive Spirit".

Jesse has been a songwriter all his life but has directed the main focus of his attention to the writing of two novels over the last 5 years.

ALL THINGS THAT MATTER PRESS ™

FOR MORE INFORMATION ON TITLES AVAILABLE FROM
ALL THINGS THAT MATTER PRESS, GO TO
http://allthingsthatmatterpress.com
or contact us at
allthingsthatmatterpress@gmail.com

www.ingramcontent.com/pod-product-compliance
Lightning Source LLC
Chambersburg PA
CBHW051638260626
47170CB00004B/1230